IN THIS SPECIAL EDITION OF DROWNED HOPES, the author offers up both the full-length novel and his adapted screenplay. So, when you finish the book portion, read on and see what the movie will be like.

...Ellen powered into the guy, swinging her high heels like twin tomahawks. She pounded at him furiously, blood spattering everywhere.

Caught by surprise, the thief fell back, cowering to protect himself. "Goddamn," he shouted. "You're killing me."

But Ellen showed no mercy, slashing away at him with those deadly heels. Years of pent-up emotion pouring out. "Fuck you," she screamed. "Fuck you... Fuck you..."

Finally, the thief broke free, threw the purse at her and hauled ass out of there.

Ellen started after him... stopped. She recovered her purse, then overcome by sudden weariness, she nearly fell. She forced herself upright, fighting for breath.

A group of tourists exited the elevator. They saw Ellen and wondered what the hell had been going on. One of the men approached her. "Can I help you, lady?" he asked.

Ellen gave him a withering look. "Piss on your help," she said.

Shocked, the man moved back to his friends. Ellen looked them all over – scorn burning in her eyes.

"Piss on all your help," she said.

The tourists hurried off, trying to get away from this crazy lady as fast as they could.

Ellen got to her feet. She shouted at them, "That's right. Run for your lives. Ellen Berman just woke up. And she's not going be anybody's victim again.

"You hear me? Never fucking again."

About The Author

Allan Cole is a best-selling author, screenwriter and former prize-winning newsman who brings a rich background in travel and personal experience to his imaginative work.

Son of a CIA operative, Cole was raised in the Middle East, Europe, and the Far East. He attended thirty-two schools and visited or lived in as many countries. He recalls hearing Othello for the first time as a child sitting on an ancient fortress wall in Cyprus - the island Shakespeare had in mind when he wrote the play.

Rejecting invitations to join the CIA, Cole became an award-winning investigative reporter and editor who dealt with everything from landmark murder cases to thieving government officials.

Since that time he's concentrated on books and screenplays. His novels include the landmark science fiction series, "Sten," coauthored with the late Chris Bunch, which have sold upwards of 25 million books worldwide and have been published in 13 languages, and "The Timura Trilogy." His latest books include "The Hate Parallax," co-authored with Russian fantasy master, Nick Perumov, "Lucky In Cyprus," "Tales Of The Blue Meanie," as well as "MacGregor," and "Drowned Hopes," thrillers set in Boca Raton, Florida. "Parallax" is the first and only novel written by American and Russian collaborators.

Allan has sold more than a hundred and fifty television dramas, ranging from "Quincy" and "The Rockford Files" to and "Walker, Texas Ranger." He lives in Boca Raton, Florida, with his wife, Kathryn.

Here's what critics have said about Cole's other works: Lucky In Cyprus: A haunting, humbling, and sobering experience ; - J. A. Kaszuba Locke, Bookloons; A Reckoning For Kings: Classic war novel - San Francisco Chronicle; The Timura Trilogy: Page turner of the year - Locus Magazine; The Sten Adventures: Landmark science fiction series – Publishers Weekly; A Cop's Life: Must-read for anyone with a badge – Philadelphia Fraternal Order Of Police.

For more information about Allan's life and work see his homepage at http://www.acole.com, or his biographical entries at http://www.IMBD.com (International Movie Data Base) and Wikipedia.com. Visit his bookstore at http://www.tinyurl.com/l9mpr5, and be sure to drop by his popular blog: My Hollywood MisAdventures at http://www.allan-cole.blogspot.com/

Drowned Hopes

The Novel

By Allan Cole

For Kathryn
My Always And Forever
And
Aunt Rita & Uncle Avi – For Their Loving Support
And
Aunt Cassie & Uncle Tommy - Who Always Believed

Hope is the thing with feathers
That perches in the soul;
And sings the tune without the words;
And never stops at all.
- Emily Dickenson

CHAPTER ONE

THE SOUTH FLORIDA night was steamy, the music sizzling as the young couple exited the Rum Runners Club. It was too early to leave the trendy night spot and the girl lagged behind her date, sexy as she could be in her micro-mini dance outfit.

She did some impromptu bumps and grinds to the music, trying to entice her boyfriend back inside. But all it did was inflame his already overheated libido and he coaxed her deeper into the parking lot.

"I wanna dance some more," the girl said, sulky and so drop dead gorgeous she drove him crazy.

"Sure, baby, sure," her boyfriend said, soothing as he could. "But let's rest in the car for awhile first, okay?"

"Rest. Ha!" the girl said, knowing what was up.

But the kid persisted and the girl let herself be drawn onward until they reached a flashy new Jeep. The boyfriend got the door open and started pulling the girl in after him, putting a liplock on her to end all liplocks. At the same time his hands were groping under that fabulous micro-mini. The girl started to – what the hell – go for it. Thinking that he was her boyfriend after all, and if she made it quick they could get back to the dance band.

Then her heart jumped, and her eyes went Bambi wide as suddenly, the meanest, dirtiest, mugger in the world made his appearance, face as wild and crazy as the gun he was waving. He exposed yellow teeth at the boyfriend's semi-erotic antics and the girl was scared spitless at the things she saw in the mugger's eyes.

Her boyfriend was oblivious, still groping. She pushed at him.

"Stop," she demanded. "Stop."

The kid paused, eyes glazed. "What's the matter, baby?" he said.

The mugger made himself known – shoving the gun in the guy's face. "You heard the bitch," he snarled.

Drowned Hopes

The boyfriend finally realized what was happening and his libido descended to the seventh level of hell. Even so, he tried to be brave, pushing the girl to the side.

"No problem, man," he said. "Take it easy, okay?"

The mugger fished a black trash bag from his back pocket and shook it out. Shoved it at the kid. "Put it in there, shit for brains," he snarled. "And I mean everything."

While the boyfriend clumsily fished for his wallet, the girl opened her purse. "Don't hurt us," she pleaded.

The mugger just shook the bag, promising nothing, threatening everything. The kids did what they were told, stripping off jewelry, watches, getting out their wallets. Dumping it all in the bag.

"Hurry it up, assholes," the mugger said.

Looking the girl over, he was getting really impatient to spring his next act. But then the girl saw something else – just over the mugger's shoulder. He caught her reaction and started to turn, but there was a sudden shock as something jammed into his back.

A hand shot forward, covering his mouth, cutting off his squeal of pain and surprise. And then another shocking blow rammed into his kidney.

The girl saw the mugger yanked back into darkness and heard two heavy thumps, followed by the thief's muffled groans. Then the hand came away from the thief's mouth and he slammed face forward onto the tarmac.

He remained there, motionless.

The boyfriend and the girl looked down at the still form, then up at their savior as he stepped into the single dim yellow light that hung over the parking lot.

Although they would never learn his name, the man they were staring at was Sam Barr and he was as big as a mountain and crafty as a fox. A breaker of heads and hearts. Few had who met him were ever lucky enough to escape unscathed. But the kids didn't know that - they were just scared and grateful.

Barr leaned down and plucked the gun from the mugger's fist and put it in his pocket.

8

Allan Cole

"Thanks, man," the boyfriend said. "I thought he was gonna kill us or something."

But the girl knew that things were far from being fine. She shivered as if it were cold, instead of an eighty-degree Florida night.

She looked down at the still form. "Is he... he... you know...?"

"Dead?" Sam said for her.

The girl gulped and nodded.

Sam kicked the mugger. There was no reaction. He chuckled. "Guess I don't know my own strength," he said.

The girl gave a little squeak. The boyfriend just stood there, totally out of his element.

Still chuckling, Sam fished a handful of pills from his pocket and popped them into his mouth. He chewed, thinking things over. Then he indicated the bag of loot in the boyfriend's hand. "I'll take that," he said.

The boyfriend frowned. Puzzled. "What?"

"The bag," Sam said. "Give it here."

It suddenly dawned on the girl what was happening. "You mean... you're... you're... like, robbing us?"

"Nope," Sam said. "I'm robbing the guy who was robbing you." He stretched his mouth into a wide grin, amused at his own joke. "You know – mugging the mugger."

Then he reached out and gently took the bag of loot from the boyfriend's hand. Turned to the girl, looking down at her. She was too spooked to move and just stood there under his steady gaze.

In the long silence that followed, her boyfriend said not a word. All bravery had drained from him, like a plug jerked from the sink.

Sam leaned down and sniffed the girl's hair. "Hmm," he said softly. "Nice."

He leaned in deeper, touching the top of her breasts with a single finger. The girl shivered, but didn't move. "Like ice cream," he said. "Vanilla."

The girl remained silent, just jumped a bit as he moved his finger up to stroke her face. "Maybe I'll give you a call a little later on," Sam said.

9

Allan Cole

Drowned Hopes

The girl didn't move, scared of what might happen, but determined not to do anything that might encourage him.

Grinning, Sam leaned in and kissed her on the lips. The girl trembled, but didn't flinch. Accepting the kiss, but being careful not to respond. Feeling like he could explode at any second.

Then Sam suddenly turned and strode off into the night.

The girl watched him go and when he was out of sight she scrubbed furiously at her lips. "Get me out of here," she told the boyfriend. "Right now."

But her boyfriend was looking down at the corpse. "Shit," he said. "We gotta call the cops."

"Are you crazy?" the girl said. "He's got our wallets. Our addresses. Let's get before he changes his mind and comes back."

At long last, the boyfriend came unstuck and the two leaped into the Jeep. He started it up in a panic, almost flooding the engine.

Then he jammed it into the wrong gear and the Jeep jerked backwards, bumping over the mugger's body.

"Shit, shit, shit," the girl said.

Then the kid finally got the Jeep straightened out and sped off into the night.

Allan Cole

CHAPTER TWO

THE STREET WAS JUMPIN' when the sleek limo cruised over the bridge and started to edge its way through the neighborhood crowd.

It was the beginning of a hot, summer weekend and the good people of Spanish Oaks Drive were putting on a block party to celebrate two days off from the perpetual blue collar grind of trading sweat for a precarious living.

Although it wasn't even noon, friends and neighbors were already out, getting ready for the night's festivities. Banners were being strung across the street, a bandstand was being set up at one end, and food booths were being knocked together. Lawn sales and garage sales were springing up – people were hoping to sell enough cast-offs to pay for the beer and barbecue, and what the hell, maybe even some lottery tickets at the local KWICK STOP where the stakes were up to twenty five million dreams.

Mainly, everybody was having one helluva good time, with kids shouting and darting around and generally getting underfoot. While the adults talked and worked, sipping at beer and wine, getting in the mood for the weekend. Playing over the whole thing was music from half-a-dozen nations and sporting events of every variety – from baseball to soccer – that blared from scores of car radios, boomboxes and portable TV's.

At first, nobody really noticed the limo. They were too busy working, gossiping and having fun. Then somebody got in the way of the driver and he beeped his horn and everybody turned to look.

Spanish Oaks Drive was a working class neighborhood in a working class city – Deercreek Beach. Limos were normally only seen hauling the rich along Federal Highway on their way to and from Lauderdale Airport and the super exclusive town of Boca Raton. People were slow to react so the driver had to tap his horn again and the crowd parted, letting him through, but not obsequiously so. They moved aside slowly, almost reluctantly, and tried to peer through the darkened windows to see who was inside.

A couple of kids made so bold as to slap the car's sides. But the adults in the crowd quickly reminded them of their manners and shooed them away. It was fine to be bold when the rich strayed into your neighborhood, but not so bold as to appear like barbarians. There wasn't a man or woman on the street who didn't know exactly what he or she would buy if they won the $25 million lottery. It would almost certainly include a limo and a driver. And they would not want to be trifled with by dirty-faced children whose parents were too ignorant to teach them decent manners.

Spanish Oaks Drive was a broad cul-de-sac, with its namesake trees shading both sides. A mixture of single family homes and small apartment buildings – all with backyards, vegetable gardens and a few with above ground pools – made up the neighborhood.

A larger, older apartment building – three stories high and painted in faded Florida colors – commanded the curve of the cul-de-sac. Framed by very old and very large oak trees, it seemed almost forbidding. Especially considering the formidable figure sitting on the front steps – Sam Barr.

He seemed more muscular than ever in his cutoffs and sleeveless tee-shirt. His arms were huge – with biceps you could break rocks on. His chest was prison-yard deep and his legs were cabled with thick muscle. But his face was unlined and he had a boyish smile he could turn on when he wanted to, softening the natural hardness of his features. His dark eyes were clear and intelligent and he kept his brown hair just long enough to be bobbed in the back with a tasty leather band. He wore a simple gold earring in his right ear and no other jewelry except a chrome-faced diving watch.

Sam watched the limo coming his way with great interest, popping handfuls of pills and washing them down with a half-gallon jug of orange juice. His interest became even more keen when the limo drew up in front of the apartment house and a uniformed chauffeur emerged. The chauffeur strode to the rear of the limo and opened the door. Not only Sam, but the entire neighborhood, paused to watch as the lone passenger emerged.

12

Allan Cole

Drowned Hopes

Ellen Berman didn't think of herself as elegant, but that's how the whole neighborhood – including Sam – viewed her as she stepped out of the limousine, her jeans' clad legs long and shapely.

She was a woman of indeterminate age. With "good bones," as some like to say. She had the figure and complexion of a younger woman and the bearing and the "finishing school" manner of someone in their third or fourth decade. If she had removed her fashionable sunglasses, her eyes would have looked sad and a little tired. Ellen wore her blond hair in a short, efficient cut. And because of her long legs she appeared tall. People were surprised when they stood next to her and realized she wasn't more than 5'5".

The women on the street ogled her clothes – a casual, traveling outfit that looked like it was right out of the pages of a fancy beauty parlor magazine. But the style was nothing any of those who perused such glossy pages had ever seen before.

The clothes spoke of "one-of-a-kind." And indeed they were. Ellen had not only designed, but had hand-crafted the embroidered jeans – with the subtle flower pattern – and matching jeans vest. Along with the plain white silk shirt she'd whipped out one morning on her sewing machine and the same went for the silken, multi-colored wisp of a scarf that went about her neck.

As she stood by the car, Ellen knew she was being stared at and judged. She also knew she looked as out of place in this neighborhood as the limo. But what could she do? She was a fugitive – from what, she couldn't say.

It certainly wasn't justice.

So, here she was and there was no going back. She'd have to make the best of it.

The chauffeur said, "I'll get your things, Ms. Berman." He popped the trunk and started to unload the few pieces of luggage that made up all of what remained of her worldly goods.

Besides the three suitcases, there were several long, sturdy tubes used to transport paintings; a collapsible easel; a few paint-spattered boxes and containers; bolts of unusually patterned cloth; and a portable sewing machine in a box. Except for the sewing machine, it

13

Allan Cole

was all a very weird assortment of possessions to bring to a place like Spanish Oaks Drive.

As the driver was unloading the trunk, the front door of the apartment building opened and an attractive – if blowsy-looking – woman emerged. She glanced at the things being piled beside the limo, then went straight to Ellen.

"Hi," she said, extending her hand. "I'm Ruth Castro. You must be my new tenant."

Ellen gripped the offered hand. "Pleased to meet you, Mrs. Castro," she said.

"Just call me Ruth and forget the Castro," her new landlady said. "My husband was Cuban. But he's dead now."

Ellen didn't quite know how to take this. But she managed to hide her confused reactions.

Ruth looked at the chauffeur, then pointed at the stuff he was piling up on the lawn. "Bottom floor, front," she said, directing him to Ellen's place.

The chauffeur sneered at her. Who was this trailer trash broad to tell him what to do? "My job ends at the sidewalk," he said with a look that was pure smart ass.

Ellen, well-aware of all the neighborhood eyes on her, tried to avoid a scene. "That's okay," she said to Ruth. "I can get it myself."

Sam strode up. He'd overheard the driver's insolence. His big hand shot out and enclosed the chauffeur's shoulder in a vise-like grip. At the same time, he leaned down and picked up one of the suitcases.

"The lady said bottom floor, front," he told the driver.

The driver winced in severe pain.

"Apartment six," Ruth said.

Sam squeezed harder, almost bringing the driver to his knees. But the chauffeur was so scared, he didn't dare make a peep.

"Did you hear what the lady said?" Sam asked.

The chauffeur nodded vigorously. "Yes… sir…" he gasped. "Apartment six."

14

Allan Cole

Sam nodded, shoved the suitcase into the guy's gut and let go. Immediately, the driver started grabbing other pieces of luggage and hauled ass into the apartment building.

Ellen smiled at Sam in gratitude. "Thank you, Mister – uh..."

She looked at Ruth for help and the landlady finally collected her manners together enough to step into the breach.

"This big hunk of lovin' is Sam Barr," she said, a look of supreme proprietary interest on her face. Then to Sam she said, "This is your new neighbor, Ellen Berman."

Barr eyed Ellen with appreciation. "My pleasure," he said.

He popped more pills, brushed off his hand, then held it out. Ellen nervously took it.

Feeling awkward as hell, she said, all-too formally, "How do you do?"

Barr nodded. Released her hand, fished out some more pills, then washed them down with orange juice. Ellen eyed the pills, a little shocked. Barr noticed and chuckled at the suspicions in her mind.

"Have to get my regular doses of aminos," he said.

Ellen looked at him, puzzled. Sam flexed a huge bicep. "They're like vitamins," he said. "Help with my workouts."

Ellen understood what he was saying and blushed, embarrassed at her suspicions. "Oh, yes... workouts," she said. "You're a physical culturist, Mr. Barr?"

Sam liked that. This was one classy woman. He smiled again, saying, "That's what I am, all right. Sam Barr - physical culturist."

Sam made a slight bow, then returned to the front steps, where he took up his previous position of ease. Ellen's curious eyes followed him. It was a curiosity not appreciated by Ruth.

She ostentatiously cleared her throat. "About the rent," she said.

Ellen had a minor panic attack. "But I mailed it to you," she said. "First and last, plus the deposit you requested. It was a money order for two thousand, five hundred-"

Ruth broke in, putting on the pressure. "Never got it," she said.

Allan Cole

Now panic was really setting. "But it was a money order," Ellen said. She started digging in her purse. "I have the receipt for it in here somewhere."

Ruth gave Ellen a shrewd look. She could see that panic city was about to overtake her new tenant. For some reason, that made her feel a little better about things.

"Calm down, Ellen," she said, very soothing. "I can call you Ellen, cant' I?"

"Of course you may," Ellen said. She was still frantically digging in her purse.

Ruth stopped her. "Never mind that," she said. "Today's mail didn't come yet. It's sort of a holiday weekend, you know? But not official. It's Cinco de something down in South America, or Mexico, you know? Like the banks and post office will still be working on Monday, kind of holiday. Hey, don't worry. We'll get it cleared up later, okay?"

Ellen nodded gratefully. "Okay," she said.

Ruth took her by the arm and led her toward the building. "Come on," she said. "I'll show you your new place."

As they approached the front porch, Sam nodded at Ellen pleasantly. Ruth opened the door and motioned for Ellen to go first.

At the same time, she leaned in close to whisper, "Hand's off... He's mine."

Ellen was startled, blurting, "Oh, Sure. Sure."

As she went inside Sam eyed her trim figure wrapped in such tasty clothes. "Nice," he said softly.

Then chauffeur lumbered up the steps, bags under his arm. He gave Sam a wary look.

"Boo," Sam said.

The guy paled and rushed inside.

Sam laughed. This was getting to be a pretty damned good day.

16

Allan Cole

CHAPTER THREE

APARTMENT SIX WAS nice enough in a "For Rent-Furnished" sort of way.

The furniture was nondescript, the carpets elderly but cared for. And the walls were decorated with yard sale prints – some of which might have been okay, except they were badly framed. But the place was quite clean, Ellen noted. Not a speck of dust or cobweb in sight. And it smelled fresh, as if it had just been sprayed with a lemony scent.

"Be it ever so humble," Ruth said, waving a hand to take in the apartment.

Ellen kept a poker face as she looked around. The yard sale prints put her teeth on edge. "Very nice, thank you," she said. "I'm sure I'll be comfortable here."

She didn't entirely fool Ruth. "Used to much better, huh?" her new landlady said.

Ellen was embarrassed. "No, honestly," she said. "It really is very nice. I'll have it looking like Ellen's Place in no time."

"That a relief," Ruth said. "For minute there I thought you hated it."

And Ellen realized that her poker face hadn't really been up to snuff. "Please forgive me," she said. "I'm dirty and tired from traveling and I was only looking at the apartment as a nice clean place where I could take a nice hot shower."

Ruth nodded understanding. "I'm a clean freak, myself," she said.

"It was really the very first thing I noticed," Ellen said, making certain she nodded approvingly at dust free corners and dirt free carpets.

Ruth smiled at her, mollified. She started to speak, but then stopped so she could step aside and let the chauffeur dump the last of Ellen's stuff on the floor. Then, without word, the man got the hell out of there as fast as he could.

Ruth laughed at his undignified exit. "He's scared Sam's going to show up and criticize his work," she said.

Ellen almost said something clever, then realized Ruth probably wouldn't get it, plus there was a very good chance she'd be insulted as well.

Instead she said, "You've both been most hospitable... Thank you."

"Tell the truth," Ruth said, "I've never done a rental like this. Sight unseen on both sides. Everything by long distance phone and overseas mail."

She gave Ellen a look. "Jamaica, right?" she said. "Your last address, I mean."

"Right," Ellen said. "Jamaica."

Ruth waited a second and when nothing more was forthcoming, she said, "I didn't know you from Adam. Still don't."

Again, Ellen remained silent. She felt uncomfortable at the clumsy attempt to prod into her affairs.

Ruth laughed – silly me. Quite aware she'd made things uneasy. "On the other hand," Ruth said, trying to make a joke out of it, "I'm not acquainted with Adam, either."

Ellen smiled politely, but didn't reply.

Ruth looked at the easel and painting gear heaped by the window. "You an artist?" she asked.

"I like to think so," Ellen said, feeling a little guilty for acting so reserved. "I had a gallery in Jamaica," she continued. "It was just getting popular when I had to... uh... you know – leave."

"Had to split in a hurry, did you?" Ruth said, an all-knowing smile on her lips.

"There was just... you know... a business misunderstanding," Ellen said, clearly uncomfortable.

Ruth gave her a woman of the world look. "I hear you, honey," she said. "Didn't mean to pry. Hells bells. There's nothing Ruth Castro doesn't know about business misunderstandings. Been on my own since my husband died and I tell you, it's shameful how ready people are to cheat a woman alone. You really have to watch yourself, you know?"

18

Allan Cole

Ellen started to warm to Ruth. "Absolutely," she said. "I never realized... until.. well... recently... what some people are capable of. I suppose I was naïve."

Ruth eyed her speculatively. "That was quite a car you showed up in," she said." The neighbors have never seen anything like it. Me neither, as a matter of fact."

"I hope I didn't give them the wrong impression," Ellen said. "My brother arranged for the car to pick me up at the airport."

"By arranged, you mean he paid for it?" Ruth asked.

Ellen laughed. "He'd better," she said. "I don't have that kind of money. Especially after... well, you know... Jamaica."

"The business misunderstanding?" Ruth said.

"Yes, it was, um-"

Loud music from outside suddenly blared, interrupting her. Ellen shut the window, cutting the sound, then decided not to go on.

"There's a street party tonight," Ruth said. "Check it out, if you want. Meet some of the neighbors."

"Thanks," Ellen said. "I'll do that."

Ruth started to leave, then stopped in the doorway. "About Sam," she said. "He'll probably come on to you. You know how men are." She said that as a statement, not a question.

Ellen smiled in friendly understanding. "I should just slap his face and send him home, right?" she said.

Ruth suddenly became very serious. "Oh, honey," she said. "You don't want to slap a man like Sam Barr. Not ever."

Allan Cole

CHAPTER FOUR

RUTH WENT OUT the door, shutting it carefully behind her.

Ellen stared blankly around the room, emotion building up – piling onto her travel weariness. Her hands suddenly started to shake. Then she very deliberately forced calm.

"Come on, girl," she said. "Get a grip,"

Then she turned, really looking around the living room, now. Trying to think positive thoughts. But the place felt so closed in, she could hardly get a breath. The air conditioner thundered on and the oppression became even more unbearable.

Ellen went to the main living room window and threw it open, breathing in the breeze that flowed in – feeling stimulated, no matter how hot and humid the day. She could smell the salt air from the nearby beach and the tropical perfume of the foliage that grew along banks of the neighborhood canal. Just outside her window she was presented with a large tree, with many fern-like branches that shaded the extensive garden.. To her delight, the whole tree was shot with fabulous red blossoms. Ellen drank in the color in along with the fresh, tangy air.

Somewhere down the street a Jimmy Cliff song was playing: "You can get it if you really want. You can get it if you really want…"

Ellen smiled and turned back into the room, humming the song.

The picture over the couch caught her eye. It was a pseudo last century Saturday Evening Post thing: a boy and a dog napping under a tree. It was so ugly it made her laugh.

While she studied it and thought, she sang, "But you must try, try and try… Try and try…"

Ellen came to some sort of a decision about the print. She went to the couch, stepped up on the pillows and gingerly lifted the picture off its hanger.

Then she went to one of the mailing tubes and popped off the end. She shook out a large poster and unrolled it, revealing a fabulous tropical montage swirling with fiery colors – not too unlike the tree outside her window. She found some tacks in one of the boxes and stuck the poster up on the wall, singing as she worked.

She stood back to admire the effect. The poster was an advertisement for the opening of her former gallery in Jamaica. But advertisement or not, it wouldn't have taken more than one glance to confirm that Ellen was a very talented artist indeed.

The caption on the poster read: Catch A Fire At Ellen's World. And almost as if it were ordained, the music outside changed to Bob Marley's "Catch A Fire."

Ellen smiled as she heard the refrain, bending her head to listen to the haunting words and music float through the window. "... The table is turn, baby, now; Catch a fire...

She studied the poster, then nodded to herself. "And you don't even have a damned brain tumor, Ellen," she said. "So what the hell are you complaining about?"

She got busy, unpacking her things and putting them away, singing softly to herself: "You can get it if you really want... really want... really want..."

The block party really started heating up when night came. Barricades were set up to stop cars, colorful lights were strung across the road, smoky barbecues were crammed with good things to eat and washtubs and coolers were packed with good things to drink.

Kids were shouting, tossing balls and chasing each other. Skateboarders were doing minor tricks like curb hops, warming up their bearings. Adults were either joining in on the games, or drinking and carrying on, getting ready for the real action.

On the bandstand, a local garage band was tuning up and already several teenagers were trying out some new dance steps. And in the shadows, several others were smoking a little grass and nipping a little beer. The boys showing off, the girls laughing.

In front of Ellen's building, Sam captained a big barbecue grill, flipping oversize burgers and swigging from a bottle of orange juice. A knock-out girl in a thong bikini was nuzzling up to him and Sam was clearly enjoying her moves. He whispered something in her ear

21

Allan Cole

and she giggled and shook her head. Sam whispered again – more giggling and head shaking.

Finally, he set the spatula down, took the girl firmly by the elbow and escorted her to a little alleyway between the apartment building and the adjoining house.

She did not protest.

A moment later Ruth emerged. She looked at the untended barbecue. Then up and down the street, searching for Sam.

She called out, "Sam? Sam?"

There was no response.

She frowned at the untended burgers, some of which were starting to burn. Ruth hurried to the grill and started turning the meat over and shuffling the patties around. The fire flamed up, burning her fingers. She eeked and dropped the spatula, sucking on her fingers.

"Damn him," she said.

Inside Apartment Six, Ellen had put on a burst of energy and totally transformed the place. The walls were covered with her artwork, the easel placed by the big window that overlooked the back yard. Swatches of colorful fabric hid the ugliness of the furniture.

Pleasantly tired from her efforts, Ellen had adjourned to the shower to wash away nearly twenty-four hours of hard travel.

When she was done, she cut the water, grabbed a towel and stepped out onto the tile floor. At the mirror, she rubbed the steam off and studied her image for a minute. Then she looked very sternly at herself and shook a finger at the mirror.

"We're getting a whole new start, right, girl?" She laughed. "Even if I don't have a Mary Tyler Moore beret to throw…"

A sudden thump against the outside wall startled her and she whirled around to see what had happened. Nothing showed itself. Just the blank wall and the closed bathroom window. Then there was another loud thump. Boom. Right up against the wall. Then another.

Allan Cole

The rhythm became all too familiar and disturbing. Annoyed, Ellen went to the bathroom window and cracked it open. The thumps became louder.

"Hello," she called out. "Who's there?"

The thumps continued.

Ellen started to become angry. "Get away from there, you hear me?" she demanded. "I'll tell your mother."

Someone laughed. Ellen couldn't tell if it was a man or a woman laughing. She started to become nervous and she backed out of the bathroom, the towel pulled tight around her.

Ruth moodily filled plates for neighbors, nodding when they spoke to her, but hearing nothing that was said. She kept looking around, trying to spot Sam.

Ellen came out. She'd changed into stone-washed jeans shorts, decorated with small hand-sewn wild flowers. She wore a matching blouse, tying the ends to show off her narrow waist and girlishly flat belly. Her bare feet were shod in simple leather sandals.

For a moment, Ruth hated her for looking so good. So classy. She didn't notice the edgy look in Ellen's eyes.

"Have you seen Sam?" Ruth snapped, very accusatory.

Ellen was taken aback by her tone. "No," was all she said.

"He didn't come knocking at your door, asking if maybe you needed something," Ruth demanded.

"Certainly not," Ellen said, getting a bit miffed. "As a matter of fact I was just taking a shower, when-"

Loud laughter interrupted Ellen's complaint. It came from behind her. She and Ruth turned to see Sam and the girl emerging from the alleyway. They both spotted Ruth, who was staring daggers at them.

Sam held up several large avocados, as if they were some sort of an explanation. He strolled over to the grill, while the girl made herself scarce.

"Little Kimberly there wanted to see your avocado tree," Sam said.

"Avocados, huh?" Ruth said angrily.

23

Allan Cole

"Sure, baby," Sam said. "How else can we make guacamole?"

He chuckled, as if he'd just made some sort of a joke. He juggled the avocados, quite skillfully, Ellen thought. Then he handed them to her with a flourish. She was so surprised, she almost dropped them.

"You know how to make guacamole, don't you Ellen?" he said with a wink.

Ellen gave a nervous laugh. "I'm afraid I missed that issue of Martha Stewart Magazine," she said.

"Is that so?" Sam said, and now he was tired of his own jokes and started to lose interest. He stretched and gave an elaborate yawn. "I think I'll go take a little nap," he said.

Sam leaned forward and kissed Ruth on the cheek. Then strolled off. Ruth stared after him – absolutely furious. Ellen tried to pretend that she hadn't noticed anything out of the ordinary.

Finally, Ruth sighed philosophically, gave a little laugh and went back to flipping burgers. "I shouldn't get so mad at him," she said. "He's like a little boy. Wants everything he sees."

She shifted some patties around. "It's those bitches like Kimberly who are to blame," she said. "Wagging their bikini thong asses at him all the time. What's he gonna do? He's a man, isn't he?"

Ellen didn't say anything. She glanced at the avocados Sam had given her. For some reason or other, the sight of them made her skin crawl. She shivered – ugh – and got rid of them quickly, dumping the fruit on a fold-out camping table.

"How long have you and Sam been together?" she asked, casually as she could.

"Six months," Ruth said. "Ever since he got out of prison."

Ellen tried to hide her shocked reaction, but without much success. "Prison?"

"Sure," Ruth said. "Where'd you think he got those hunky muscles?"

Ellen didn't know how to respond to a statement like that.

"I know what you're thinking," Ruth said. "You're wondering what he was in for."

Allan Cole

"Well, I have to confess that I'm just a weenie bit curious," Ellen said with a nervous laugh.

"He was a bank robber," Ruth said. "Not a common thug, but a real class act, you know?"

"Uh... well... I suppose so... sure..." was Ellen's inept reply.

"He's not into that line of work anymore," Ruth said. "Besides making all those nice muscles, he got himself two years worth of college credits while he was in prison."

"I see," Ellen said, not really knowing what kind of comment was called for.

"Soon as he gets enough money saved, he going to get his degree," Ruth continued.' You watch and see. Sam is a determined man. He's going places, that's for sure."

"Very admirable," Ellen said.

"He's gonna get his degree in psychology," Ruth said. "Then open a clinic to help troubled kids."

"What kind of work does Sam do now?" Ellen asked.

Ruth shrugged, then waggled an open hand. "Little of this and a little of that," she said. You know... self employed. He does very well, believe me. He's a real go-getter."

"I'm sure he is," Ellen said. "Sam certainly has the appearance of... uh... an industrious man."

If Ellen had looked up right then she'd have gotten an idea of just how industrious Sam was.

Because at that very moment he was in her apartment, peering out at her through a gap in the curtains.

Allan Cole

CHAPTER FIVE

SAM CHUCKLED AT the little trick he'd played Ellen, then turned away, letting the curtains fall back in place. He strolled over to the couch and studied the "Catch A Fire" poster hanging on the wall. He checked the artist's signature on the right hand corner, noting that it was Ellen's.

"Not bad," he said, nodding approval.

Then he moved around the room, picking up things, examining them and humming a little tune to himself.

He entered the bathroom, spotted the open window and went to it, sticking his head out, looking this way and that.

When his head came back in he had a big smile on his face. "Naughty boy," he said.

Sam opened the medicine cabinet. Popped it open, picked up each item one by one, looking them over.

He even examined the toothbrush and tested the toothpaste tube to see if it were real, and not one of those hollowed out things they sold in dope shops.

Sam continued his search, moving to the two drawers in the vanity. Finally, he drew back, disappointed. "Ellen, Ellen," he said. "What do you do about birth control, woman?"

He exited the bathroom and tried her bedroom next, switching on the light. Several of Ellen's tropical paintings were hung on the walls and there was a colorful bolt of cloth thrown over the bed.

Sam tried the bureau top, opening a small jewelry case and pawing through Ellen's keepsakes – examining each item with an expert's eye. He sighed. Nothing of value there. Then he started checking out each bureau drawer. He found where she kept her underwear and fingered the filmy material.

"Better and better," he said.

He dug under the underwear and came up with something. He held it to the light and saw that it was a diaphragm case.

"That's my girl," he said.

He opened it, examined the contents, pulling out the diaphragm and snapping it like a rubber band. Sam giggled like a boy, then wet a finger and swept it around the inside of the diaphragm. Eyes closed he sucked on the finger.

"Delicious," he murmured.

Then he put everything back and returned the case to its place in the drawer. Sam perked up his ears. He heard the sound of a door opening and closing and someone coming into the apartment.

Quickly, he cut the light and flipped a long knife out, the blade gleaming in the light streaming through the open bedroom door.

Sam moved closer to the door. Through the crack, he could see Ellen moving around the room, a cellphone cradled against her ear.

Ellen paced, puffing angrily on a cigarette while the phone rang on the other side. No one answered for a time, then a machine voice came on, declaring that nobody was home.

"Pick up the damned phone, Harry," Ellen growled. "It's your sister."

She waited, but there was no response.

"Damn you, Harry," she finally said. "Answer the stupid phone. You know why I'm calling. I need my money right now. No more excuses."

She turned away from the bedroom door and Sam's face appeared in the crack, eyes glittering with interest.

Ellen stubbed out the cigarette, smashing it into an ashtray. "Jesus Christ, Harry," she said to the answering machine. "You've got me living in some dump with an ex-con and his god damned gun moll girlfriend."

Still nothing, just the beep of the answering machine.

"You hear me, Harry," Ellen demanded. "You'd better pick up the phone. I won't stand for this one more minute-"

Ellen ran out of steam in mid-sentence. She snapped the phone shut and dumped it on the couch. She lit another cigarette and started pacing again. Smoking and pacing. She stopped in front of the poster

Allan Cole

and frowned. Reached out to touch the surface as if the poster had been interfered with.

Then she shook her head. "What in hell am I going to do?" she said.

Ellen put out the cigarette, started to get another, but the pack was empty. She crumpled it and went to the bedroom. Pushed the half-closed door open and walked in. She snapped on the light, then crossed to the bureau and opened a drawer to get out another pack.

Suddenly she stopped.

Something about the jewelry box caught her attention. Frowning, she opened it and fingered the contents. Satisfied everything was there, she closed the box. Then her hand went to her underwear drawer. More frowns. As if she sensed something was amiss.

She opened the drawer, moved things around. Then shook her head. Sighing, she slid the drawer shut.

Ellen crossed to the closet, where the door was partway open. She reached out, as if to open it wider and get something from inside.

Instead she gave the door a violent shove and it slammed shut. "Harry, you asshole," she said.

Ellen hurried out of the room, snapping off the light as she exited. There were sounds of her storming across the living room, the front door opening, then slamming shut.

A moment later the closet door slowly came open and Sam stepped out, the gleaming butterfly knife in his hand.

He chuckled, flipped it shut with an expert snap of his wrist and exited the room.

Allan Cole

CHAPTER SIX

THE BLOCK PARTY was going full blast when Ellen emerged from the building.

She strolled through the crowd, trying to forget her troubles. Forcing smiles at the playing children, sniffing at the cooking food, trying to enjoy the companionship of all the happy people.

Ellen paused at the bandstand and swayed to the hot Spanish rock rhythms of the local group, really making herself get into the mood. Around her, people were dancing and down the street kids were shooting off fireworks. Lovers were ducking into the shadows of the trees to embrace and soon Ellen felt herself relax and her lips parted into a smile.

Over by the bandstand someone noticed her, and her smile, and stepped away from the crowd.

This is my natural state, Ellen thought, spreading her arms like a bird.. I'm not an old gloomy Gus. I always try to look on the bright of things.

An image from Monty Python's "Life Of Bryan," leaped into her head. The men hanging from the cross, doing Busby Berkley kicks while they whistled and sang: "Always look on the bright side of life…"

Ellen started laughing, but an old woman gave her a strange look and Ellen choked it off the best she could. You weren't allowed to look too happy. Or laugh inappropriately. They put you away for such indiscretions.

Even so, she was still grinning at her own private joke when she reached the barricade at the street's entrance. She didn't notice the shadowy figure that broke away from the crowd at the bandstand to follow her.

Ellen passed several yard sales where people were gossiping about the neighbors and bargaining good-naturedly over prices.

Drowned Hopes

It was darker near the barricade and off in the distance she heard the music of an ice cream truck. Ellen stepped out of the way when two laughing kids burst from the darkness, dripping ice cream cones in their hands.

"Yum, that looks good," she said.

One of the kids – a little girl – pointed beyond the barricade. "He's right down there," she said. "Better hurry if you want some."

The children ran off.

Ellen laughed, then stepped past the barricade, thinking she could use a little sweet stuff to maintain her cheery attitude. As she moved off in the darkness, the shadowy figure followed.

She walked over the bridge - then down a long dark avenue that ran through thick tropical foliage - and just where another street intersected she found the ice cream truck. A young man dressed in the traditional white ice cream man uniform with a cap and a bill, was serving a few kids. The requests were mostly for tropical freezes that Ellen had never heard of.

When it was her turn she gave him a little girl's smile and asked, "Do you guys still make Eskimo Pies?"

The ice cream man laughed. "Sure we do, lady," he said. "Here you go."

He dug an Eskimo pie out of the freezer and handed it over. Ellen paid him. "Enjoy," he said.

Then he hopped in the truck and drove off, music playing. Ellen watched him go. She unwrapped the ice cream and took a large bite.

"Ambrosia, thy name is Eskimo Pie," she said.

Then she started back toward the bridge and Spanish Oaks Drive.

But as she passed a thick clump of bushes, someone leaped out and grabbed her from behind.

Ellen struggled and tried to scream, but the attacker was too strong, muffling her cries with a dirty towel. He dragged her back into the bushes. Ellen kicked and thrashed, but it was no use.

Deep in the underbrush, her attacker forced her to the ground. Finding her chance, she raked the son of a bitch's face with her nails, drawing blood.

30

Allan Cole

Pissed, the guy reared back to punch her. He was gonna mash her face, knock out her teeth, bust her dirty bitch's nose.

But before he could strike, a muscular hand shot out of the darkness, grabbing the attacker by the offending arm and jerking him to his feet. Ellen heard several loud thumps and then she saw the man hanging there, held up by the enormous fist of Sam Barr.

Sam punched the would-be rapist with his other hand and blood spurted from the man's mouth.

"Goddamn freak," Sam said. He hit the guy again and it was so hard Ellen could hear the sound of bones breaking.

Sam dropped the guy and gave him a kick. The man groaned. Sam kicked him again. Then his slender butterfly knife came out and he grabbed the man by the hair and pulled his head back, exposing his throat.

Ellen gasped, "Sam, don't."

Surprised, Sam let the rapist go.

Immediately, the man scrambled to his feet and limped away as fast as he could.

Sam stared after him, wanting to follow. "Nothing I hate more than a pervert," he said.

Then he looked over at Ellen. She was trying to straighten her clothes, but to little avail. They were ripped and torn and looked – well, like somebody had just tried to rape her.

Sam took pity on her. He was wearing an oversized Hawaiian shirt. He stripped it off and handed it Ellen. His big chest and arm muscles gleamed in the moonlight. Sam flexed just a little, showing them off.

To his disappointment, Ellen took no notice of his physique. Gratefully, she pulled his shirt on over the tattered clothes. It was so big she could wear it as a very roomy dress.

"I don't know how I can..." she started to say, but then her voice broke and she wept. Sam knelt beside her. Ellen waved him away. Then got herself under control. "I'll be okay," she said.

"Sure you will," Sam agreed. Then he said, "Look, I'm sorry about this. It's really not a bad neighborhood. Nice people. I guess

Allan Cole

the party drew that creep onto our turf." He grimaced. "Like mosquitoes hunt a crowd, but worse."

Ellen climbed to her feet, determined to get her act together. She brushed the shirt down, straightening out the wrinkles she'd made. It fell well below her knees.

She looked up at the big man. "I'm sure they are all absolutely wonderful people," she said firmly.

Ellen took a deep, shuddering breath. "It's a good thing you happened along," she said.

Sam shrugged. "Spotted that creep spookin' up the path," he said. "Figured he was up to something. Guess I figured right."

He offered Ellen his arm. She took it and they started to walk back toward the block party. The music and crowd sounds grew louder and Ellen gave a shaky little laugh.

"I really owe you an apology," she said.

"For what?" Sam asked.

"When we met I made a snap judgment," she said. "And I was wrong."

Sam smiled. "Ruth probably helped you along with that snap judgment," he said. Told you about my ill-spent youth, right? And you were wondering what you'd gotten yourself into. Moving next door to an ex-con."

Ellen grimaced. "Something like that," she said.

"It's not a bad way to think," he said. "Very few ex-cons remain 'exes' for long. I could tell you stories that would… Well, it's no time to talk about Sam Barr's theories on the criminal justice system."

"For a minute there I thought you were going to kill that man," Ellen said.

Sam shrugged. "For a minute there, so did I," he said.

"I wanted you to, I'm ashamed to admit," Ellen said. She gave a nervous laugh. "But only for that theoretical minute."

"Nothing to be ashamed of, theoretical or otherwise," Sam said.

They reached the apartment house again and Ruth frowned when she saw that Sam was bare-chested and Ellen was wearing Sam's shirt.

32

Allan Cole

She looked Ellen up and down, noting her tousled appearance. "What's going on here?" she said suspiciously.

"Ellen just met some asshole on the way to the ice cream truck," Sam said. "Nearly got herself raped, is what is going on." He snorted. "Jesus, Ruthie," he said. "You gotta lighten up."

Ruth was embarrassed. She went to Ellen, concerned as hell and feeling like shit for behaving the way she had. "Are you okay, honey?" she asked in her most sisterly tones.

Ellen nodded, but tears welled up. She was starting to feel sorry for herself.

"Come on, honey," Ruth said, pulling Ellen toward the front door. "Let's get rid of those things and put on something fresh. And then we'll get you a nice, strong drink."

Soothed by Ruth's mothering, Ellen let her take command. "Thanks, Ruthie," she said.

Then she stopped, remembering – "Did the money come?"

"What money?" Ruth asked.

"The money order," Ellen said. "For the rent."

Ruth gave her a big smile. "Oh, sure it did," she said. "See. I told you. Nothing to worry about at all."

Then she led Ellen through the front door, Sam staring thoughtfully after them.

"You are one lucky son of a bitch, Sam Barr," he murmured.

Allan Cole

CHAPTER SEVEN

ELLEN SPENT THE remainder of the weekend restlessly pacing the apartment. She unpacked her paints, stretched and prepared a new canvas, which she set up on the easel. The she cleaned her brushes, wiped off her palette, rinsed out a spare water glass. When she was finished she did the whole thing over again.

Anything to avoid actual work.

She even considered reorganizing her paint boxes, then admonished herself for acting like an amateur - an artist wannabe with not an ounce of courage and certainly lacking focus.

Monday morning she finally took the large step of loading one of her brushes with color, then standing before the picture window, to stare out at the large tree in the backyard. She didn't know what kind it was – only that it appeared very old, with a thick trunk and heavy, twisted limbs.

Despite its age, the tree's canopy was healthy and bright tropical green. But more amazing still were the hundreds upon hundreds of bright red blossoms that stood out from all that green. It was almost like a kid's painting of a fruit tree, with big daubs of red among the green.

Ellen looked closer, noting that the blossoms had yellow centers.

Then she pulled back, looking again at the basic structure of the tree. Undressing it, until it was only an old tree. She leaned forward and touched the paintbrush to the glass and sketched a faint outline of the tree on the window. Suddenly, she broke away and moved quickly to her easel, where the blank canvas sat, waiting… impatient for Ellen to take charge.

Ellen hesitated, intimidated by that unblemished expanse. Then a determined look transformed her face and then her body language. And she sprang at that canvas – at first, as if it were an opponent.

But then as a lover, stroking, smoothing, adding and subtracting…
until after a long time it seemed nearly complete.

She stepped back.

A fabulous still of vibrant tropical life had emerged from the
canvas after three long hours of labor.

Ellen smiled at first, then frowned. Her brush hand kept going to
back to the tree. Something was missing. Something was wrong.

She felt terribly frustrated. "What damn, you?" she said to the
painting. "What are you trying to tell me?"

The cell phone rang, jarring her. She looked around the room,
bewildered at first, then spotted her cell phone sitting on a nearby
table. Mood broken and disgusted, she threw the brush down and
strode over to the table.

She picked up the phone and flipped it open. "Yes?" she said,
very abrupt.

Then her eyes widened in surprise as she heard the voice. "Oh,
it's you, Harry," she said.

She listened some more, face full of suspicion. "I don't need
lunch at your club, Harry," she said. "What I need is my money. "

More listening. Frown marks creasing her forehead. The anger
building. Then –"Don't start with me, Harry," she said. "Just do the
right thing for a change."

But Harry started to motormouth, cutting her off. Finally, she
sighed. "Okay, Harry," she said, she said. "As always, you win. I'll
see you at one o'clock. And never mind the stupid limo. I'll get
myself there, if you don't mind."

She cut the connection.

Then she stood there – very still – emotions boiling.

Ellen closed her eyes, holding the cell phone to her breast like a
child. Breathing in and out, getting herself under control.

Then she looked at the painting. Sudden hatred flared. "What
shit," she said.

And she grabbed a brush loaded with red pigment and slashed a
large "X" across the painting.

"Not," she shouted.

"Not. Not. Not."

35

Allan Cole

CHAPTER EIGHT

SAM HAD A CLASSIC 1973 Mustang convertible pulled up in front of the building.

He had the hood popped, his hands and arms deep in the engine, singing along to a Charlie Ryan rock-a-billy song on the stereo: "Well, I wound it up to 110; Twisted the speedometer cable right off the end...."

Barr swiveled his hips like Elvis as he sang, getting in the groove for a day he was certain was filled with opportunity. "Had my foot glued right to the floor; I said, "That's all there is - there ain't no more..."

The Mustang had been ripped off an antique dealer's lot up in Alabama by a car thief Sam had met in the slammer. When the guy had come around to brag about his score, Sam had in turn ripped the car thief off, thumping him liberally about the head and shoulders until he made himself scarce. Remembering the look on the asshole's bloody face, Sam choked with laughter. Then he stepped back and viewed his handiwork with more than a little pride.

All he had to now do was monkey with the numbers, fix some stuff the asshole dealer in Alabama had tried to foist off on the unsuspecting public, and he'd clear a good ten grand, no questions asked, from a Broward County deputy he knew who had a hard-on for old Mustangs.

He was about to let loose with another verse of "Hot Rod Lincoln," when he heard the front door of the apartment building bang open and looked up to see Ellen charge out, very pissed looking. Before the door closed, there was light streaming in from the hall behind her and with her thin summer dress Ellen was revealed as if she'd been stripped naked.

What a sexy lady, Sam thought. He wouldn't mind making time with her. Jesus but it'd be intriguing to get past that classy armor she wore. Dig down, see what kind of a woman she was beneath it all.

Drowned Hopes

Then he decided to pretend he didn't notice her and really give Ellen a hip-swingin' rock 'n roll show. He leaned over to turn up the music but to his disappointment, a cab pulled up in front – horn beeping - and Ellen ran across the lawn to it... feminine as could be with a gracefully arced wrist... fabulous legs set off in high heels... and that the frothy summer frock that floated around her sweet figure.

Ellen spotted Sam, waved to him and jumped in. She was so gorgeous – so innocent and ready to be fleeced by a man like him, that Sam almost groaned aloud.

He made up his mind on the spot. As the cab pulled away, making a U turn to get out of the cul-de-sac, he slammed the hood shut, jumped in the Mustang and fired it up. The engine boomed deep and rich. Damn, you had to love Old Shelby.

Sam waited until the cab reached the turn, saw it go left, then followed.

Ellen looked out the window as the cab cruised north along A1A. The coastal road went past some of the most exclusive seashore developments in the world, including gated mansions owned by corporate chieftains presently defending themselves before the U.S. Congress and many, many Federal courts.

There were also fabulous glimpses of the Atlantic sparkling under the noonday sun, with surfers playing on the waves, and surfer girls in skimpy bikinis prancing along the shoreline.

It gratified Ellen to see that a good many of those tiny bikinis were now being presented on surfboards, instead of solely in the cheer-leading sand zone. She envied the new generation. But then again – when she thought about it – she would have hated to go through the whole young adult routine again just to join the current, "grrls must have fun" craze.

Then the taxi turned off the highway onto a broad, private road that led up to the Boca Raton Country Club. There were two clubs, actually. One on the beach that looked like it was out of the pages of the Arabian Nights, and this one – a tower peering out over the

37

Allan Cole

Intercoastal waterway, which meandered from the Keys to the Carolinas.

Ellen had been here before – but it was long ago, and with her parents – so she looked to see if anything had changed. The guard shack, standing under the flowered trees was the same. Only the guards had changed – handsome-looking black men, smart in their tailored uniforms. Ellen thought they looked like islanders – to her the men and women from the islands always seemed to have a wistful, look on their faces when they were away from home.

The long, winding drive to the club was the same as before. As was the shocking first view of the Boca Club: The tower was, pink! pink! pink! The most glorious example of bad taste in architecture that Ellen had ever seen.

The alleged architect – one Addison Mizner – had been one of those early Twentieth Century rogues who had a talent for charming respectable people out of their money for the most appalling mounds of construction. Although Mizner had no professional standing as an architect he'd managed to bribe a license from the State of Florida – a special bill was passed by the Legislature making allowances that only applied to Mizner – and he'd parlayed this, plus the friendship of a Singer sewing machine heir, to a fortune of his own in real estate.

At that time Boca was only accessible by sea and the land was virtually worthless – but Mizner was such a salesmen that the town soon became a Mecca for rich Easterners. Ellen recalled that Mizner had excused his choice of a perfidious life to a comely magazine reporter as follows: "You don't necessarily have to work hard at making money legitimately… but you do have to work continuously. And I despise working hard, much less harder than my fellow."

Whenever she thought of Mizner – which wasn't that often, to be sure – she had to admire him for his cunning. For example: Boca Raton sounded like such a romantic name for a city. A name created for the tourist trade. But in fact, it was Spanish for "Rat's Mouth," because that was what the rough-edged bay had looked like to the Spanish pirates who had plagued the area for years.

Allan Cole

Drowned Hopes

That's your trouble, Ellen, she thought as the cab pulled up to the entrance, and a doorman rushed over to help her out – always stuck in the middle; afraid to get off the fence.

With a little guts and very few scruples, you too could transform a disgusting name into a glamorous retreat for rich tourists.

When Sam saw Ellen's cab turn off to the Boca Club he felt well-rewarded for his spur of the moment decision to follow her.

He pulled up to the curb some distance from the guard shack that watched over the entrance and observed the security man check his list for Ellen's name, then wave the cab through.

"Getting better and better," Sam muttered, shutting off his engine.

Sexy though this lady may be, he had to remember that she most assuredly represented a business opportunity – an opportunity he was still examining. Sam popped a handful of amino tabs and washed them down with a jug of orange juice from the little cooler sitting next to him on the seat.

He double-checked the cooler and smiled. There was plenty of OJ.

Sam hit the MP3 player button and punched up another car song, Sir Mack Rice's "Mustang Sally."

He sang along with the music: "All you wanna do is ride around, Sally - Ride Sally ride… "

The maitre-de escorted Ellen across a luxurious dining room, with ice sculpted swans decorating the long buffet tables and chefs with tall hats helping people to their food.

The room looked out over the Intercoastal and through the big windows, Ellen could see yachts and sailboats cruising the sparkling waters, all with beautiful people aboard.

But the fabulous view was lost on Ellen and her mood took a sharp, nasty turn as the maitre-de came to a stop. The table she'd been escorted to held only a single person – one Rachel Berman.

Rachel was posed like she was waiting for a movie close-up. About Ellen's age, she had trophy wife written all over her. Rachel

Allan Cole

was expensively – and tastefully – dressed, coifed and jeweled. Her face and body were tight as tight could be, from hard exercise and the skills of Brazilian surgeons. But she had the slightly desperate look of a woman who knows she once replaced a younger wife and may already be past that same replacement age herself.

Rachel spotted Ellen, gave her a supercilious smile and raised a glass of white wine in a welcoming toast. "What a treat to see you again, Ellen," she said.

Ellen came unstuck from any pretense of politeness and stalked over. She looked down at the table, noting the place settings. "It's only set for two, Rachel," she said. "I guess that means Harry isn't in the men's room, powdering his whatsit. Instead, he's decided to take a powder of his own."

Rachel sipped her wine and nodded. "Yes… Well, unfortunately Harry's on his way to Hawaii, Ellen," she said. "Important business, you know. Quite sudden. But he does send his regrets."

Ellen was stunned. "Hawaii?" she said. "But… but… I just spoke to him on the telephone."

Rachel gave a embarrassed shrug. "He called from the airport," she said.

Ellen was furious. "This is just so much bullshit. Harry can't even be bothered to have it out with his own sister. Instead he sends his wife. What a coward. I'm out of here, Rachel. Tell Harry – the man you married - that Ellen said to go screw himself."

Before she could storm away, Rachel held up an envelope. "Please, Ellen," she said. "I know this is awkward. But Harry did give me a check for you."

Ellen looked at the envelope, then at Rachel, whose façade of superiority had cracked. She could see that the woman really felt bad about the situation.

"This is so humiliating, Rachel," Ellen said.

"I know, I know," Rachel replied, squirming in her seat. "Harry can be infuriating." She absently rearranged cutlery that was already perfectly placed. "Come on, Ellen. Sit with me. There's important things to discuss."

Ellen, warily: "What important things?"

Allan Cole

"Well, your mother to start with," Rachel said.

Ellen's eyes widened. "My mother," she said. "Is there something wrong-"

Rachael broke in. "Nothing urgent," she said. "But we have to talk. Please, Ellen. Sit."

Ellen sat.

Rachel motioned to a passing waiter, who paused and then hoisted the wine from the ice bucket to pour a trickle into Ruth's glass, then Ellen's.

Ellen gestured impatiently at him. "More," she said.

He filled it to the top. Ellen drank it down and gestured for more.

"Very well, Ruth," she said. "What is it exactly that my dear brother is up to? Hmm?"

Allan Cole

CHAPTER NINE

WHEN HE REALIZED it might be a bit of a wait, Sam moved the Mustang's new paint job into the shade of an old oak tree. Shame to see blisters mess with such a perfect finish.

He was chilling out now, playing his tunes and perusing a restoration manual while he waited for Ellen to emerge.

Sam could see everything that was happening on both sides of the street, with an especially good view of the entry road to the hotel.

A loud backfire caught his attention and he looked up to catch a city bus pulling into the curb. The door opened and men and women poured out. They were mostly black and Hispanic and from the look of them, Sam figured they were hotel employees.

He was about to go back to his manual, when he saw a huge white man emerge from a clump of bushes. He wore a ratty Hawaiian shirt, khaki cargo shorts, a Panama hat and a generally mean attitude.

Sam figured him for a redneck of the lowest, Florida cracker order. Definite trailer trash. He saw the man approach the emerging passengers.

"What's this?" he said, putting the manual aside and clicking off the player.

The answer was soon apparent, because as each worker got off the bus, they reached into pockets or purses, handed the Cracker some money, then hurried off to their jobs.

"Smart," Sam said, admiring the redneck's enterprise.

One worker in a waiter's uniform tried to push past the Cracker. Shaking his head and telling him no deal. A quick flurry of thumps followed and the waiter was knocked on his ass.

"Not so smart," Sam said.

He got out of the Mustang and moseyed over to the Cracker just as the waiter got up, handed over some money and was sent on his way with a kick in the butt. The Cracker saw Sam and turned, glowering at him.

Sam grinned. The guy had his Prison Exercise Yard glare down pretty damned good.

"What the fuck you want, boy?" he growled.

Sam chuckled. "Everything you got, pal," he said.

He reached out a hand, snapping his fingers for the Cracker to give over. Instead of obeying, the redneck exploded into motion, hurling an enormous fist at Sam.

Sam slipped gracefully to the side, grabbed the man's hand and slammed down on the forearm with his own big fist.

There was a loud snap! and the Cracker fell to his knees, screaming in agony.

Sam shook his head at the sorry sight. "Jesus," he said. "What a baby."

He ripped the collar right off the guy's shirt – holding him by the hair with one hand while he did the deed. He stuffed the collar into the Cracker's mouth, muffling the screams, while he patted the man down, pulling out wads of money and shoving the bills into his own pockets.

When he was done, Sam turned and strolled away, whistling an old tune, leaving the Cracker kneeling there.

A black security guard came running out of the shack. He saw the Cracker and stopped. A big grin spread across his face. He turned and gave Sam a questioning look.

Sam shrugged. "Drunk, I guess," he said. "Some guys get weepy, you know?"

He stick some bills into the guard's pocket. The man's grin got bigger still. "That's my guess, too," the guard said.

In the country club dining room, Ellen toyed with a shrimp salad, while Rachel attacked her blackened Mahi-Mahi with dainty gusto.

"Everyone's still talking about you in New York," Rachel said. "You've always been so much more adventurous than the rest of us.

Allan Cole

I simply don't know how you managed the courage to run off with that handsome beach boy. All of us were dying with envy."

"He wasn't a beach boy, Rachel," Ellen said. "He was an attorney. A Jamaican attorney."

"But...he was... well, black, wasn't he?" Rachel asked.

Ellen's anger got the better of her. "As the ace of spades," she said. "Any other details you want to know? Shirt size? Penis size?"

Rachel raised a hand in surrender. "Please, Ellen," she said. "I didn't mean anything. It was just stupid nervous talk."

Ellen relented. "I'm not in the greatest of shape, myself, Rachel," she said. "Sorry I blew up."

She sipped wine, getting it together. Then: "To be honest, I'm damned embarrassed," she said. "My Jamaica adventure went to hell. Along with the man of my so called dreams. My gallery, my paintings, my commissions – poof... Up in smoke."

"Harry mentioned there was some trouble with the authorities," Rachel said.

"Authorities," Ellen exclaimed. "Please. Let's call them what they truly are. Thieves. It's as simple as that. I didn't know that I was basically living – and working – there under the protection of Andre."

"The man of your so called dreams?" Rachel asked.

"Well, yes," Ellen replied, feeling very uncomfortable. "But I shouldn't give you the idea it was Andre's fault. We broke up. Compatibility problems... The sex was great – Oh, god, it was great. But he had certain ideas about a woman's place... and I had others."

Rachel smiled and took a deep drink of her own wine. "Sounds familiar," she said. Shakes her head. "God, men are such dogs."

Ellen nodded agreement. "In my case," she said, "the dog dumped me and split for France. The moment he was gone, the wolves moved in... stealing all my paintings, my furniture... my money... In retrospect, I suppose Andre tried to warn me, but I was too broken up about our dissolved relationship to pay attention."

She made a face. "Jesus, I hate that word," she said. "Relationship."

Allan Cole

Drowned Hopes

Ellen started to say more on, then cut herself short. This was not a subject for lunch – especially for a proxy business lunch. Time to get on with it.

She said, "Anyway, they – the wolves, I mean - devoured everything I owned, then barred me from the country on some trumped up excuse."

"But now you're back home, right?" Rachel said. "You can start over again. A new leaf, as they say."

"As they say," Ellen replied.

She looked pointedly at the envelope next to Rachel's elbow. "Not to be crass, Rachel, old buddy," she said, "but new leaves are expensive, you know?"

Rachel nodded, then picked up the envelope. She started to hand it over, but held onto one corner as Ellen tried to take it.

"There are certain conditions, Ellen," she said ominously. "Harry's conditions."

She let the envelope go. Ellen snatched it up – she hated it that she was acting this way, but she was so angry at Harry that all politeness had deserted her.

Ellen ripped the envelope open then, without preamble withdrew the check. When it was half out she became anxious and plucked it the from the envelope. She unfolded the check, letting her eyes run across the numbers, reacting in shocked disbelief when she came to the total.

Her eyes snapped up to meet Rachel's – on fire and totally pissed.

"What the hell is this?" she demanded. "It's not even half."

"I know, I know," Rachel said, doing her damnedest to make peace. "I pleaded with Harry not to do this. At the very least not force me to be the bearer of such bad tidings." She sighed. "But you know how he is."

"Cut to the chase, Rachel," Ellen said. "What's Harry's pound of flesh? What do I have to do to get what's rightfully mine?"

Rachel hesitated, clearly uncomfortable about her mission. Then she gathered her nerve and plunged into forward. "He wants you to assume more responsibility for your mother," she said.

45

Allan Cole

Ellen was appalled. "My mother?" she said. "He doesn't have to pay me to help my mother."

She was so upset that she almost got up to leave, then sat back down. Caught her breath. Took a sip of wine. And tried again.

"My mother is why I came back to Florida, instead of New York," she said. "So I could be near her."

Ellen's momentary calmness was just that. She suddenly lost it. She slammed her hand down on the table. Glasses toppled. Water and wine spilled. People reacted and stared. Waiters and restaurant personnel rushed this way and that.

"What the hell is wrong with Harry?" she demanded in a loud voice. "She's his mother too..." Ellen's voice broke, she almost cried, but got her scattered thoughts together and she said, "And after all this, Harry still can't talk to me – his sister – face-to-face? About his own mother?"

Soothingly, Rachel said, "I know, Ellen. I know," trying not to glace around to confirm just how much of a spectacle they were making. She kept repeating soothing "I knows" until Ellen got her act together.

Finally, Ellen railed, "No, you don't know... Harry turned our father against me. And... and... and when our father died, Harry did everything he could to dominate me. To take control of my life. For God's sake, he and dad even forbid me to divorce Jim."

She slammed the table again and Rachel rescued her wine glass just in time. She drank from it, sucking up courage to face Ellen's wrath.

"Is that out of the Middle Ages, or what?" Ellen demanded. "A brother ordering his sister to remain in a marriage with an absolute bastard?"

She deepened her voice, mimicking Harry: "Don't be so hasty, Ellen. Jim's an important client."

Her voice returned to semi-normal. "Not only that," she continued, "he brainwashed our father and made him put anything that was to be mine into a trust.

"A trust that Harry controls."

Allan Cole

The anger suddenly went out of Ellen. She sagged back in her seat. "Never mind, Rachel," she said. "I'm so tired I could cry. Just get it over with. What does Harry want?"

In the renewed calm, a waiter rushed over to repair the table settings and people went back to eating.

Rachael repaired herself with the help of several deep swallows of wine. "Your mother is getting worse," she finally said. "I hate to put it this way, but she's not with us anymore." She tapped her head for emphasis. "The Alzheimer's, you know?"

Ellen nodded. She knew.

Rachel took another drink of wine, trying not to look at Ellen's stricken face. "I found a nice home for her right here in Boca Raton," she said. "She's getting good care... excellent care... They're really very professional. But, somebody has to be there as often as possible because even professional people may let things slip if the family isn't around. I've been going over once a week. That's really not enough. But I don't have time to do more."

"What about Harry?" Ellen asked. "How often does he go?"

Rachel squirmed. "Well, he, uh... Well... You know how uncomfortable Harry is around sick people and he, uh..."

Ellen broke in. "Never mind, Rachel," she said. "I get the picture."

She quickly digested the situation, then said, "Of course, I'll go see her and relieve you of that responsibility. I'll go every single day if I can. But I would have done that anyway. Why is Harry trying to make me feel like an uncaring daughter by trying to bribe me?"

Ellen waved an impatient hand. "If that's even possible," she added. "The money's mine, after all. Oh, Jesus Christ, Rachel, why is he doing this?"

Rachel shrugged helplessly. Ellen took pity on her and patted her hand. "That's not fair of me," she said. "I know why. Because he wants to drag me down to his level.

Ellen suddenly got to her feet. She slipped the envelope into her purse. "I'd better go, Rachel," she said. "Or I am going to lose it so badly that they'll send for the police."

Allan Cole

She leaned over and give Rachel a quick peck on the cheek. "Thanks for lunch," she said. "And for your empathy. Harry doesn't know what a prize he has in you."

Ellen turned and strode away on those long elegant legs, poor Rachel staring after her.

When Ellen's cab exited the country club, Sam was ready. He quickly started up the Mustang and fell in behind the taxi, wondering where his wandering girl was going to take him next.

Fifteen minutes later, Sam was most pleased when he saw the taxi pull up in front of a bank.

Like Willie Sutton said, that's where the money is.

Allan Cole

CHAPTER TEN

THE WOMAN BANK officer looked up as Ellen approached, a snotty expression on her face.

Ellen thought she must have some kind of aura of failure emanating from her to deserve such an expression. She'd dressed well for the country club luncheon and her jewelry – although not made of precious stones – was of her own design and quite pricey when sold at her old boutique.

Maybe I have the letter "L" for loser tattooed on my forehead, Ellen thought as the bank officer waved an imperious hand at a chair across from her desk.

"How may I help you?" the woman asked as Ellen sat down and opened her purse.

"I'd like to open a savings account, please," Ellen said.

She handed over Harry's check. The bank officer studied it, her lip lifting in a slight curl. "This is a personal check," she said.

"Yes, it's from my brother," Ellen said. "Harold Berman. He has an account here. So there shouldn't be any problem."

The bank officer sighed. Ellen didn't like the sound of that sigh. "May I see some identification, please?" the bank officer said – almost sharply.

A little taken aback, Ellen dug into her purse. It wasn't the request that startled her, but the abrupt manner. "Certainly," she said. "Right here."

She handed over some documents. "Here's my passport. Driver's license. My Social Security card."

"Social Security isn't valid ID," the bank officer said.

"Oh, uh… fine, then," Ellen said. "You've got my passport and driver's license. I'm sure they'll do."

The bank officer studied the license, checking Ellen's face to see if it was the same as the one pictured. Ellen sat up straighter, as if that would make the likeness closer.

"This is a Jamaican driver's license," the bank officer said. "We can't accept that as valid ID."

"But the passport is American," Ellen said, a little exasperated. "You can use that, can't you?" She snapped her purse shut. "You see, I just arrived in the States after closing down my business in Jamaica and-"

The bank officer rose abruptly from her chair, cutting Ellen off. "I'll be right back," she said.

She strolled away, taking Ellen's documents with her. Ellen started to worry. What was wrong with this bank?

More importantly, she was starting to wonder if maybe there really was something wrong with her.

Outside, Sam was taking his ease at a sidewalk café down from the bank, drinking herbal tea and reading the Miami Herald. He favored the business section, which in recent days had become almost like the Policeman's Gazette, with all the corporate executives being indicted and mostly dodging jail. You could get a lot of good tips, if you studied those guys.

As he waited for Ellen to emerge, a middle aged couple strolled by. Sam's sharp eyes noted that the woman's purse was open, her wallet revealed. At that moment, a clean cut young man exited the café and bumped into the woman.

He was immediately apologetic. "I'm so sorry," he said with great contriteness. "How clumsy of me."

As he spoke, Sam saw the young man's fingers dip into the purse. At the same time a second young man passed by and the wallet was handed off, with no one but Sam the wiser.

The woman said, "That's quite all right, young man. No harm done."

The young man bobbed his head, smiling a most charming smile of boyish innocence. It brought a blush to the woman's cheek,

Allan Cole

making her feel quite motherly toward him. Then the young man strolled away.

"Such a polite young man," the woman said. "That's so rare these days."

The couple moved onward. But Sam wasn't watching them any longer. His eyes were on the polite young man, who had crossed the street the moment he left the couple and as Sam watched, he was ducking into an alley. A few seconds later the second young man walked casually toward the alley, then slipped inside when he thought he was unobserved.

"Lucky day," Sam murmured.

In the bank, Ellen was still at the desk, cooling her heels. Finally, the bank office returned, frostier than ever.

"I'm sorry, Ms. Berman," she said, "but with your credit record I'm afraid we'll have to reject your request for an account."

Ellen was startled. "What's wrong with my credit record?" she asked.

The bank officer slid a document across the desk. "If you want to see your credit report," she said, "you'll have to fill out this request form. Processing usually takes ten working days."

Ellen pushed the form back. She'd had it with these people. "Never mind the account," she said. "Just cash the check please and I'll get out of your hair."

"Very well," the bank officer said, "but, I'll have to call your… ahem… brother to verify the transaction."

Ellen was alarmed. "He's in Hawaii," she said. "On business."

"How unfortunate for you," the bank officer said. "Perhaps when he returns… Hmmm?"

"I need this money now," Ellen said, totally frustrated.

But all the bank officer wanted at that moment was shut of her. "Why don't you try our main branch?" she said. "Perhaps they can help. It's on North West 13th Street and Glades."

Ellen took the check and climbed to her feet. "Thank you so much for your assistance," she said, putting as much deliberate sarcasm as she could in her voice.

51

Allan Cole

But the bank officer one-trumped her with an equally sarcastic, "Service with a smile. That's our motto."

Ellen wanted nothing more than to rip the bitch's lungs out. Instead she turned and walked as calmly as she could to the front door.

In the alley across from the bank, Sam had the two pickpockets spread-eagled against the wall. Blood smeared their faces and stained their shirt fronts.

Sam, meanwhile, was looking over the sheaf of bills and credit cards in his big hand. "Not bad," he said. "Not bad at all."

He pocketed the loot, then slapped one of the men across the back of the head. The guy yelped in fear and pain. "Where's the rest?" Sam demanded.

"That's all there is," the guy said.

Sam punched him in the kidneys. The young man groaned and nearly fell. But Sam steadied him against the wall.

"If I hit you again," he said, "you'll be pissing blood for a month. So don't bullshit a bullshitter. I know how you guys operate. Where's your stash?"

The second guy was so scared he was wetting his pants. "Jesus, Rich, tell him," he said.

Rich said, with a squeak in his voice: "Look in the trash bin."

Sam turned to a nearby dumpster. Lifted the lid. "There's a Burdine's Department Store bag right on top," Rich directed.

Sam found the Burdine's bag, pulled it out and looked inside. A big smile spread across his face. "I could tell you two were hard workers," he said, as he examined the big wad of cash and cards. "But this is impressive. It really is."

He turned his head slightly and said, "Okay. You can go now."

Immediately, the two pickpockets spun around and walked very quickly toward the mouth of the alley. Sam grinned at them, enjoying the whole scene.

But then the grin faded when he saw Ellen coming out of the bank. She was in a hurry, moving fast and no sooner had she raised a hand to signal, than a cab pulled up.

Allan Cole

Cursing, Sam took off for his car. The two pickpockets thought he was after them. They squealed in terror and raced away.

Out on the main drag, Sam vaulted into his Mustang and started to peel away from the curb.

Up ahead, Ellen's cab beat out a yellow light. Before Sam could follow, a bus pulled in front of him, blocking the Mustang.

Sam sounded the horn, but it was no good. Damned city drivers. He slammed the car into reverse and rammed the vehicle behind him. They were phony bumpers anyway, so fuck 'em. There were shouts and he mashed the accelerator to the floor and kept pushing with his bumper.

A space opened up.

He shifted into first, came forward a bit, then reversed the hell out of there at top speed, nearly hitting another car. There were more shouted curses and blaring horns, but Sam just flipped them the finger and sped off, nearly colliding with several other vehicles.

Then he was by God out of there, screeching down the street and through the red light.

Almost immediately, he spotted Ellen's cab and slowed down.

Patience, Sammy, boy, he admonished himself. Patience. Like the guy said – "Follow the money."

Allan Cole

CHAPTER ELEVEN

SAM STARTED TO get the general drift of what was happening to Ellen by the time she cleared the second bank.

He followed her to a third, saw her emerge after a long time, even more angry than before, and made up his mind that the time was getting definitely ripe.

The fourth bank was only a few doors from an auto supply shop for old cars – Glenn's Classic Auto Parts – that he sometimes frequented. He pulled up in front of it and shut off the engine.

Sam chewed thoughtfully on some of his aminos, swigging down orange juice, running the whole thing over. Then a big grin lit up his face as a lightbulb went on. He hopped out of the Mustang and hurried into Glenn's.

In the bank, Ellen was squaring off with yet another manager – a smiley-faced suit who looked like he was too young to smoke, much less run a bank.

"I've only been out of the country for two years," Ellen said. "I know September Eleven changed a lot of things. I know we all have to be more watchful and secure. But could things have changed that much? I'm an American, for crying out loud. Not a naturalized American, but an American-American. My family practically goes back to the Mayflower. So why are you denying me access to my own money?"

The kid banker gave her an annoying smile. "Ellen, Ellen," he said, which was more annoying still. "You must understand. Technically it isn't your money until we cash the check. Until that time it still belongs to…" he glanced at the card… "Mr. Harold Berman."

"My brother," Ellen said.

"So you tell us," the kid said, with a TV ad smile.

Drowned Hopes

Ellen jumped to her feet. Enough was enough. "This is too much," she shouted. "How dare you judge me? You aren't even old enough to be away from your mother. Have you no respect? Have you no empathy? My God, where are you people from – Rude-ville USA?"

Suddenly there was a bank guard at Ellen's shoulder. An older black man with a genteel manner, he seemed more on Ellen's side than the bank's.

"Excuse me, ma'am?" the guard said.

Ellen whirled on him, ready for battle. "What's this?" she said. "Have you come to arrest me? Well, go right ahead. Why spare me this last indignity?"

The bank guard replied, as politely as he could, "No, ma'am, I'm not here to arrest you. Nobody's going to arrest you. But, you see I have to keep it peaceful here. That's my job. And if you don't leave, well..." he gave a sad shrug... "Please don't force me to make a fool out of both of us, ma'am."

Ellen sagged in defeat. "Okay, I'll go," she said.

She started to leave, but then suddenly turned for one last parting shot at the kid banker.

"Look at this face," she demanded.

The kid banker looked.

"Look at this finger," she said, and she shot him the bird. "I promise you, the day you die, this face and this finger are going to be the last things you remember."

The kid banker turned white as a Canadian tourist. Well satisfied, Ellen stalked away, the bank guard at her side.

He leaned close to whisper, "That was some curse."

Ellen said, "Learned it in Jamaica from a voodoo queen."

"Is that a fact?" the bank guard said, thinking she was fooling. But when he saw the look on her face he glanced back at the kid banker and felt a little sorry for him.

The moment Ellen was out of the bank, her anger – and with it all her spirits – collapsed. She was suddenly very tired. All she

55

Allan Cole

wanted to do was crawl into some hole and feel sorry for herself for a very long time.

She looked up and down the street for a cab, but didn't see one. Ellen fished out her cell phone and speed dialed, but then her face suddenly screwed up in fury. She smacked the phone against her thigh.

"Damn. Damn. Damn." she said.

Ellen put the phone to her ear again. Still no good. Service had been cut off, according to the voice.

At that moment, a horn beeped and as Ellen looked up, Sam guided his Mustang to the curb.

"Hi, neighbor," he said. "Need a lift?"

Ellen frowned. What the hell was Sam doing here? As if guessing what she was thinking, Sam held up a large bag. The label read: Glenn's Classic Auto Parts.

"Had to pick up a distributor," Sam said. He indicated Glenn's Classic Auto Parts store down the street and Ellen's suspicions vanished. "That's my favorite toy store," Sam said. "Can always find what I need."

He grinned a sheepish grin. "Besides," he said. "Had a little accident with my rear bumper."

Sam jerked a thumb back to indicate and Ellen saw a small dent in the metal. "I had to order a new one," he said with a shrug. "No big deal. The other was a counterfeit part and I'm trying to get this baby back to a true original." He gave the Mustang's dash a fond pat.

Ellen smiled, feeling a little foolish for being suspicious. This was no weird stalker.

"I'd love a ride home," she said. "I've spent a small fortune on cabs and all my patience on banks today."

Sam leaned over, popped the passenger-side door and Ellen got in. He drove smoothly away from the curb, taking it easy, not gunning it, chilling the lady out with his easy personality and the nice music he already had set up on the player.

Having already seen her mini-collection in her apartment, he had a pretty good idea what her tastes were. He clicked on Peter

Allan Cole

Tosh singing, "Stop that train: I'm leavin' today; stop that train: I'm leavin' anyway..."

Soon he had her smiling, feeling just a little easier about things – especially herself - whisper-singing, "Stop that train: I'm leavin' and I said: It won't be too long whether I'm right or wrong... Stop that train..."

He took a couple of short streets, then was out on the beach road. With the top down, there was a nice breeze blowing.

Ellen leaned back in the seat, listening to the music, letting the breeze blow over her, enjoying the feel of the wind whipping her hair around.

"God that feels good," she said. "I don't know what it is about banks, but I always feel dirty when I leave them."

Sam laughed. "Nothing filthier than money," he said. "Think about all the places the stuff's been and the places it's gonna go before it meets its Maker in the big Federal Reserve Incinerator In The Sky."

"Are you speaking as an expert?" Ellen said, teasing. Then she realized what she was doing and was aghast. "Oh, please, I shouldn't have said that. I'm so sorry."

She got herself together again. "It's no excuse, but I've met so many rude people today that I guess some of it has rubbed off."

"No big deal," Sam said. "Actually, I thought it was pretty funny. I mean, who knows more about banks than the people who rob them, right?"

Ellen became very grim. "Well, I know some perfect candidates for robbing," she said. "It'd serve them right, by God."

Sam glanced over at her. Consummate con man that he was, he had a look of sincere concern all ready for her. "They been giving you a bad time?" he asked.

"That's certainly an understatement," Ellen replied.

"I don't mean to pry," Sam said. "But if you don't mind me asking - what's it all about?"

Ellen patted her purse. "I've got a perfectly good check. It's from my brother for goodness sakes and he's richer than King Midas, so you just know it's good."

57

Allan Cole

She turned to Sam, getting angry all over again. "They won't let me deposit it," she said. "And they won't even let me cash it. Not without waiting ten days for the check to clear, that is."

Ellen shook her head in disgust. "As if I had ten days worth of living expenses stashed away somewhere."

Sam said, "Let me guess – credit problems?"

Ellen gave a bitter laugh. "You'd better believe it," she said. "I don't know what's happening, but somehow from one day to the next my credit rating's gone to hell. I mean, I always pay my bills on time. Somehow, and some way, I manage. My father taught that your credit rating was next to a government security clearance in importance. So, I've always been careful."

A bitter laugh. "Probably the only thing my father said that I ever paid attention to. But then it all went away – poof! And I'm magically tainted."

Ellen sighed. "It's like somebody's stalking me on a computer," she said. Then it suddenly occurred to her.

She slapped the dashboard with an open hand. "Harry." she exclaimed. Another slap on the dashboard. "What a bastard."

"Harry's your brother?" Sam said.

Ellen was astonished. "You're good," she said. "How'd you guess that?"

"I got to be a pretty decent judge of human nature in prison," Sam said. "And you did mention his name."

Ellen nodded. "That's right," she said. "You're studying to be a psychologist."

Sam shrugged. "Never mind that just now," he said. "What about the check? How are you gonna get your money? You have to live, right?"

Ellen slumped back in the seat. Tears welled up. God knows," she said. "Everything seems so... so against me lately. Damn it. I actually know what feeling overwhelmed really means, now. Before it was just a mood description in one of those Jane Austen rip-offs they're pushing these days."

Sam had never read Jane Austen. But he'd read about her in a quickie lit survey course in prison – the kind that impressed hell out

Allan Cole

of female members of the parole board. Ellen's comment about what he guessed were literary rip-offs was a little obscure, but he intuitively knew what she was talking about. A con is a con in any game. So he could give Ellen a sincere nod of understanding with the light in his eyes of knowing who Jane Austen was.

And in his most soothing manner, Sam said, "It just feels that way because you're new to town and haven't made any real friends yet. Somebody to argue with you – take the opposite view. Then put it together again. Yin and Yang, you know? Like Jane Austen.

"Although, I'm probably reaching there. Getting way over my head and making myself a fool. Because the only thing of Miss Austen's I got through was a beat up copy of 'Pride And Prejudice' in the prison library. But it seemed like her point, you know what I mean? Yin and Yang? Opposites that show what it's all about so you can put things together again?"

Sam laughed in a self-depreciating manner. "Of course, I was reading some Zen stuff then too, so I probably got it all mixed up with Miss Austen."

Ellen wiped her eyes. She was not the crying sort and didn't like giving way like that. She was also mightily impressed.

Of course, he had a pretty weird view of Jane Austen. But it was damned impressive that a macho sort – let's face it, Ellen, a lower class sort - even knew who Jane Austen was, much less having read her most important book.

"I guess..." she said, feeling it was a pretty weak reply to a guy who had just been reeling out handmade theories about the literature of Jane Austen.

Sam's eyes widened – and he reacted as if a thought of great brilliance had just hit him. He slapped the dash, much like Ellen had, but with his strength it was with greater force and made her jump.

"Hey, I know," Sam said. "My buddy Danny manages one of those check cashing joints. And boy, does he owe me big time."

He glanced over at Ellen. "Maybe he can help." He shrugged. "Danny's been on the wrong side of bill collector's himself, so he knows what it's like."

Allan Cole

Ellen looked doubtful. "I don't know," she said. "It's a pretty big check. And a private party one at that."

"All Danny can do is say no," Sam said.

He flashed a wolfish grin. "And Sam Barr is not a guy you can say no to lightly."

60

Allan Cole

CHAPTER TWELVE

ELLEN WAS INTRODUCED to the poor man's banking system in a formidable place on the south-western most edge of Deercreek Beach.

The building was long and squat and made of stacked concrete blocks, topped with a flat tar roof, which had a squalling antique air-conditioning unit jutting out of it.

Since the business was arguably in an unincorporated area, jurisdiction was questionable and the only cops who ever stopped by were those who were down on their divorce luck and trying to cash checks before the audit board clipped them for child support.

Ellen found herself standing in one of several very long lines of people of various nationalities, dress and sanitary habits. Sam stood guard beside her, looking over the crowd.

The place was loud, hot and very democratic. At the head of each line people were yelling at cashiers in fenced-over cages. And the cashiers were yelling back.

Eventually, money was exchanged for paper and the customer went away semi-satisfied and the line moved up a notch.

"Might be a bit," Sam said.

"Okay by me," Ellen said. "At least they're getting the job done."

Then she looked up at the big signs on the wall, where the rates were posted for cashing checks. Sam saw her visibly pale.

"Oh, my God," she said, "this is usury."

"But perfectly legal," Sam said.

"I won't have anything left," Ellen said. "Not enough to live on, anyway."

"Welcome to the Poor Man's First National Bank," Sam said. "After your boss screws you, we get in a poke of our own." Then he grew serious. "Don't worry about it, Ellen," he said. "Remember what I told you – Danny owes me."

Ellen lowered her voice. "But the check's for four thousand dollars, Sam," she said. She indicated one of the offending signs. "That's a five hundred dollar commission he'd be giving up."

Sam gave her a quizzical look, that she couldn't read. "How long is that supposed to last you?" he asked.

"Three months," Ellen said. "I'm supposed to get eight thousand every quarter, but that'll never happen as long as Harry's got his hand on the till. So four thousand it is."

"Leave it to me," Sam said. "You just hold on. I'll be back."

Sam headed for the center cashier window, pushing through and passing by the lined up people.

Several of them objected to him butting in, but Sam only had to give them a look with those flat convict eyes of his and the objections died.

When he reached his goal Sam elbowed his way in front of a bored clerk – Laura, her nametag said – who was getting ready to cash out the first guy in line. The man bristled, blowing himself up. He was already a pretty big guy and was practiced in the poor man's art of making himself appear bigger.

"I need to get in here, Big Guy," Sam said diminishing him by recognizing his game.

Then to Laura, he said, "Get Danny for me."

Big Guy became righteously angry. He'd been waiting for a fuck of a long time. He inflated himself even more, eyes bugging with the effort.

"Hey," he said. "The hell you doin'?"

And the sucker reached out to push Sam away.

Sam just smiled and grabbed the Big Guy's hand. He pulled it below counter level and squeezed – very, very hard. Like he was cracking Christmas walnuts.

Big Guy's face became stricken. "Jesus," he said. "Stop. Stop." Sam stopped.

Without another word, Big Guy moved back several places in line.

62

Allan Cole

Sam returned his attention to Laura, who was staring at him in awe. He snapped his fingers and she jumped. "Danny. Remember?" he said. "Tell him Sam's waiting."

"Sure, Sam, right away," Laura said. And she hustled off to find Danny.

Sam turned to face the line next to him – which was between him and the big iron door that led into the main offices.

He pointed at the first guy in line, who had seen everything that had gone on and gulped. "Coming through," Sam said.

The guy jumped out of the way. As did several other people, shrinking up like cheap woolen sweaters in a hot Laundromat drier.

Sam strolled easily to the iron door, the lines parting like the Red Sea before Moses.

At the far end of the room, Ellen watched Sam's progress, frowning, wondering how he did it.

People moved out of his way with no argument that she could see. Sure, he was big and tough-looking – but he didn't seem to be threatening anyone. What was this magic that Sam Barr had that made people do what he asked?

At the cashier's window she caught some kind of an exchange between Sam and the first man in line, but then people got in the way and she couldn't make out what happened next. Apparently everybody here was a friend of Sam's and let him get his business done without trouble. A lot of people besides this Danny person must owe him favors.

Witness the fact that Sam was now going to the big iron door, which had security signs and warnings all around it, and the door was opening up despite the posted rules forbidding such a thing.

She saw a hard-looking young man in a grubby white shirt and dirty tie talking to Sam, his brow furrowed in worry.

Sam's friend, Danny, no doubt.

Danny nodded at whatever Sam was saying, but then, at the last instant, shook his head negatively. A few seconds later Danny firmly closed the door.

63

Allan Cole

Ellen's spirits fell. People – even friends – have a way of disappointing you.

Sam made his leisurely way back through the crowd.

"I knew it," Ellen said when he'd returned, "Too much money to take a chance on, right?"

Sam chuckled. "You've gotta have more faith in your new friends, Ellen," he said. "Danny will cash it, no problem."

Ellen's face lit up. What a relief. She started to dig the check out of her purse. "Oh, my God," she said. "You're a miracle worker, Sam."

"Hang on," Sam admonished. "There's only one little catch. A hurdle we have to clear."

Ellen raised an eyebrow. "You mean, he's going to charge me five hundred dollars after all?" she said. "Well, at this point, I'm so grateful to just-"

Sam jumped in, cutting her off. "Wait up, Ellen," he said. "You've got to let a guy finish. It isn't going to cost any five hundred dollars. Fifty, maybe. Seventy five at the most."

He paused for effect, then said, "The thing is, he needs an hour to clear the check through his own sources, know what I mean?"

Ellen shook her head. "No, I don't."

"You have to trust him to hold the check," Sam said. "For about an hour, hour and a half. No more."

Ellen became very hesitant. "I don't know..." she started to say.

Sam nodded, quite firmly. "You're right to be suspicious," he said. "Hell, there's about a dozen con games that are spun on this very same situation."

He let that sink in then added, "But Danny isn't conning us."

"Still..." Ellen said, reluctant.

"Okay, tell you what," Sam said. "If Danny screws around I promise that I will personally bust down that door and beat him to within an inch of his life."

Then, most disarmingly, he gave her the most charming, boyish smile she'd seen in her life. "How's that for a guarantee?" he said.

There was a long uncomfortable pause as Ellen considered. She remembered the would-be-rapist and Sam's knife at the guy's throat.

64

Allan Cole

If she hadn't protested...

Sam shrugged, as if a negative decision had already been made. "No problem," he said. "I understand. I can drive you around to some more banks if you like."

And now he added just a touch of emphasis: "I've got plenty of time this afternoon."

That's what decided it for Ellen. Reluctantly, she handed Sam the check.

Sam said, "That's fine, Ellen. But you have to endorse it."

And he turned around and offered his broad back as a desk. Ellen smiled, fished out a pen and put the check on his proffered back. She scribbled her signature.

Sam laughed.

"Does it tickle?" Ellen said, teasing.

"Oh, yeah, Ellen," Sam said. "It tickles like hell."

"Wish it were ten thousand dollars," Ellen said. "Or even an hundred thousand. Can you imagine how much that would tickle."

"I certainly could, Ellen," Sam said with a laugh. "I certainly could."

Allan Cole

CHAPTER THIRTEEN

WHILE THEY WAITED for Danny to come through, Sam treated Ellen to a little mini-tour of the area.

He drove past what he called the "Butterfly Ranch," where a person could stroll among tens of thousands – maybe even hundreds of thousands - of exotic butterflies flitting around in an enormous enclosed garden filled with jungle plants. A rare passion flower had bloomed there recently, he said. One that hadn't been seen in over a hundred years.

Sam promised to take her and Ruth there in the near future. "Maybe get Ruthie to pack a picnic," he said.

Then he showed her the Gumbo Limbo Museum, where the sea turtle volunteers gathered. Sam stopped long enough for Ellen to grab some printed material and buy a jar of local honey.

Again, Sam said he'd take Ellen and Ruth there at a later date. He seemed quite knowledgeable about the place. He told Ellen there were canoe trips of the Everglades that could be arranged at the center.

"You should see me in a canoe, Ellen," Sam said, going for his boyish, smiley charm. "I can churn up the water like nobody's business." Then he chuckled. "Of course, everybody wants to go slow to see the nature sights… Not get splashed by me," he said. "But I'm a little hyper, you know?"

Ellen laughed. Sure, she knew. Sam was starting to seem more like a normal guy to her. He was just a big hyper kid from a bad background who had rushed off in the wrong direction because it seemed too exciting to resist.

Finally, Sam introduced Ellen to a little place called Paradise Cove, which sat between Boca Raton and Deercreek Beach. It was a small marina, with shops and eateries on one side and professional fishing boats and short-cruise boats berthed at the docks.

Drowned Hopes

To Ellen, Paradise Cove was an Old Florida place, struggling to maintain its presence between the pressures of big city Miami, and burgeoning super class of Palm Beach. Ellen found the shops and restaurants to be middle-class tourist – but the fishing boats for charter at the docks were the real thing, as were the men and women who ran them.

She promised herself that she'd come back and talk to them. Her years in the Caribbean had made her particularly sensitive to people who made their living from the sea.

Inspiration peeped out from every corner of the waterfront and Ellen determined right there and then to return someday and make good use of it. But she didn't tell Sam any of this while they strolled through Paradise Cove proper, perusing the boutiques and art shops.

To her surprise, some of the shops were amazingly good. They were places that gave Ellen new hope for setting up business for herself one day in a gallery she could afford and where knowledgeable customers might find her – drawn by the ambience of the area, not expensive advertising.

She even stopped to write down the number of a real estate agent, whose sign claimed to have rentals available in the center.

"You don't want that guy," Sam advised. "Ruth knows him. Says he charges a nonrefundable fee, then it turns out the only places he has listed aren't fit for business."

Ellen tore up the scrap of paper. She said, a little ruefully, "I'm getting quite an education today. A regular crash course in the school of hard knocks."

"It's not so hard from my point of view," Sam said. "Of course, like the man said, I've been down so long everything looks up to me."

He glanced at her. "But then I wasn't brought up rich," he said rather pointedly.

Ellen didn't take offense. "We weren't rich," she said, with the assurance of the class that knows what true wealth consists of. But we were certainly well off."

"What happened?" Sam asked, asking the question that jumped years.

Allan Cole

"I fell in love with an inappropriate person," Ellen said. "And I was declared unclean by my entire family. They thought I was crazy. I guess, maybe I was. I left my husband. A very important, very rich New York investment broker. My father and brother considered it a personal betrayal."

She hunched her shoulders and ducked her head down as she walked, determined to get the rest out. For herself – not Sam.

"So they ganged up on me," she said. "Had me declared insane and put in an asylum. I lost my gallery. All my paintings. My reputation. My... everything."

Sam watched her with great interest as she spoke, taking note not just of what she said, but of her body language, mannerisms – the way she held herself. She was a woman, he thought, very near collapse. Which for his purposes, made her the perfect mark.

Ellen said, "Then my father died, which is how I got out of the asylum." Bitter laughter. "He – and only he – had the legal authority to keep me there. I was actually happy when he died. A terrible thing for a daughter to say about her own father."

"I know all about screwed up fathers," Sam said, "so don't feel entirely like the Lone Ranger. The main thing is that you got your freedom."

Ellen nodded. "I got my freedom," she said. "And I flew off to Jamaica to be with my knight in shining armor. I got another gallery going. It was quite successful until my knight's armor developed a bad case of rust."

She gave another bitter laugh. "Anyway, I'm not sure who left whom," she said. "But the upshot was that when Andre and I split up, the authorities descended on me and..."

Her voice trailed off. This was not a place she wanted to visit again. She shook her head, as if the thoughts could be scattered away like water drops.

"I get the picture," Sam said.

He waited a moment, then asked – "So you live off, what, your trust fund?"

"Not until recently," Ellen said. "Unfortunately, my brother controls said trust find." She sighed. "Which made me so pissed off

Allan Cole

that I didn't touch the money for ages. I made my own way with my art. Something I was very proud of. Not a lot of artists can be self-supporting, you know?"

"But then Jamaica hit the fan?" Sam guessed. Of course, it really wasn't a guess. He'd pumped Ruth for the information.

"Yeah – boy did it the fan," Ellen said, weariness returning. "Anyway, when I tried to get my money – my inheritance - Harry got his hooks in me again. Practically making me beg for what's rightfully mine. Then doling it out, penny by penny."

Sam asked, "Nobody else in the family to take your side?"

Ellen shook her head. "My mother used to speak up for me," she said. "But she was pretty beaten down by my father. And now she's… Well, sick. Like in Alzheimer's sick."

Sam brought the stroll to a halt. They were in front of the Rum Runner's Club.

The lunch hour was over and it was still a bit before the happy hour "two-for" madness advertised on the posters outside.

He checked his watch. "Let's get a drink," he suggested. "Get out of the sun."

This was more than okay with Ellen and he escorted her inside.

A definite party place at night – the Rum Runner's Club was relatively quiet this time of day.

The bandstand was empty, soft background music played on the stereo, and a few people were scattered around talking quietly and eating peel-your-own shrimp – one of the off-hour specialties at the Rum Runners.

Sam and Ellen took their seats at a long empty bar. A tall, silver-haired bartender came over to them to see what they wanted. His nametag read: Phil. Ellen got a white wine spritzer, Sam stuck with his plain OJ.

After Phil had delivered the drinks, he moved away to give them privacy. But as Sam spun his web, Phil kept glancing over at Ellen, concerned.

After awhile Sam looked at his watch again and said, "I'll give Danny a call and see what's up." He patted his pockets. "Damn," he said. "Left my cell at home." He held out a hand. "Can I borrow yours?"

Ellen blushed. "That's another thing," she said. "They cut off my service for nonpayment. Which is pure baloney. I always pay my bills."

She shook her head with great disgust. "But what I'm really worried about is getting a phone at home. They'll probably give me the same run around the bank did. And I need to keep in close touch with my mom's nursing home."

Sam grinned one of his con man grins and dug into his pocket to fish out a thick wad of prepaid phone cards.

"Let me introduce you to the Poor Man's phone service," he said. Then he handed her a card. "They're prepaid. Get 'em at any drugstore… whatever. Never have to worry about the bill, because when the card runs out, so do you. Works on a cell phone and if you get basic service at home – which, since you have a sick mother and there could be an emergency, they have to provide by law, – you can use the pre-paids there as well."

He gave her one of his broadest smiles and said, "Used to be folks who couldn't afford a regular phone used the pay telephone on the corner, feeding it dimes and quarters. Now they're either impossible to find, or when you do find them, they cost more than your rent."

Ellen looked at thick wad of cards in his hand. "Why do you buy so many at a time?" she asked."

Sam laughed. "Buy?" he said. "You must be kidding." But when he saw the shocked look on her face, he pretended it was a joke. Laughing, he said, "I was just being stupidly clever," he said. "Let's just say that I have my ways."

Ellen gave a nervous laugh. "Well, I guess it's better than robbing banks," she said.

"Actually, I never really robbed that many," Sam said. He saw the doubtful look on her face and moved on. "Oh, sure, that's what I was busted for," he continued. "And I tell people that's what I did. Bank robbing is considered one of the classier crimes. Like jewel

Allan Cole

thieves and cat burglars. But the truth is, that was only my third bank."

He took a long drink of his OJ and gave Ellen a rueful grin. "I was helping a friend," he said. "A friend who ended up being not such a good friend after all."

Ellen said, with much feeling – "I know how that goes."

She drank a little of her wine, then asked shyly: "So… if it wasn't banks…"

She let it trail off. But Sam nodded, getting her drift. "Mainly, I robbed other crooks," he said.

Ellen was puzzled. "Come again?" she asked.

"I specialized in taking out strong arm men, pick pockets, muggers, con men, even armed robbers," he said. "I got pretty good spotting them. I'd follow them until they did the deed. Then I'd liberate the money they'd just stolen from some honest citizen."

He grinned that boyish grin of his. Like, how could I have been so stupid? "Of course, I realize now I was only rationalizing," he said. "And that by putting a middle man, so to speak, between the innocent victim and me, I was trying to distance myself from moral responsibility."

Sam laughed and said, "Before I was cured, my prison shrink thought I was a sociopath's sociopath. Which I always thought was a pretty good line, you know? Something he could probably put in a book about oddballs like me."

Despite herself, Ellen felt a little in awe at a criminal who only robbed other criminals. She said, awkwardly, "But… wasn't that, you know… dangerous."

Sam nodded. "Sort of," he said.

Then he couldn't help but add a brag, which was one of his weak points, he knew. One he was working on it.

Even so, he slipped and added: "But they usually gave it up pretty fast when I explained how things were." And he held up a fist that looked like sledge hammer.

Ellen shuddered and Sam realized he'd gone too far. So he did a quick verbal tap dance around his error. "But, I'm not the same man, Ellen," he said, sincere as could be, stirring his OJ with his finger,

71

Allan Cole

making the threatening hand seem smaller. "I've not only had extensive therapy, but I plan to become a psychologist myself. My dream is to open a clinic for ex-cons to help them stay straight and build a good life for themselves."

He gave a self-depreciating laugh. "Who better to cure a thief," he said, "than a man who was one?"

This got a smile from Ellen. "That's an admirable goal," she said. "Ruth must be proud of you."

Sam frowned a little. "Ruth?" he said. Then his face cleared. "Oh... sure... Ruthie has been very, you know, supportive."

He held up a hand to catch the bartender's attention. "Yo, Phil," he called. "Two more of the same, my friend."

He turned back to Ellen. "Hold the fort while I use the gent's room," he said. "And I'll call Danny and see where we're at with the check cashing."

As he headed for the rest room Phil fetched another round. Ellen smiled at him politely and took a sip of her wine spritzer.

"You pour a decent house wine," she said.

"Oh, that's not our house wine," Phil said. "The house wine is what we get when I drain the sink. This is the good stuff. It comes from Chile in steamed out gasoline cans."

Ellen laughed. She toasted Phil and took another sip. "Thank God for the people of Chile," she said.

Phil looked her over without being obvious about it. If someone had been watching they could see that he liked how she handled herself. And also that something was worrying him.

Finally, he went for it. But not before testing the waters. "Are you and Sam coming back for the dance party tonight?" he asked. "We've got a pretty good group booked."

Ellen hastened to correct Phil's error. "Oh, no," she said. "I'm not with Sam."

Then she realized that might sound a little odd. "I mean, I'm here with him now," she said. "But just as a friend."

Ellen drank some of her wine, then added, "He's helping me with a personal matter."

Allan Cole

She smiled. "If he goes dancing," she said, "I'm sure it'll be Ruth he brings along."

Phil looked at her speculatively. Then nodded. "That's right," he said, "Ruth's his lady friend."

He polished the bar, then asked, "I suppose you're new to the area?"

Ellen nodded. "I just moved into Ruth's building a few days ago," she said. "Sam and I are neighbors."

"So, you and… uh… Sam… just met, huh?" Phil asked.

Ellen frowned. "What of it?" she asked.

Phil started to answer, but then he saw Sam coming out of the rest room.

He moved away, but not before saying, in a very low voice: "You seem like a nice lady. So be careful, huh?"

Ellen didn't know what to make of that. But before she could reply, Sam was at her side.

"Danny came through," he said.

Ellen clapped her hands in glee. "That's wonderful news," she said.

"Let's go," Sam said. "He's waiting for us."

As he hurried Ellen out of the bar Phil stared after them, sadly shaking his head.

Allan Cole

CHAPTER FOURTEEN

ELLEN WAITED IN the Mustang while Sam went into the check cashing center to collect her money. She kept twisting her scarf, nervous as hell, expecting something to go wrong.

Phil's parting words of caution had her worried and she kept imagining Sam inside with Danny laughing at the stupid broad they'd just conned. They were probably splitting up her money now and Sam would bolt out the back door, never to be seen again. Or he could just tell everybody she was a liar and a crazy person and he'd never seen the check, much less touched her money.

What could she do about it?

Call Harry for help?

She'd rather die in pauper's prison. Except they didn't have pauper's prisons anymore. The world was much less civilized. You just died in an alley, or something. She'd end up being a bag lady in faded rags of her own design.

Then Sam came walking out of the place, waving a thick manila envelope at her and her heart jumped as all the suspicions vanished. He tossed the envelope to her then vaulted into his seat and sped away.

Excited, Ellen ripped the envelope open and dug out a handful of greenbacks. She waved them about and then let out a whoop of glee. She – Ellen Berman – had just beaten the system.

"Screw you, Harry," she shouted into the wind.

"You tell 'em, girl," Sam shouted back, laughing with her. Enjoying her pleasure.

Ellen hugged the fat envelope to her breast. "My brother's going to have a fit when he realizes that I've gotten around him," she said. "I'll bet he told the bank people to give me a hard time. But now I've beaten him at his own game."

She turned to Sam. "How can I ever repay you?" she said.

"Don't try," Sam said. "Like the man said, pay ahead, not back. Help somebody else out of a jam someday."

Ellen nodded. "I like that," she said. "Pay ahead, not back."

She stuffed the money back into the envelope and fastened it. "Listen, if it's not too much trouble," she said, "could you drop me off at my mother's place? I was dreading seeing her before because I was already so damned depressed I was practically suicidal. But now – hell, I can take anything."

"Can't keep a good woman down, right?" Sam said.

"Right," Ellen said, with deep, deep feeling.

A little later Sam pulled up in front of a pleasant-looking South Florida nursing home on the northern edge of Boca Raton.

As Ellen got out of the car, Sam asked, "Want me hang around?"

"Thanks, but no," Ellen said. "I don't know how long I'll be."

Sam nodded pleasantly. "Later," he said.

He drove slowly off, checking his rear view mirror – watching Ellen enter the nursing home.

The moment she vanished inside he stopped the car. He made sure she wasn't coming back out again, then he did a fast U-turn and tucked his car beneath a large oak tree where he could see the entrance, but nobody could see him.

Sam popped some pills and chewed. Turned on the radio. A Beatles song was playing: "Lady Madonna."

He hummed along with the music, tapping time on the dash. After a few bars he suddenly grinned and started singing along: "… Who finds the money, When you pay the rent? Did you think that money was… Hea-ven sent?"

Vivian Berman was glued to the television set – a rather elderly model – where a Perry Mason episode was just beginning. The volume was up loud – blasting out the show's distinctive theme music.

Mrs. Berman – who at seventy five was the picture of health – sat primly in a chair in front of the set. She was dressed as if she

Allan Cole

were about to go shopping. There was even a purse looped over one arm.

The door opened and a nurse – Betty – escorted Ellen in. Ellen immediately went to her mother, then stood there awkwardly, not know what to say or do.

Finally, she blurted, "Hello, Ma."

She leaned down to kiss her, but this blocked Vivian's view. Mrs. Berman gently edged Ellen away, craning her head to see the TV.

"That's nice, dear," her mother said absently.

Ellen looked up at the nurse, bewildered. Betty smiled. "Your mom loves Perry Mason," she said. "Watches it faithfully this time every day."

Ellen gave a shaky laugh. "She can remember when a TV show's on," she said, "but not her own daughter."

"You'll break your heart if you take it personally, Ellen," the nurse said. "It's plaque on the brain instead of the teeth. Nothing more."

Ellen sighed. "I know," she said. "I'll just sit here and keep her company."

Betty nodded approvingly. "She likes company," she said, "Even though she doesn't always know who people are, their presence seems to perk her up. And sometimes she surprises you and remembers certain people. You sister-in-law, for instance."

"Rachel," Ellen said.

"Yes, Rachel," Betty replied. "She's very popular with your mother. A loving woman, she is."

"What about Harry?" Ellen couldn't help but ask as sibling rivalry reared its homely head. "Does she recognize my brother?"

Betty thought a minute, then said, "I don't think Mr. Berman's ever been here," she said. Then, realizing this might be a touchy subject, she added, "Not during my shift, at any rate. He probably comes later in the day – after work. Or on the weekends."

"Sure he does," Ellen said, feeling pleased at the answer, and mean-spirited at the same time for thinking that way.

Allan Cole

Betty started to close the door. "Just ring if you need me," she said.

Ellen nodded. After the door closed, she pulled another chair next to her mother and sat. She looked around – it was quite a nice room. Comfortable. Decorated with some of her mother's favorite things.

Then a commercial came on and Mrs. Berman cut the sound with her remote. Even so, she kept her eyes on the tube, not Ellen.

"Rachel doesn't like the commercials," she said. "But I don't mind. Sometimes you see something you need. Then you can turn the sound up with the remote."

Ellen leaned close, giving it a try. "It's me, Ma," she said. "Ellen... Your daughter."

"Ellen went away to Jamaica," Mrs. Berman said. "Harry says she's not coming back."

"But, I'm here, Ma," Ellen protested. "Right here."

"I keep thinking that maybe Harry's wrong," Mrs. Berman said. "Or just being spiteful. He and Ellen never did get along." She sighed. "I miss Ellen." Another sigh. "She's an artist. A real artist. And she's so pretty too." She turned to Ellen and said, "She' my daughter, you know."

Tears streamed down Ellen's face. She nodded. "Yes, Ma, I know," she said.

Mrs. Berman rose from her chair. "Do you want to see my book of secrets?" she asked."

"I'd love to, Ma," Ellen said.

Mrs. Berman opened a bureau drawer and drew out a photo album. Clippings and loose photos stuck out of the sides.

She resumed her seat and spread the book open on her lap. She pointed at a picture. "This is my Ellen," she said. "See how pretty she is?"

Ellen leaned down to see a picture of herself when she was younger.

"It's before Ellen went crazy," Mrs. Berman said. "I didn't think she was crazy. But Frank and Harry said she was. So we had to put

Allan Cole

her away so she couldn't hurt herself. That's what Frank and Harry said she wanted to do... hurt herself."

"Oh, Ma," Ellen said in a soft voice. "I never did."

Oblivious, Mrs. Berman turned the page. "Here's Frank," she said.

It was a picture on an older man, quite handsome.

Ellen nodded. "Daddy," she said in a little voice.

More pages were turned.

"And here's Harry... That's when he was captain of the Yale boxing team."

The picture showed a muscular young man in boxing togs, fists raised in the classic pose of a pugilist.

Mrs. Berman turned to a graduation picture of the same young man. "That's when he graduated," she said. She smiled proudly. "Top of his class, you know."

"I know," Ellen said in that tiny voice.

Mrs. Berman shut the book. She indicated the TV where Perry Mason was boring in on a suspect on the witness stand. "Perry's going to get him, now," she said. "Then I have to take my nap. If you come back, I'll show you some more secrets. And maybe... I'll show the biggest secret of all."

Ellen got the hint. She leaned over and kissed her mother on the cheek. Mrs. Berman pulled her head away – not rudely. But she clearly didn't want to be touched.

"If you see Ellen," she said, "tell her to come and visit me, will you?"

Ellen choked back tears. "Sure, Ma," she said. "I'll tell Ellen."

As she left, Mrs. Berman clicked the remote and the Perry Mason theme song boomed from the set.

Outside, Sam looked up from a dog track racing form as a cab pulled in front of the nursing home. The horn honked and Ellen came running out.

Sam thought she looked upset. The observation made him smile.

Then she scrambled in and the cabbie drove away.

78

Allan Cole

Drowned Hopes

When the taxi was out of sight, Sam slipped the racing form into the glove compartment, then climbed out of the car.

Whistling "Lady Madonna," he walked to the front entrance of the nursing home, opened the door like he owned the joint, and strolled inside.

Allan Cole

CHAPTER FIFTEEN

DRESSED IN PAINT-SPATTERED cutoffs and a halter top, Ellen restlessly paced her living room, glass of wine in hand.

It was night, and except for some faint sounds coming from TV sets or radios, the apartment building was silent.

She went into the kitchen, opened the refrigerator and looked in. There was nothing in there but a bottle of wine and a head of lettuce. Ellen fetched out the wine, refreshed her glass, then broke off some lettuce.

Nibbling leaves and sipping wine, she resumed pacing – looking frequently over at the easel sitting by the window.

A large blank canvas glared back at her like an accusing eye.

Finally, Ellen could take no more. "Shut up," she said to the canvas.

She resumed her pacing. Then she turned her MP3 on. Hit the "random" button to let it surprise her.

A Desmond Decker song came on: "Where Did It Go?"

Ellen grinned, as if greeting an old friend. She hummed along, sipping wine, sometimes dunking hunks of lettuce in her glass, swaying to the music: "There was a song we used to sing, whenever this life got us down…"

She started dancing. Singing along with Desmond. Spinning around and around. Really getting into it: "…Then it would give us hope again, help pull ourselves up from the ground…"

The song went on and on, Ellen dancing to the tune. Finally it ended – a little sooner than she'd recalled - and she bumped into the easel. She steadied it, so it wouldn't tip over.

"We really have to stop meeting like this," she said to the easel.

Then her mood made an abrupt change. She stared at the blank canvas, long and hard. As if willing it to reveal some deeply held secret. She was a little drunk, but not so drunk that she couldn't paint up a storm, if conditions were right. And tonight, the conditions were erratic. She needed to paint – desperately so. But the subject was maddeningly eluding her.

"Why do I always have to do all the work?" she demanded of the blank canvas. "Aren't you going to even give me one little hint? Just one, hmm? For old time's sake?"

Naturally, there was no reply. Ellen's temper flared. "When are you going to be satisfied?" she said. "I give and give, but you're never happy. My husband. My family. My lover. I don't have anything left, damn you.

"What more do you want? Do you want to turn me into a drunk? Ellen the god damned crazy drunk?"

She hurled the glass to the floor, shattering it.

"Well, I refuse, do you hear?" she proclaimed to the canvas. "I – Ellen Berman – will not allow you to destroy me."

She grabbed a piece of charcoal and began drawing with a fury. In the background, the radio started playing Jimmy Cliff's "The Harder They Fall."

Ellen drew and drew, streaking the canvas with charcoal and perspiration. After a long time, a picture began to emerge. To her surprise, it was of Sam Barr. Not the charming con man mask that has been presented to Ellen all along. But someone powerfully evil.

Ellen stopped drawing. She stepped back to study her work, reacting - more than a little shocked. Pulling away as if the half-finished portrait of Sam was going to attack her.

"My God, Ellen," she said. "What the hell's in your head, girl?"

Confused, she started to move away. There was a crunching sound under foot and she winced, hurt.

Looking down, she saw that she'd stepped on the remains of the wine glass in her bare feet. A tiny sliver of glass protruded from one toe and she was bleeding all over the rug.

"Shit, Ruthie's rug," she said. "She'll kill me."

She hopped awkwardly into the kitchen on one foot. She picked out the glass, then tore off a thick handful of paper towels and wrapped them around her wounded foot. Then she grabbed the bottle of wine from the fridge and another glass and hopped into the bedroom.

81

Allan Cole

Drowned Hopes

After finding her first aid kit, Ellen got her foot properly disinfected and bandaged. After disinfecting her insides with a little more wine, she returned the kit to the dresser drawer beside her bed.

The envelope of money was in there. She frowned at it, more than a little tipsy from the wine and stressful work at the easel.

"It's not right, Harry," she said. "It's not right and you god damned know it. So why do you do it, then, huh? I know. Because you can, you bastard."

She replaced the envelope and grabbed her cell phone. She started to punch numbers then shook her head as she remembered that she'd been cut off.

Then she laughed, remembering something else. Ellen got out the phone card Sam had given her and resumed punching numbers.

Ellen listened to the phone ring on the other side. Then, when she heard the machine voice, she said: "It's your sister, Harry. With one more message for your fucking answering machine.

"And you know that that message is? Listen real close, Harry... Put your ear right up next to the god damn machine so you won't miss a word."

She gave it a second then: "Okay, here it is. From me to you, big shot." And she blasted the phone with a big fat raspberry.

Giggling she snapped the cell shut.

Then she leaned back into her pillows and took a large hit off her wine.

"What a life," she said to nobody in particular.

Allan Cole

CHAPTER SIXTEEN

THE MOON STREAMED through the window, pooling around Ellen, who was asleep in her bed. She'd slept restlessly, and the covers were pushed aside. She wore a plain white cotton nightgown and her bandaged foot was pushed slightly off the edge of the mattress for comfort.

In the other room, there was the sound of feet crunching broken glass. Ellen stirred. There was another crunching noise and Ellen's eyes snapped open.

She stayed very still, listening to faint sounds of someone moving about her living room. The footsteps came nearer and Ellen almost stopped breathing, she was so frightened.

Then a dark figure slipped into her bedroom. A pencil flashlight snapped on, the beam sweeping slowly over the room. Just before the light passed over Ellen's face, she closed her eyes.

The light finally moved to the bedstead, where it found the money envelope in the open drawer. The dark figure came closer leaning over the bedstead.

A hand closed over the envelope.

Ellen exploded out of the bed. "That's mine," she shouted.

After struggling so hard to collect the money, there was no way she was going to be ripped off without a fight. She grabbed the envelope and there was a furious tug-of-war.

The thief cracked Ellen across the head with one hand, while still hanging on to the envelope with the other. But Ellen was like a tiger. She wouldn't give up. She kicked and screamed and raked the thief with her nails.

Then her hand encountered the wine bottle and closed over it. She smashed the thief across the head.

The bottle exploded, sending glass everywhere.

The thief staggered back, still gripping the envelope. Dragging Ellen out of the bed.

"Bitch," he shouted.

He slammed a fist into her head, knocking her away. Then he spun about and fled the room.

Ellen leaped up and ran after him. "You can't have it," she shouted. "It's mine."

She pursued the man into the living room, but he got to the door first, flinging it open and rushing outside, then slamming it in her face.

Ellen went down again, but she quickly scrambled to her feet, sobbing and yanking at the door, her hand slipping off the knob. Then she got it open and raced into the hallway just in time to see the thief escape out the front door.

Ellen slipped and fell, but was up again, continuing her pursuit. But as she reached the front door she heard the roar of a motorcycle engine. She jerked the door open and ran into the night, only to come to a stop when she saw a motorcycle speeding down the street.

Ellen whirled and raced back inside. She ran to the manager's office and hammered on the door. "Ruth," she cried. "Help me, Ruthie."

The door came open to reveal Ruth standing there in her nightclothes. Sam was behind her, wearing only a pair of boxer shorts.

A crazy part of Ellen's mind thought - then it couldn't have been Sam. He wasn't dressed.

Ruth was aghast when she saw Ellen's bruised face, wild hair and tousled clothes.

"I was robbed," Ellen said, pointing down the hallway. "He… he… took all my money, Ruthie. Every damned cent."

Sam pushed forward. "Where is the son of a bitch?" he growled, his big muscles bunching.

Ellen shook her head. "Gone," she said. "Took off on a motorcycle."

Ruth's face softened. "Come on in, honey," she said.

She and Sam coaxed Ellen inside.

Allan Cole

Drowned Hopes

Ruth's place was rather garish – like the owner's unit in a trailer park. But Ellen didn't look around. The moment she got into the room, she went to the phone.

"Who are you calling?" Sam asked.

"The police," Ellen said. She became impatient. "Didn't you hear me? I was robbed."

"Hold on a second, Ellen," Sam said. "The cops won't do shit. Let's think things out on our own."

Ellen shook her head stubbornly and took a firmer grip on the phone. "I'm calling the damned police," she said. "That's what they're for."

Ruth gave her a sisterly hug. "You go right ahead and call, honey," she said. She turned to Sam. "Better make yourself scarce, baby."

Sam nodded, then went into the bedroom and returned with his clothes.

Ellen was confused. "Why's he leaving?" she asked.

"With my record," Sam said, "it's best to avoid the police."

And he was out the door. Ellen lifted the received and dialed 911.

When somebody answered, she said: "I want to report a robbery..."

Allan Cole

CHAPTER SEVENTEEN

A ROBE WRAPPED around her, Ellen huddled on the couch near the easel that held the drawing of Sam.

She was still pretty shook up, a condition that was not improved by the presence of the detective who was parked on a chair across from her, notebook in hand, a bored look on his craggy face.

He'd introduced himself as Sergeant Bill Propp, of the Deercreek Beach Police. He was an older cop, with sarcastic eyes and a grim mouth. He had a look about him that did not engender trust.

"Okay… the suspect fled on a motorcycle," Propp said, "but you don't know what kind."

Ellen gave a helpless shrug. "I don't know anything about motorcycles," she said.

The cop didn't respond. He looked over his notes. "Okay, let's back up a minute," he said.

Propp indicated the broken glass on the carpet. "The first time you were aware of the perp was when you heard him step in the glass, right?" he asked.

Ellen nodded at the debris on the living room floor. "See how it was ground in by his big fat foot," she said bitterly.

"Yeah," Propp said. "But what I want to know is how the glass got there in the first place."

Ellen blushed. "Oh… uh… It was a wine glass that I broke earlier," she said. "I was, uh… tired. And decided to clean it up in the morning."

"You always leave things like that until the next day?" Propp asked.

He didn't quite sneer, but Ellen got a definite sense of disapproval. Instead of getting angry, she was puzzled by his behavior.

"No," she said. "Not usually. But this time I did."

"Drinking a little were you?" Propp said.

"I had some wine after dinner," Ellen said, getting irritated. "I was drawing… making an under-painting. And sipping wine in the privacy of my own living room." Then, exasperated – "So what?"

Propp shrugged. "Just trying to get the picture, Ellen." He pointed at the easel. "Speaking of which… Is that what you were working on?"

"Yes," Ellen said, getting even more irritated now. Who said he could call her Ellen? "But what does that-"

"Who's the guy?" Propp said, cutting her off.

"A friend," Ellen said.

"A Deercreek Beach friend, or an old friend?"

"A Deercreek Beach friend," Ellen said. Then for some reason she couldn't fathom she added, "I don't work from photographs."

Jesus, Ellen. Why'd you say that? This clod doesn't know, or care, about the difference.

"Deercreek, huh?" Propp said, making a note.

He flipped pages, examining them. Then he said, "I guess you make friends pretty fast. You only arrived in town last Saturday morning, right?"

For reasons she couldn't fathom, the question rang alarm bells in Ellen's head. But she kept a blank face and only nodded. "Right. It was a Saturday."

"From Jamaica?" Propp asked.

"Right again, sergeant," Ellen said. "I arrived in Fort Lauderdale on a direct flight from Jamaica."

Her temper flared. She couldn't understand the purpose of these silly questions. Questions that all seemed aimed at her, instead of finding the son of bitch who had stolen her money. All the money she had in this fucking Harry-benighted world.

She sat up straighter. "Pardon me, Sergeant Propp," she said. "I don't know what you're after, but-"

Propp butted in once more. "Your friend," he said… "Your new friend you just met last Saturday… looks kind of familiar to me."

"He's a neighbor," Ellen said. "The owner's fiancé. He helped me get situated."

Allan Cole

"Is that right?" Propp said. "Situated, huh?"

"What are you implying," Ellen said, getting frosty.

"Only sorting through the details," he replied.

Ellen said, "Well, I'll have you know that when I went to Ruth's for help, Mister Barr was right there with her."

She took a deep breath, then added, quite firmly, "He couldn't have been involved in the theft, because I saw the thief flee on a motorcycle not two minutes before."

"Mister Barr, huh?" Propp said, scribbling in his notes. He looked up at Ellen. "Would that be Sam Barr, but any chance?"

Remembering Sam's worries, Ellen became concerned. "Please don't bother the poor man, sergeant," she said. "He's been a great help to me. And so has Ruth."

Propp shut his notebook and got to his feet. "You ought to be careful who you get your help from, Ellen," he said.

He started for the door. "Well, I'll just stroll on down the hall and see what your friends have to say for themselves."

Ellen didn't reply and carefully avoided his eyes. Even so, she could tell that Propp was looking her over as if she were a piece of meat. Mentally stripping her.

Propp grinned and let himself out, closing the door softly behind him. Ellen shuddered. Went straight to the door and shot all the locks.

Her encounter with the police made her feel like she'd made herself more vulnerable than safe.

Might as well be in Jamaica, she thought.

Things did not improve with the new day.

The next morning, Ellen was at Ruth's breakfast table, adding more coffee to an already coffee-soured stomach, when they heard a key turn in the front door lock. Alarmed, Ellen started to get up.

But then Ruth said, "Thank God, there's Sam now."

Then the door came open and Sam walked in. Unshaven, bleary-eyed and in none too good a mood.

Allan Cole

Ruth rushed to him and tried to give him a hug but Sam pushed her away. "Aw, Jesus, Ruthie," he said. "I smell like a pig." Shook his head in disgust. "Damned cop shops get filthier by the day."

Ellen felt terrible. "I'm so sorry, Sam," she said. "I didn't know."

"Nothing to be sorry about, Ellen," Sam said. "You're the victim, here, not me. So they kept me all night. Least they didn't lay into me too much."

He found a chair and sat at the table. Ruth fetched him a tall, frosty glass of orange juice.

Ellen was shocked at what he'd implied. She gasped, "They… they… beat you?"

Sam shrugged. Then downed his juice in one long swallow. "Just a rap on the skull bones every now and then to let me know they were serious," he said.

"That's awful," Ellen said, really feeling like shit now.

"No big deal," Sam said. "The main thing is, what about your money? Seems to me they're too busy circling their own rectums to find it."

"What can I do?" Ellen said, totally hopeless.

Sam said, "Hell, we don't need Sherlock Holmes, here. Just a little common sense."

He held up his glass. Ruth poured more OJ and handed him big jar of aminos. "I mean, who knew about the money?" Sam said, shaking out some aminos. "Did you tell anybody at the nursing home? Or the cab driver on the way back here?"

"Certainly not," Ellen said.

"So, the only people who knew," Sam said, "were me, Ruth and…"

The light bulb switched on for Ellen. "Danny," she exclaimed.

"Bingo," Sam said.

He popped the aminos into his mouth and washed them down with a huge slug of orange juice. Sam closed his eyes to the bitter taste, then kept them closed, as if drawing strength.

The he sighed, saying, "Fucking Danny. I can't believe he'd have the nerve to fuck with one of my friends, but Jesus, he's a pill

89

Allan Cole

freak, you know?" He shook his head, mourning the vagaries of pill addicts. Sam said, "Can't ever tell what's happening in a pill freak's head."

Sam fell silent, thinking. Ruth and Ellen didn't say a word as he rolled it over, clenching his big fists, making his muscles jump as he did his isometric exercises.

Ellen found herself becoming fascinated. Sam wasn't a blown up muscle man, like a one of the Hollywood action stars. His muscles were long and thick and ropy and bursting with animal-like power. But Sam didn't appear to be an animal at all. He was deep, had read Jane Austen, and in his way was respectful of women. Hadn't he been ready to kill the man who tried to rape her? And wasn't he trying to help her now?

Sam suddenly brightened. Once again, Ellen saw a light dawn on his face. "Okay, I know how to get your money back," he said. Then he paused, looking her over, doubtful. "But you have to go along with what I say."

Ellen had her own misgivings. Sam, she'd learned, could be a nearly uncontrollable force. "You're not going to hurt him, are you?" she asked.

The moment she said it, she was sorry that she did. She'd practically peed her panties when Danny had crept into her room.

"Nah," Sam said. He shrugged. "Danny can't help himself, you know. There'd be no point in busting his chops. Like I said, he's a pill freak."

He grimaced, as if not liking what he had to say next. "But what I have to do," he said, "is scare the holy bejesus out of him."

"Good," Ellen said firmly. "He sure scared more than that out of me."

90

Allan Cole

CHAPTER EIGHTEEN

IT WAS QUITTING time at the check cashing store and Danny was whistling tunelessly as he flipped the sign to closed, then exited and locked up.

He touched the bandage on his head and winced. The bitch, he thought. Then he jumped a mile as a voice came from behind him:

"Looks like she really clocked you a good one, Danny, boy."

Danny came around to find Sam grinning at him. Over Sam's shoulder, Danny could see Ellen waiting at the mouth of the alley. He barely had time to react before Sam sledgehammered a fist into his gut, driving the air out of him like a curb-shot tire.

As Danny went down, hands gripped over his injured belly, Sam grabbed him by the collar and cake-walked him to the alley.

Several passersby look at them in alarm. "Bleeding ulcer," Sam explained. And he kept going, leaving them gawking in his wake.

In the alley, Ellen hopped behind the wheel of the Mustang. Sam forced Danny inside and piled in next to him.

"Go," Sam commanded.

Ellen went, burning rubber all the way.

Sam directed Ellen generally west and south from Deercreek Beach until they were driving along a frighteningly empty rural road. Nothing but deep ditches and thick woods on either side, with an occasional break for a mobile home or a barn.

"We're way out in Crackerland now," Sam said to nobody in particular.

He pointed to a battered sign advertising an I-Hop ten miles up ahead. "Can't even get syrup on your overhauls for another ten miles," he said. "But there's plenty of opportunity for gator poachers and frog giggers."

"Jesus, Sam," Danny said. "I'm no cracker, you know that."

Sam clapped him on the shoulder. "If you say so, Danny boy," he said.

A dirt road loomed up ahead on the right. Sam pointed it out to Ellen. "Here we go," he said.

Ellen made the turn. Instantly they were bumping over a busted track that jerked the Mustang all over the place. She down shifted. An experienced driver over such roads during her Jamaica sojourn, she knew how to avoid busted axels and pierced oil pans.

Sam nodded at her approvingly. "Not bad," he said.

Ellen grinned, feeling exhilarated. But that quickly changed to foreboding when Sam pointed to a turnout that overlooked a wide canal. She pulled up to it and stopped the car.

Sam vaulted from the car, popped the door and dragged Danny out with him. Ellen started to protest the treatment, but a look from Sam silenced her.

"For chrissakes, Sam," Danny said. "I told the lady I was sorry."

Sam ignored him. He went to the trunk, popped it and hoisted out several hefty cement blocks. He fished out a long heavy chain that rattled like a metallic snake as it slid over the rim of the trunk.

Danny stared at them warily. "What're you doin', man?" he asked.

Sam gestured at the canal. "Some cracker told me these canals can get twenty, thirty feet deep," he said. "Think they're lyin' Danny boy?"

Danny licked his lips, then slowly shook his head. Sam smiled at the response. "Well, I'm not too sure myself," Sam admitted. "Nobody likes to twist the truth more than a Florida cracker. It's his nature, you know?"

Danny didn't say a word in reply. Ellen looked from one man to the other. Wondering what Sam was up to.

"I say we find out for ourselves just how deep this canal is," Sam said.

He started looping the chain around Danny's neck. Danny tried to shrug the coils off, but they kept gathering around him like a huge snake.

Allan Cole

"This ain't necessary, man," he said. "I told you- I blew the money at the dog track."

"Yeah, that's what you said," Sam replied, throwing more coils of chain over Danny.

Then he got out a large padlock from his pocket. Danny started to struggle, but Sam gave him a sharp slap across his face. Ellen winced at the sound of it.

"Hold still," Sam said quite calmly, as if it had only been a friendly tap.

Danny obeyed and Sam slipped the chain through the cement blocks. Ellen was pale as a ghost. Despite Sam's promise to not hurt Danny, she was afraid that things were going too far.

"Sam, please," she blurted.

Sam gave her a warning look and once again she shut up. Not feeling too good about herself as she complied.

"Listen to her, Sam," Danny pleaded. "You don't want to do this. I mean, how am I going to pay her back if I'm… you know… in the canal?"

He looked at Ellen pleadingly. "What would you rather have, lady. Money or satisfaction?"

Ellen nodded in agreement. "Satisfaction doesn't pay the rent," she said.

Sam hesitated, then nodded. "How true," he said. He gave the chain a shake, rocking Danny back and forth. "Do you hear what she said, Danny, boy? Satisfaction doesn't pay the rent?"

Danny got eager as hell. "I can get the four thousand up by the first of the month, okay?" he said.

Sam looked disappointed. "Why, that's almost four weeks away, Danny," he said. "What's the lady going to do meanwhile? I mean, you wiped her out, you greedy little prick. Not only that, but if she's short the rent, that means my old lady, Ruth, is fucked too." Shook his head in disgust. "But you didn't think about that, did you? How your criminal act might impact innocent people like Ruthie."

He slapped Danny across the head with an open palm. "With you it's 'me, me, me.' Never mind the consequences for somebody else," he said.

Allan Cole

Suddenly he reached out and slapped Danny's face really hard. So hard that it left the man's cheek stained deep red, like a palm print birthmark. Danny cowered, whimpering, but Sam only grinned at him as if it had been a friendly swat from a couple of kids playing grab ass.

"What I want to know, Danny boy," he said, "is how much you can give this lady today. And in case you're wondering, I don't give a damn what you have to do or who you have to fuck over to get it."

"I don't know, Sam-" Danny started.

Sam's growl cut him off. "How much?" He raised a threatening fist.

"Five hundred dollars," Danny blurted. "I can get her five hundred dollars. Tonight, man. Tonight."

Sam suddenly smiled and patted Danny's cheek. "See how easy that was?" he said.

Danny smiled, relieved. But Sam soon wiped that off his face. "What about next week?" he demanded.

Danny way jolted. "What?" he asked. "Whaddya mean, next week?"

Sam sighed with exaggerated exasperation. Danny finally got it.

"I give her five hundred more," he said.

Sam rolled his hand. "And so on and so on," he said.

Danny was alarmed. "Jesus, man," he said.

Sam jerked the chain.

"Okay, okay," Danny said. "I'll give her five hundred a week until she's paid off."

Sam shook his head. "Bullshit, Danny boy," he said. "The five hundred is the vig. The interest. She gets five hundred a week for four weeks. And on the fourth week you also pay her the four thousand dollars you stole from her."

He raised his balled up fist. It looked like a five-pound sledge. "Got it?"

Danny ducked his head. "Yeah, man," he cried. "I fucking got it."

94

Allan Cole

Sam stepped back, well satisfied. Ellen looked at him in amazement. Sam gave Danny a shove. "Start walking," he said. "It's only ten miles to that I-Hop."

He checked his watch. "And you can come on over to my house about… oh… eight thirty. And bring that five hundred dollars, you hear?"

Danny spun around and started trotting toward the road, dragging the long chain behind him. Too scared to stop and take it off.

Sam laughed at the sight, then turned back to an astonished Ellen. "So now you're a big time loan shark, Ellen," he said. "Got four thousand out on the street earning five bills a week."

Ellen gave a nervous laugh. "That's me," she said. "Public Enemy Number One."

Allan Cole

CHAPTER NINETEEN

PERRY MASON WAS up to his old tricks again on Mrs. Berman's TV. The theme music was blaring and the cast regulars were being introduced, but before the story could start, bars of white shot through the picture and the screen went blank.

"Oh, dear," Mrs. Berman said. "There it goes again." She poked buttons on her remote, but to no avail.

"Let me try, Ma," Ellen said, going to the set and fiddling with various knobs.

Her mother watched as Ellen tried to restore her favorite show, trying first one thing, then another. But it wasn't much use. "I think you need a new TV set, Ma," Ellen said.

"Harry's buying me one," Mrs. Berman said.

This surprised the hell out of Ellen. "You talked to Harry?" she asked.

"I certainly did," her mother replied. "He's my son, isn't he? He's not like Ellen. She never calls, or writes, or comes to visit me."

Exasperated, Ellen said, "But I'm Ellen, Ma. And I'm right here."

Mrs. Berman didn't respond. Instead she asked, "Would you like to see more of my secrets?"

Ellen sighed. "That'd be nice, Ma," she said.

She fetched the scrap book from the bureau and sat beside her mother, pretending great interest while the old woman slowly turned the pages.

Outside the home, Sam was parked in his old place under the tree, watching the entrance. Danny sat next to him, feeling generally lousy.

He touched his banged up head and face. "Christ, Sam," he said, "couldn't you have gone easier on me?"

Drowned Hopes

Sam shrugged. "Had to look real," he said. "That Ellen's no dummy. And you sure as shit aren't any kind of an actor. Jesus, the phony way you whined I thought maybe you got some tips watching old Scooby Doo reruns."

Danny rubbed his head again, wincing. "Yeah, yeah, yeah," he said. "But you didn't have smack me so hard on my sore head." Then he suddenly grinned. "Pretty cool move, man," he said. "Using the bitch's own money to salt the mine. Serves her right for hitting people with wine bottles."

Sam grunted – uninterested in small talk. Then his eyes widened as he saw Ellen exit the nursing home. She walked swiftly to a waiting cab, got in, and drove off.

"Show time, folks," Sam said, suddenly full of good cheer again.

The two men got out of the car and went to the trunk. Sam opened it and motioned to Danny. "Get the TV," he said.

Danny nodded, lifted out a large box containing a portable television set.

"Come on," Sam said.

He hurried toward the home, Danny staggering after him with the big box in his arms.

In the nursing home, Mrs. Berman sat sadly in the chair, staring at the blank TV screen. Then the nurse opened the door. The towering figure of Sam was right behind her.

"Look who's here, Mrs. Berman," Betty said.

Mrs. Berman spotted Sam and beamed with delight. "Harry," she cried, her voice full of joy.

Sam bounded into the room, charm turned up full blast. "Hi, ya, Mom," he said.

He gave Mrs. Berman a big kiss and a hug. "How's my girl, huh?" he said. "When are we gonna blow this joint and go dancing?"

Mrs. Berman laughed and gave him a playful slap on the arm. "Oh, Harry," she said. "You're so fresh."

Allan Cole

Betty smiled at the nice scene. "You sure have been popular lately, Mrs. Berman," she said. "Two visitors and it isn't even time for lunch yet.

Sam gave Mrs. Berman yet another hug. "Of course, she's popular," he said. "A regular heartbreaker, that's my Mom." He turned back to Mrs. Berman. "Hey, wait until you see what I got you," he said.

Mrs. Berman squirmed with excitement. "The TV?" she asks.

"Just like I promised," Sam said. "But better."

He waived to Danny, who was out in the hallway. "Bring it in, Danny," he said.

Betty made herself scarce while Danny lugged in the TV box.

"Let's get the sucker open," Sam said.

Mrs. Berman watched with rapt attention as Sam flicked out his deadly knife and slit the box open. He did it carefully, slitting all along the box. He folded the knife, put in his pocket.

Then he remembered Danny. He motioned to him. "Get lost," he said. "I wanna be alone with my mom."

Danny got lost. Sam turned back to the task at hand. "Now, wait until you see what we got here, Mom," he said. "A real super duper deal."

And he lifted out a portable TV/VCR combination. "Ta Da," he exclaimed with a flourish.

Quickly he removed the old set and put the new one on its stand. Plugged it in, turned it on and bingo! an episode of Mayberry RFD faded into view.

Mrs. Berman was ecstatic. She clapped her hands and hooted in glee. Sam stepped away from the set, watching her watch the TV. Then he flicked the set off.

"But, Harry," Mrs. Berman complained. "Perry Mason's coming on soon."

"In a minute, mom," Sam said. "We have to do something else, first. We'll tape the episode, then you can watch all you want."

Mrs. Berman nodded wisely. "You want to see my book of secrets again, right?" she said.

"What a mind reader you are, Mom," Sam said.

98

Allan Cole

He clicked the remote and got the VHS going to tape the show, then he fetched the scrap book and sat down beside Mrs. Berman.

"This time I want you to concentrate on Harry, Mom," he said. "Never mind everybody else. Just Harry."

Mrs. Berman looked confused. "But, you're Harry," she said.

"Sure I am," Sam agreed.

He leaned over and gave her yet another big kiss. "I just was to relive the old times, Mom," he said. "The good times I had with you."

Mrs. Berman gave him a look of pure love. "You could always get anything you wanted from me, Harry," she said.

She started flipping pages.

Ellen had been working steadily on the portrait of Sam. She'd finished the preliminaries and was deep into the painting itself. Daubing the oils on so thick it was almost like she was working in clay.

She stepped back to study the painting. In color, Sam looked even more foreboding than before. "Where are you going with this, Ellen?" she said aloud. "And why does he look so damned mean?"

Ellen picked up the brush again, but before she could continue there was a knock at the door. She groaned with impatience.

A voice called out: "It's Ruth, Ellen."

Ellen put the brush down and started for the door. A sudden thought made her stop and go back to the painting. She turned it to the wall, so Ruth couldn't see. "She wouldn't get it," Ellen said. Then, grimacing, "Hell, I don't get it."

She hurried to the door and opened it. Ruth craned her neck, trying to look into the room.

"I thought I heard you talking to somebody," she said.

Ellen gave a small laugh. "Nobody here but us crazy people," she said. Then: "Don't tell anyone, but I talk to my paintings."

Ruth forced a smile. "I thought Sam might be here."

Ellen was surprised. "I haven't seen Sam since yesterday," she said.

Allan Cole

Ruth wasn't quite satisfied. But she didn't press the point. She indicated the reversed easel. "What are you painting?" she asked.

Ellen hesitated, realizing that the green-eyed monster had a firm hold on Ruth. "Nothing I want to brag about," she said. "I swear, I'm about to paint over the thing and start on something else."

Then realizing – "But, please. I'm being rude keeping you out in the hall. Come on in. Have a glass of wine, or something."

Ruth shook her head. "You have somebody asking for you outside," she said.

Ellen frowned. "For me?"

"Yeah. It's that limo guy again," Ruth said. "Lazy jerk. Couldn't fetch you himself. Instead he honked until I came out to see what all the fuss was about."

Exasperated, Ellen said, "I'm sorry Ruthie. I'll go see what he wants."

She glanced back at the reversed easel, then headed out the door.

Outside, she found the limo pulled up and the chauffeur lounging against it, listening to country music on the radio.

Ellen stalked over to him, pissed. "What's with all the honking?" she demanded. "Are you trying to get me evicted?"

The chauffeur ignored her complaint. "Your brother wants to see you," he said flatly.

Ellen was taken aback. "What is this?" she demanded. "Has Harry joined the Mafia? Summoning people with a snap of his fingers?" She snapped her fingers by way of illustration.

The chauffeur shrugged. "I'll tell him you refused to come," he said.

Ellen started to give the chauffeur a real piece of her mind. Then she calmed herself. In reality, there was nothing she wanted more than a face-to-face showdown with one Harold Berman, alleged brother.

She indicated her painting outfit. "You'll have to wait until I change," she said.

100

Allan Cole

"Whatever," the chauffeur said. "I'm paid by the hour on this gig."

Barely keeping her temper in check, Ellen spun around and stalked away. Fucking Harry was going to get a piece of her fucking mind.

And this time she wouldn't let him hide behind Rachel's skirts.

Allan Cole

CHAPTER TWENTY

ELLEN COOLED HER heels in Harry's outer office, flipping through an old issue of U.S. News And World Report, trying not to listen to the humming of the electric motor in Harry's inner office, and the steady, thump, thump of running feet.

Harry's secretary – Linda – sat at her desk trying to look occupied, but she was becoming increasingly uncomfortable at Ellen's long wait.

In her forties, Linda was a woman who dressed well and took care of herself. Ellen remembered when she was much younger and about to become Harry's mistress. That episode hadn't lasted long – but it did provide Linda with infinite job security. She knew where Harry had buried all the bodies.

Linda glanced at her watch. "Two more miles," she said, with a weak laugh. "He always tries to get in at least five this time of day."

"The way the chauffeur acted, it seemed like a matter of life and death," Ellen said.

Linda made a face. "The chauffeur," she said with heavy sarcasm. "He's just some dork Harry got out of jail and is making work off his fee." She shrugged. "Look, instead of reading that right wing propaganda Harry's too cheap to even get a new subscription to, why don't you just tell me to go fuck myself and barge right in."

Ellen got up from her chair. "Do I really have to say something rude to you?", she said.

"I'll make something up," Linda said. She indicated the office clock on the wall. "He has to leave in a little bit, so what he's doing is playing the filibuster game… dragging things out until the last possible second. If he follows his usual MO, he'll give you a ration of garbage, then leave in a hurry. This way – the if you barge in, way – you'll maybe have a chance to get in the last word."

"Sounds like a plan to me," Ellen said. "Consider yourself told to fuck off."

Linda put a hand over her heart, as if wounded. "I've been told," she said.

Ellen barged in.

Her entrance, however dramatically intended, fell flat. Mainly because Harry didn't notice her. Earphones clamped to his head, sound turned up full volume, he was jogging at a fairly fast clip on his running machine.

A powerful looking man several years older than Ellen, he wore a form-fitting runner's outfit that showed off his build. Despite his attempts at masculinity, Ellen thought he looked a little… well, fey… the way he ran. Waving his hands about to the time of the music as if directing an ethereal orchestra.

What a nerd, she thought as she plopped herself in a client's chair and looked about his office. It was a large room, expensively decorated in leather and dark wood. Besides the usual law books, one wall was devoted to pictures of Harry in various athletic pursuits. Running, biking, tennis, rock climbing, etc. There was even a blown up picture of the younger Harry in a pugilist's pose from his Yale boxing team days.

The jock oddness continued in other areas of the room. Besides the running machine there was a weight rack, folded up exercise machines, a crunch board, and so on. In one corner he even had a speed bag.

Ellen rolled her eyes at all the macho weirdness. He really was a nerd, she thought. And not for the first time. It seemed to her that Harry had gone to many extremes over the years to shake off his inherent nerdiness. That was what the boxing team business was all about. And all the hours at the gym making muscle to cover over the wimp inside. Like fleshy armor, she thought

Then she turned, cupped her hands around her mouth to make a megaphone and shouted: "Turn the damn thing off, Harry."

The shout was loud enough to cut through and Harry jumped as if goosed. He palmed the off button, straddled the running boards, and removed the headphones. He looked around until he found Ellen.

"So you made yourself at home, did you?" he said.

103

Allan Cole

"I told Linda to fuck off and barged right in," Ellen said.

Harry, shrugged – that figures - and got off the machine. He drank some water from a fancy bottle and wiped himself down with a towel.

"Got my five miles in," he said. Then he struck a pose, flexing his arms, sucking in his gut, etc. "Pretty good for forty two, huh?"

He picked up some 35-pound barbells and started doing biceps exercises.

"Forty two, are you?" Ellen said sarcastically. "Talk about forever young. One of these days I'm going to wake up and find my older brother is suddenly younger than I am."

"Still a bitch, aren't you, Ellen," Harry said. "You'll never change."

"God knows it's not for want of you trying, brother dear," Ellen said. "You've gone out of your way to brainwash me. Up to and including throwing me into a loony bin for electric shock treatments."

She gave him a withering look. "And now I have been summoned, O Lord And Master Of Morality," she said. "I tremble to hear what great crime I have committed that has so offended thee that thou hast found it necessary to send thy chariot to fetch this lowly bitch."

Harry snorted. "Piss on it, Ellen," he said. "It seems that a certain detective came to visit me… A Sergeant Bill Propp…"

Ellen frowned. "I don't know why he bothered you about my robbery," she said. "Unless he thinks you're one of the suspects, that is."

"Don't be ridiculous, Ellen," Harry said. "Sergeant Propp was only following orders." He gave her a meaningful look, "I've asked the local authorities to keep an eye on you," he said.

Harry put down the weights and started doing stretches. "The Deercreek Chief Of Police and I golf together with some regularity," he said.

While Ellen thought this over, Harry went to an exercise machine – one of Chuck Norris' Total Gyms. He dropped it down,

104

Allan Cole

stretched out on the board and started working the cables, pulling himself up and down the board.

"Listen, Harry," Ellen said. "I'm not going to get into it with you. Yes, I was robbed. Which can happen to anybody these days."

"I know, Ellen," Harry said. "But why is it that everything always seems to be happening to you? I swear to God, if I heard that your nude body had been pulled out of some rural ditch I wouldn't be surprised one bit."

"Well, until that happy day, Harry," Ellen said, "what is it you exactly want to know about the robbery? I'd be glad to fill you in on the thrilling details, even though the incident really is none of your damned business."

"I'm afraid it is my business, sister, dear," Harry replied. "As the executor of our father's estate and overseer of your trust, I have certain fiduciary duties. Which include being what you believe is nothing more than a common snoop."

Ellen's laughter was bitter. "Peeping Tom is more like it, Harry," she said.

"Let's get to the point," Harry said, "I have a busy afternoon."

"I certainly don't want to impede your progress," Ellen said. "How exactly do you intend to screw me this time, brother dear? I'm dying to hear the details."

Harry only shook his head at her sarcasm. "Apparently you've carelessly lost the money I gave you," he said. "I also wanted to make it plain that I will think carefully about the amount I disperse when the next payment comes due."

"Bullshit and double bullshit, Harry," Ellen retorted. "You shorted me on the one and only check I managed to squeeze out of you. Every time I ask for what is rightfully mine, you always come up with some ridiculous, self-righteous excuse."

She gave him a penetrating look. "Sometimes I wonder if you're trying to cover something up."

Harry frowned and stopped working the cables. "What are you implying?" he demanded.

"That maybe you've been dipping into the fiduciary till, Harry," she said. "Tell me it isn't so."

105

Allan Cole

"That's just like you, Ellen," Harry said. "You blow it – and you blow it big time – and immediately look around for someone else to blame."

Ellen became weary of the sibling game. "Let's not fight," she said. "The stolen money is no long an issue. My friends found the man responsible and I'm being paid back."

Harry stared at her a moment, then went to his speed bag and started punching. "Did you notify the police?" he asked. "That's the proper course of action."

"You mean Sergeant Propp?" Ellen scoffed. "Give me a break. He was ready to arrest me for stealing the money from myself."

"I don't like what I'm hearing," Harry said. "And I'm telling you right now that I do not approve of the course of action you have chosen."

"Well, there are certain things I don't approve of, Harry," Ellen said, "that are far more important than my robbery, or your efforts to humiliate me. I'm speaking of our mother."

Harry stopped punching and turned to Ellen. "What about her?" he demanded. "I've placed our mother in the best facility available. And have provided her with the very best medical care. You can't believe the astronomical bills-"

Ellen was fed up and jumped in. "Shut up with your bullshit, Harry," she said. "You don't pay the bills, so just shut up. You know very well that the money comes from mother's inheritance from father. Plus her own money – which is plenty. Don't pretend otherwise."

"This conversation has gone far enough, Ellen," Harry said. "I'm putting you on warning right now. I'm very influential in Palm Beach County. And if you get out of line I'll… Well, let me put it this way - you'll rue the day that your crossed me."

Ellen got to her feet. "Just remember, do right by our mother," she said, "or you might be the one who ends up doing a little ruing for a change."

She boiled out of the room, slamming the door behind her. Harry stared at the door for a long time, then shrugged – fuck her. And he went at it on the speed bag again. Pounding at it for all he

Allan Cole

was worth – but instead of calming down he got angrier, really ripping into the bag.

The intercom buzzed. Harry sighed and held onto the speed bag, panting. It buzzed again. Harry grabbed a towel and wiped the sweat away as he to his desk and hit the button.

"Yes, Linda?" he said.

"It's time for your appointment at Fist City, Harry," Linda said.

A big smile creased Harry's face. "Thank God, Linda," he said. "After dealing with my sister I need to work off a little steam."

Allan Cole

CHAPTER TWENTY-ONE

SAM WAS PARKED in the Deercreek Beach library lot – which was just across from Harry's office. It was an ideal spot, with plenty of trees for shade, no parking meters to feed, and an easy exit if he had to follow somebody fast.

Better still, with all the pretty young mothers in halter tops and shorts, or thin summer dresses going back and forth from the library with their pre-school charges, the view was full of many bonuses. He got a hard on just looking at all that fecundity.

Sam had tailed Ellen's limo to the office, wondering what was up. Danny was with him – Sam had made him take some time off for his injuries, figuring he - Sam - might need an errand boy with a small mind and an obedient attitude.

It was fairly obvious what Ellen's business was when Sam had slipped into the building after her and checked the office directory. The Harold Berman, Attorney At Law sign had made things Crystal City clear.

This was the glass-bottomed boat Sam had been looking for ever since he'd overheard Ellen giving her brother's answering machine a piece of her mind. Now he was getting a close-up look at how the Berman family worked.

He'd returned from Harry's office building with a light heart, sliding behind the wheel, flicking on the air conditioning and preparing to wait for as long as it took.

"What's happening, man?" Danny wanted to know. "We gonna eat soon, or what? I'm fucking starving."

Sam looked up and down the street. Then he spotted a health food store. He pointed it out to Danny. "I'm feeling peckish, myself," he said. "Go get me a pound or so of their mixed nuts – the nut barrels are in the back. Another pound of their mixed dried fruit – and dig in deep, the stale shit's at the top."

He thought a minute, then, "Yeah, and maybe a quart of egg whites for a little protein pick me up and a couple of jugs of orange juice. Fresh as they got, so check the wear dates."

Then he turned back to watching the office building. Danny didn't move. Sam looked over at him and saw the worried expression on his face.

"Why are you still here?" he asked. "When we split, it'll almost certainly be fast."

"I don't have enough money for all that shit," Danny whined.

Sam gave a long sigh. "I don't give a shit about your money problems, Danny boy," he said. "You're a fucking pill freak and I'm giving you a chance here. Now, go get my shit. And whatever you want, if anything. And for fuck's sake don't get yourself busted for shoplifting, because not only will I cut you out of this deal, but I will kick your ass from here to Mars when you get out of county lockup."

He leaned over and pushed the passenger door open. "Now, fucking get."

Danny got.

He returned about twenty minutes later, his shirt and pants bulging. He'd managed to boost everything Sam had asked for, plus a few oatmeal cookies for himself. Even so, Sam pissed in his ear about the nuts being stale, just to keep him straight.

He was just mixing an egg white and OJ cocktail when Ellen emerged. He reached for the key to start the engine, but then relaxed.

"Ain't you gonna follow her, man?" Danny asked.

Sam didn't answer. Instead, he watched her hail a cab, get in and leave. He settled back.

"Guess not," Danny said.

Sam finished his cocktail. Drank it down – smooth, real smooth.

Then he turned on the radio and listened to some oldies but goodies for awhile, tapping the dash to the time of the music.

Beside him, Danny squirmed and sighed like a restless kid. Sam was seriously considering smacking him, to make him stay still, when he saw the limo pull up in front.

"Here we go," he said.

"Here we go, what?" Danny wanted to know.

109

Allan Cole

Sam didn't bother answering. He pushed the food and shit off his lap and fired up the Mustang.

A minute later a tall, muscular looking man in a lawyer's suit emerged and got into the limo.

That must be Harry, Sam thought.

"Are we gonna follow them?" Danny asked.

The limo moved smoothly away from the curb. Sam tucked in behind the limo, one hand easy on the wheel, the other holding his OJ bottle ready for the next toke of vitamin C and egg whites.

"Guess we are," Danny said.

Sam followed the limo all the way to Lauderdale, then lost it in afternoon traffic. Munching aminos to maintain his calm, he made a wide circle, then narrowed the circle until Danny finally spotted the limo.

"Over there," he said, pointing.

There was a large, flashy gym/entertainment center for well-to-do sports wannabes. A big garish sign, framed with neon boxing gloves read: FIST CITY. The limo was parked out front with the driver lounging against it, smoking a cigarette and nipping from a half-pint.

"What's this shit?" Danny wondered. "Workouts for candy asses."

Sam didn't answer. He just found a good place to park, got out and headed for the joint – Danny in tow, jabbering about absolute bullshit.

Sam tuned him out, not hearing a word. It was a trick he'd learned in jail. Bullshitters have to bullshit, was the universal rule. But that didn't mean you had to listen. Sometimes you shut them up. Sometimes it wasn't worth it, or politically expedient. In which case, you just switched off that part of your brain. The bullshit part.

They strolled into the gym, which was a huge place – almost hotel size with several floors of activity.

They moved past racket ball courts, wall climbing rooms, two big swimming pools, rooms full of exercise equipment, other rooms full of women in leotards doing aerobics, or yoga, or dancing, or

110

Allan Cole

sprawling across huge balls – whatever the latest craze was in exercise.

They also went past health food bars, juice bars, and even a big cocktail lounge with a dozen or more big screen TV's scattered around tuned to the sports channels and waitresses in skimpy outfits serving drinks like carrot juice and Stoli.

"If this is how the other half lives," Danny commented, "They can keep their half."

"I don't know," Sam said. "Sure beats the shit out of the prison exercise yard."

Then they came to the boxing center – a large room containing two professional-size boxing rings, plus plenty of room for punching bags, speed bags and whatever else a boxer might require.

Two men were going at it in the center ring. Sam and Danny stood there watching them for awhile.

"Is that the guy?" Danny finally asked. "Hard to tell with the head gear. Plus, last time we saw him was in a suit."

Sam nodded. "That's him," he said. "His mom's got a picture of him in the same getup."

In the ring, they saw Harry hit his opponent with a nice combination, and the guy went back into the ropes.

"Not bad," Danny said.

But the guy wasn't going down that easily. He exploded back at Harry, driving him across the ring with a flurry of blows. Sam saw Harry's legs wobble and wondered if he was about to fold. Then, all of a sudden, Harry drove a powerful left into his opponent's groin.

The man doubled over and Harry slammed a right into the back of his head. And his opponent went down for the long count.

"Shit, you see that?" Danny said. "The son of a bitch cheats."

Sam grinned wolfishly. "Shoot, for awhile there I thought old Harry was just another dime-a-dozen bulked up wimp," he said. "I mean, what's up with that Yale Boxing Team business?"

"Now we know better," Danny said.

Sam eyed Harry. "Uh, huh," he said. "We surely do."

111

Allan Cole

CHAPTER TWENTY-TWO

THE INTRUDER CAME in through the garden, pausing in the deep shadows of the trees while he peered into Ellen's apartment through the big picture window.

The lights were on, but there was no one around. He heard music playing faintly – she was either home, or had gone out and left the TV or radio on.

It was a cloudy night, so not even his shadow could be seen as he moved swiftly out of the cover of the trees and went to the window.

Again he paused, watching and listening.

The music – although still faint – was a bit more recognizable. It had an island beat – Reggae, the guy guessed. He shook his head in disgust. He hated that stuff. They should keep it in the islands where it belonged.

The intruder slipped a long piece of plastic from his pocket – a device used by locksmiths to open car doors. Also suitable for bullshit window locks. He slipped it through the cracks, wriggled the plastic strip around until the hook on the end caught the bar, then gave a sharp yank.

The lock slid easily aside.

Thank God it wasn't painted over, which was typical in these low class neighborhoods.

The intruder pushed at the glass with gloved fingers and the window slid up with the same ease as the lock. He smiled. Pretty good landlady. She'd even kept the window runner lubricated with bar soap.

With the window open he could hear the music loud and clear: It was Harry Nilsson's Reggae song, "Put Da Lime In De Coconut."

The intruder frowned. Was she here, or wasn't she? Then he heard Ellen's voice singing along with the music: "She put da lime in da coconut, Drank dem both up.."

Drowned Hopes

He hesitated. Okay, she was home? But where, exactly? He pushed his head through the window, looking and listening. And he heard, "... She called the doctor woke 'em up... Doctor... Ain't there nothing I can take to relieve this belly ache..."

But he also heard the sound of splashing water over the music. His eyes went to the partly open bathroom door. The splashing seemed to be timed to the beat of the music. He grinned. She was in the tub, singing along to music that was turned up to nine and her window was unlocked... the dumb bitch.

The intruder slid through the open window, then turned to shut it behind him. He looked around the room and immediately spotted the painting on the easel. He studied it for a time. It was nearly complete and the portrait of Sam was even more brooding and evil than before.

"Jesus Christ," the intruder said under his breath. Hate to meet that guy in a dark alley.

Then he moved to the bathroom door and peered through the small gap. Ellen was happily ensconced in her tub, glass of wine in hand, and singing along at the top of her lungs. Soaking and singing her troubles away. An MP3 player hooked up to with two speakers was set up on a chair next to the tub.

The intruder thought Ellen looked pretty damned good in the tub. Wet flesh gleaming. Boobs bouncing up and down in the water as she moved to the time of the music. Nice long legs, too, he noted. He tried to see more, but there was a washcloth in the way.

He felt the warm and familiar stir in his britches of what he like to call his "trouser snake." Rising up to strike.

The intruder's hand came forward, almost pushing the door open. The urge was almost overwhelming.

But then he regained control of himself. First things first, by God.

Business before pleasure.

He moved away from the door and crept into Ellen's bedroom. At first, the intruder kept his search quiet and professional. Sliding open drawers, shuffling through the contents, replacing the drawers.

113

Allan Cole

Drowned Hopes

But the woman's sexy singing voice started to really get to him, especially when she apparently hit the repeat button on her player and the same song started played: "Doctor! Ain't der nothin' I can take... To relieve this belly ache... Doctor! You such a silly woman!"

Getting angry, and also fixating on the memory of those long legs in the tub and the tantalizing washcloth curtain over what he was certain was a mound of curly gold, he started not really giving a shit.

Damn but he'd love to relieve that friggin' belly ache.

He ripped drawers open, dumping them on the floor. Dragged clothes from the closet. Getting hotter and hotter as that song kept going on – the lime in fucking coconut. Shit, he knew what he was gonna put in her damned coconut before this night was through.

In the bathroom, Ellen thought she heard noises in the other room. She reached for the volume control, then hesitated. Why draw attention to herself?

Instead, she got out of the tub, pulled on a robe and went to the wall that adjoined her bedroom. She placed her an ear against the wall. Her eyes widened when she heard the faint sound of something falling on the floor.

Her heart went off like a trip hammer. So many things – terrible things – raced through her mind that it was difficult to concentrate on what was happening to her here and now. An intruder was in her house.

Again.

The last time it was a robbery. But that had only been Danny, whom she'd seen humiliated and basically unmanned by Sam. She didn't think the guy in the other room was Danny. Maybe it was the rapist from the other night.

Maybe it was-

She stopped herself. Calmed herself. This was bad. Really, really bad. How she behaved in the next few minutes might determine everything that happened in the future. If there was a future.

Allan Cole

Now, cut that out, she demanded of herself. Bottom line – she had nails and goddamned teeth and she could kick and hit and do whatever it took to stop whoever he was. This asshole was not going to get Ellen Berman.

She crept to the door and very slowly and very quietly, closed it and locked it. Then she went to the bathroom window. She opened it, but it was too high to climb out.

Ellen fetched the wastebasket that sat next to the toilet, upended it, and made it into a stool under the window. She climbed up on the wastebasket, but it was still a long reach, and as she clambered up onto the sill the wastebasket crashed over.

Immediately, Ellen grabbed for some sort of handhold outside the window, but all her fingertips met was the rough stucco surface of the building. Even so, she dug in, and felt the skin peel off her fingers and she pulled herself out.

But then she heard the door crash open and she screamed as loud as she could, trying to kick herself through the window.

Strong hands grabbed her legs and pulled her back inside. She screamed and kicked and flipped over on her belly, trying to crawl out like a kid scrambling back into her hiding place. She screamed again, but then a gloved hand went across her mouth, cutting it off.

And a strong arm wrapped itself around her waist and she was dragged back into the bathroom, flailing and kicking, but feeling ridiculous and helpless.

Which instead of discouraging her, made her even madder. She was forced into the bedroom and hurled onto the bed. Legs splaying wide, showing her nakedness, which made her madder still. Ellen used the bounce of the bed to roll over backwards, and never mind the robe going up over her bare ass.

As she tumbled over, she grabbed up the tableside lamp, raising it like a bludgeon to strike the blurred figure standing across the bed from her.

But then a familiar voice snapped out: "Hold it right there."

Even so, she almost didn't hold it. She almost smashed the son of a bitch in the fucking mouth for what he'd done and what he might do. Get in one good shot and never fucking mind what

115

Allan Cole

happened next. At least the asshole would know he'd messed with Ellen Berman.

But then the guy came into focus and she gasped as she saw who was standing in front of her.

"Jesus Christ," Sergeant Propp said, "I'm not here to rape anybody."

Ellen suddenly felt so calm it was almost ethereal. She looked around her destroyed room, then back at Propp – her fear distilled into pure fury.

"Just what are you here for, Sergeant?" she demanded.

To her surprise, Propp seemed unaffected. He gave a casual shrug. "Your brother wanted the place checked out," he said. "So I tossed it."

Ellen's face showed no reaction. Nothing Harry did surprised her anymore. "Taking a big chance, weren't you?" she said, emboldened by the sheer effrontery of the whole thing. "No warrant. No cause for one."

Propp gave another one of his uncaring shrugs. "Oh, if I wanted cause," he said, "I could make one. Just as if I wanted evidence…" He reached into his pocket and pulled out a bag of white powder. "… I could manufacture it."

He dumped the baggie on the table, completing his demonstration.

Ellen raised an eyebrow. "Was that your intention?" she asked. "To incriminate me."

Her attitude was very sophisticated and very cool and the way she primly drew her robe about her and tied it drove Propp nuts with desire to dominate her.

"Maybe later," he said. "Or maybe I'll come back when you get this mess cleaned up and we can make some other arrangements…"

And he gave her his nastiest, you are my bitch, grin. Then he completed the thought: "Private arrangements, if you get my drift."

Ellen's temper blew. She hurled the lamp and it smashed into Propp. He staggered back, his hand going to his face.

"What the fuck?" he cried. "You crazy?"

116

Allan Cole

He examined his hand. There was blood on it and more blood was dribbling from a wound in his cheek.

Ellen grabbed another lamp and reared back. Propp jumped away, nearly falling, and pulled his gun.

"Put it down you dumb bitch," he said. "Before I fucking blow you away."

Still too angry to really feel fear, Ellen lowered the lamp, but held it ready – like a missile.

"Okay, I'm leaving now," Propp said. "But I'll be back. That I guarantee. And you'd better start thinking about what you've got that I want, bitch. And you'd better make me want it real bad. Or, I'll put you in a world of hurt. Hear me? A world of hurt."

Propp backed out of the room.

Ellen stared at the empty doorway, listening to heavy footsteps retreating. The sound of the front door opening, then slamming shut.

She drew in a long shuddering breath – fighting back the mountain that would crush her and turn her into jelly. She swiped at her eyes, angry at the moisture gathering there.

"This time you don't break, Ellen," she said.

Allan Cole

CHAPTER TWENTY-THREE

THE TWO MEN watched with more than mere prurient interest as Harry Berman fucked a woman who was definitely not his wife.

To make the picture divorce court complete, the men were peering through the window of a fancy yacht named the Freebooter, which was berthed at one of the best slips Paradise Cove had to offer.

Raucous music played on Harry's super expensive stereo and while the two men watched, Harry and the girl paused in their love-making to knock back a couple of shooters. Then, to make matters even more felonious, Harry offered the girl a mirror containing several lines of what appeared to be an illicit white powder.

The girl, who had a body that would make the editors of Penthouse weep, snorted two of them and Harry shorted two of his own. Then dived back into those pulchritudinous charms. Fortunately for Harry, the men watching didn't have his wife's interests at heart.

Sam and Danny looked at each other, much impressed with what they had seen.

"I like his style, you know?" Sam said to Danny. "We've been following him all damned day and he is an honest to friggin' God, 'Take No Prisoners' kind of guy if I've ever seen one. We've watched him fuck more people – one by one – than the average Joe can do in a lifetime. And now he's playing around the world with the kind of pussy that makes you know there really is a God."

He turned to Danny. "Enough messing about," he said. "I've made up my mind. Let's do this deal."

Danny had no argument. The two men quietly retreated across the dock, then went to the parking lot where they'd left the Mustang.

Which is when Danny asked, "You got any of that money left we took off the bitch? My old lady's all over my ass for the rent money, man."

Sam gave him a look. "No can do," he said. "I paid out another five bills to Ellen today. We'd best keep the rest of her dough for expenses on this gig."

"Expenses?" Danny wanted to know. "What expenses?"

Sam was in a good mood and didn't slap him. He just said, "Don't push it, Danny boy. I'm stressed out as it is with all I've got on my mind."

Danny wisely didn't push it.

Allan Cole

CHAPTER TWENTY-FOUR

ELLEN DECIDED THAT it was time to quit screwing around and get the hell out of Dodge.

She packed one small bag and one large purse and fled to Fort Lauderdale Airport. Next stop, by God Paris.

Just down from Air France's main ticket desk, she stopped at a bank of pay phones to complete her arrangements. She fed the prepaid card into the phone's slot and punched many buttons. She waited, then waited some more.

The machine burped and a mechanical voice told her to do the whole thing again and so she did. Finally, the damned thing rang with that peculiar ring foreign phones have. Somebody answered. It was a man. Ellen came up straight.

"Hello, Andre, is that you?" she said. With that question in her voice that everybody has when they are scared spitless and know very well who is on the phone. "It's me... Ellen," she said. Knowing damned well that Andre knew who the hell belonged to that voice.

She listened as Andre talked, glancing at her watch and grimacing. "I'm sorry," she said. "I thought it'd be morning there." She laughed nervously. "I mean, like eight o'clock morning, not four o'clock morning," she said.

Ellen lapsed into silence to do penance and hear more cranky words cross international lines.

Then she said, "I'm calling because I was thinking of visiting Paris." She glanced at the Air France ticket counter. "You know how artists are, darling," she said. "We get these sudden... you know... whims."

More listening was required. And more glances at the Air France booth and the clock above it.

"The thing is, Andre," she said, "the air fare won't leave much left over for a hotel room. And I thought maybe –" She stopped, cut off by a voluble Andre. She listened patiently, nodding here and there.

"Yeah, I realize that it's kind of sudden," she finally said when there was a break. "And believe me there are reasons. For being so sudden, I mean. I'll tell you all about it when –"

Andre cut in and Ellen stubbornly bulled through. "Damn it, Andre," she said. "It is important that I get the hell out of here right now. I mean like right this very minute."

Then she curbed herself in. She didn't want to beg, for crying out loud. But she was ready too. Damn but she wanted to cry and sob and beg Andre to protect her. No, no, Ellen, she warned herself. You must keep it together at all costs.

While Ellen talked with her former lover, just down from the phone bank a young man was looking her way. He was a Sam wannabe, a child of opportunity. And from the whole airport crowd he'd picked out Ellen as the one most vulnerable. He couldn't hear what she was saying on the phone, but he only had to watch her face and look at the single bag at her side and the fat purse over her arm, to know that this was a very vulnerable target indeed.

Ellen said, "Anyway… I was hoping that since we parted friends – well, we are, aren't we? Friends, I mean? Anyway, as my friend I was hoping that maybe you could put me up for a little while. No strings attached. You'd just be helping out an old… you know… friend."

The young opportunist moved closer to Ellen, picking up phones as he went along, pretending to punch buttons and make calls. Now he was close enough to hear the anxiety in her voice. He looked at the baggage, then the purse, then Ellen.

A small mental voice told him to wait. He picked up a phone and pretended to talk into it, while he listened in to Ellen's conversation.

"Oh, I see," Ellen was saying, her voice strained. "You don't think your fiancé would understand."

She bit her lip, thinking that was certainly a quick romance. The guy had leaped directly from her bed into pledges of matrimony with another woman. This was not good for a girl's ego.

121

Allan Cole

She gritted her teeth. She was not to be fucked with, was her new mantra.

"Okay, Andre," she said as pleasantly and carefree as she could. "No hard feelings. Have a nice life."

She hung up the phone.

Ellen took several very deep breaths, getting her head screwed on straight again. Never mind Andre. Concentrate on here and now. She fed the prepaid into the slot again and punched out a number. Waited for the pickup and then:

"Ruth? This is Ellen. Is Sam there?" She listened, her face registering disappointment. "That's okay," she finally said[. "I just wanted his advice about something."

Then she added, to ease the green monster of jealousy – "A police matter kind of something, Ruth. I don't want to screw up like I did before."

Ruth had some things to say, but from the young thug's point of view they were inconsequential.

The phrase "police matter" had gotten his attention, but after glancing around the immediate vicinity it was apparent that cops were not of imminent concern.

Ellen said, "No, there's no message, Ruth. Too late for that now. Sorry to bother you... Night."

She hung up. Ellen stood there for a few moments, eyes shut, thinking.

The young opportunist watched her, getting more and more certain that this was his target.

Her eyes came open and he quickly turned his head away. His former mentor, an older boy he'd been forced to pleasure in Juvie had told him to never look directly at a mark. That they could sense you.

Not noticing the young thug a few booths down, Ellen looked around the airport at all the international signs. She bit her lip in frustration – she could be anywhere in the world in a matter of hours. Away from Sgt. Propp. Away from her brother. And, yes, away from her mother too.

Allan Cole

Drowned Hopes

She opened her big purse and checked inside. Pulled out a
manila envelope like the one Danny's money came in. Reached
inside and pulled out a thin bundle of bills.

Shook her head. Way short, Ellen.

She shoved the money back inside.

Ellen laughed at herself and said, "So much for a life as an
international fugitive."

Decision made – a thousand other previous decisions tossed
aside – Ellen picked up her suitcase and headed for the exit.

The young opportunist fell in place behind her, visions of
envelopes full of money dancing in his head.

Outside, Ellen was confronted with several lanes of traffic and
scores of confusing signs. She spotted what she thought was a sign
directing her to the cab stand and tottered over to it on high heels.

The heels made her supremely angry at herself. Why hadn't she
put on some regular traveling flats, for crying out loud? The only
thing she could think of for an excuse was some sort of subconscious
bullshit involving threatening men like Sergeant Bill Propp.

Did she want to be eye level with danger, was that it? Jesus,
Ellen. Get a grip. She tottered onward, leaning forward with a
definite don't screw with me attitude.

The young opportunist didn't give a shit about her attitude. All
he saw was the swinging purse, filled with money. So there was no
mystery about it.

He darted toward her. Running at full speed. Grabbing her purse
as he ran, nearly throwing her to the ground as he ripped it from her
shoulder.

She tried to hold onto a tiny piece of the leather – even went to
her knees in the effort.

But he twisted it expertly from her grasp and kept running.

There were several bystanders walking past at that moment.
Ellen saw them and shouted: "Stop him. He's got my purse."

The bystanders ostentatiously ignored her. No way were they
getting involved.

"Fuck you," Ellen shouted.

Allan Cole

Drowned Hopes

She jumped to her feet, scooped up her high heels and took off after the purse snatcher.

Ellen ran across several lanes of traffic and an airport bus nearly hit her. She dodged it, swiveling her hips like a backfield runner, and plunged across the path of two other cars, hot on the trail of the man who robbed her.

Horns honked, curses were hurled, but not one person answered her pleading shouts: "He robbed me. Stop him, he stole my purse."

The thief ran into a parking structure, trying to lose himself among the parked cars.

Amazingly, Ellen had been gaining on him and saw him vault over a rail and run up the next floor.

"Stop, damn, you," Ellen shouted, then ducked under the rail and took off up the ramp.

The thief glanced over his shoulder, just about freaking when he realized the bitch had followed him. He put on a burst of speed, but so did Ellen. The thief skidded around the next corner and raced up a ramp that led to the roof.

Ellen doggedly charged onward.

Getting really tired now and panting like an old dog, the thief grabbed another quick look and saw that the bitch was actually gaining on his ass.

"Shit," he said.

Then he was on the roof of the parking structure, barely able to breathe he was so exhausted. Feeling his legs cramping the hell up.

He paused to look around – lots of cars, but no people. Then he looked back and nodded in satisfaction when he saw that Ellen was still there.

Time to end this shit.

He turned, motioning for her to keep coming. "Come on, you dumb bitch," he shouted.

But instead of being intimidated, Ellen charged onward, shouting, "Don't you bitch me."

And she powered into the guy, swinging her high heels like twin tomahawks. She pounded at him furiously, blood spattering everywhere.

124

Allan Cole

Caught by surprise, the thief fell back, cowering to protect himself. "Goddamn," he shouted. "You're killing me."

But Ellen showed no mercy, slashing away at him with those deadly heels. Years of pent-up emotion pouring out. "Fuck you," she screamed. "Fuck you... Fuck you..."

Finally, the thief broke free, threw the purse at her and hauled ass out of there.

Ellen started after him... stopped. She recovered her purse, then overcome by sudden weariness, she nearly fell. She forced herself upright, fighting for breath.

A group of tourists exited the elevator. They saw Ellen and wondered what the hell had been going on. One of the men approached her. "Can I help you, lady?" he asked.

Ellen gave him a withering look. "Piss on your help," she said.

Shocked, the man moved back to his friends. Ellen looked them all over – scorn burning in her eyes.

"Piss on all your help," she said.

The tourists hurried off, trying to get away from this crazy lady as fast as they could.

Ellen got to her feet. She shouted at them, "That's right. Run for your lives. Ellen Berman just woke up. And she's not going be anybody's victim ever again.

"You hear me? Never fucking again."

Allan Cole

CHAPTER TWENTY-FIVE

ELLEN WAS SLUMPED in the back seat of the cab, feeling despondent to the extreme as the taxi made its way out of the airport. All her plans had gone right down the toilet, plus she'd made a fool of herself with Andre. And now she was back in the same mess, with even fewer options than before.

She looked out the window at the passing scene – fast food joints, liquor stores, all night markets. All very depressing.

Then a billboard caught her eye and she sat up straight. The billboard showed a young woman with a gun, crouched, pistol aimed, as if she was about to blow somebody away.

Beneath the picture were the words: STOP BEING A VICTIM! BE-SECURE!

Ellen tapped the driver on the shoulder. "What's that sign all about?" she asked, pointing it out. "Be-Secure?"

The driver didn't have to look, he knew the sign. "Sort of a fancy gun store," he said. "Over where you're going – in Deercreek Beach." He chuckled. "They cater to paranoid people – like me."

The cabbie popped the glove compartment and indicated a nasty-looking gun inside. "It's all about protection these days, you know?" he said. "Everybody figures, if the muggers don't get you, the terrorists will."

Ellen shuddered. "I could never shoot anyone," she said.

"Well, you might not say that," the cabbie said, "if the right – or maybe I should say, wrong – circumstances came along. Course, they've got other stuff at Be-Secure's besides guns. Stuff that'll knock you average guy on his fundamentals, but not damage him permanently, if you get my meaning."

Ellen thought about that. "Maybe I'll go by there tomorrow," she said.

"I can drop you there now, if you want," the cabbie said. "They're open until midnight. You'd be surprised how many people get freaked out at night and find themselves wanting some protection fast."

"I wouldn't be surprised at all," Ellen said. "Take me there. Please."

The cab delivered Ellen to a well-lit, upscale shopping area of Deercreek Beach.

The Be-Secure gun store was a trendy-looking place, its front window display making it look more like a sporting-goods store than a weapons shop.

But once Ellen was inside, the rows of weapons sitting in racks behind armored glass were all-too apparent. As she looked them over, the in-your-face- violence they represented intimidated her.

She started to turn and go back out the door, when a familiar voice called out: "Excuse me, ma'am. But don't I know you?"

Ellen turned back and was surprised to see Phil, the bartender from Rum Runners. "Oh... Well, yes," she said, confused. "We met at Rum Runner's."

She laughed nervously. "Well, not exactly met," she said. "We weren't formally introduced."

Grinning, Phil extended a hand. "I'm Phil Collins," he said. "Bartender by day, part owner of Be-Secure by night."

Ellen took his hand. "Ellen Berman," she said. "Painter by day and I can't think of anything clever to say about night."

The two laughed. Phil subtly guiding her around the store, moving past the many displays.

"You looked like you were about to depart our fine establishment," he said. "Are we doing something wrong?"

"Well, to be honest," Ellen said, "I was kind of intimidated. I came here on the spur of the moment, but then when I started looking..."

Her voice trailed off and she shook her head, not sure how to describe her feelings.

"Suddenly you were looking at racks of guns," Phil said, "and wondering if the problem you have requires such drastic action."

127

Drowned Hopes

Ellen was impressed by his analysis. "You seem to be an excellent student of human behavior," she said. "Years of experience behind the bar, I presume?"

Phil shook his head. "Not that many years," he said. "Actually, I spent most of my adult life in the military. Retired a few years ago and bought into this place with an old Army buddy. I took the Rum Runner's job to bring in cash until the store starts paying off."

He laughed. "Whenever that is," he said.

Phil looked at Ellen, concerned. "Don't mean to stick my nose into your business," he said. "But does this sudden impulse to visit a gun shop have anything to do with Sam Barr?"

Ellen was a little surprised. "Why, no," she said. "Not at all." Then she remembered. "Oh, that's right," she said. "When I saw you last you were trying to warn me about Sam."

Phil's smile faded. "That was not my place," he said. "I know that and I apologize. It's just that you seem to be such a nice lady. A real lady – in the old-fashioned sense, if you don't mind me saying so…"

Ellen blushed. "I don't mind," she said.

Phil tried to go on, but didn't do that well. "You see," he said… "Sam… Well, Sam has…"

He trailed off and made no attempt to continue.

Ellen tried to help him. "I know Sam's an ex-con," she said. "He didn't hide that from me. Nor did his fiancé, Ruth Castro, a local apartment building owner."

Phil looked contrite. "Listen, I shouldn't have said anything," he said. "It's just that… Well, look… Let me be perfectly straight with you. Sam doesn't know me from the man on the moon. But he used to date my sister. She wrote to me about it when I was stationed in Germany. Anyway, he didn't do well by Trish, you know? She's been in and out of rehab and off and on the streets ever since."

A long uncomfortable silence followed as Ellen took this in. Then: "I'm sorry to hear that," Ellen said. "I truly am. But – in my case I first met Sam when he saved me from a rapist."

Allan Cole

Drowned Hopes

She shuddered at the memory. "He pulled the creep off me and beat him to within an inch of his life. And I'm not ashamed to admit that I enjoyed every blow he struck in my behalf."

Now it was Phil's turn to take the long pause. Finally: "Enough said."

Then he smiled that nice smile of his – friendly, not pushy, with just a touch of a question if things could go farther. "Maybe we can agree to disagree about Sam Barr and go on from there," he said.

He put out his hand. "Shake?"

Laughing, Ellen again took his hand. "Shake," she said. A small moment passed between them. Then, shyly, Ellen withdrew her hand. Phil cleared his throat, then pressed on with his tour.

He stopped before a display on non-explosive weapons – stun guns, mace, things like that. "Now to return to your reasons for visiting Be-Secure," he said.

Quickly, Ellen said, "I'd rather not talk about it. The reasons, I mean."

"I understand," Phil said. "None of my business. But I'm assuming they are perfectly good and legitimate reasons, correct?"

"Correct," Ellen said. "But I also don't want to kill anybody, you know?"

Phil laughed. "No killing. Got it," he said. "How about simply knocking this problem of yours on its ass? And making said problem remain there while you remove yourself to safer climes?"

Climes, Ellen thought. She liked that.

"Just what the doctor ordered," she said.

Phil turned to show her a display. "Mace. Stun guns… Collapsible batons…" he said, indicating each item. He demonstrated the baton, snapping it open so that a long, thick piece of wire protruded. Phil whipped it back and forth, making the air sing.

Ellen frowned and shook her head. "I don't know…" she said. "Reminds me of sick old holy men flailing themselves for thinking about unmentionable things."

"Like sex, you mean?" Phil said.

"Yeah, like sex," Ellen said. She didn't blush. Phil liked that.

129

Allan Cole

He snapped his fingers. "I've got it," he said. He pulled what appeared to be an umbrella from a basket display.

Ellen was puzzled. "An umbrella?" she said. "What, is there a sword hidden inside, or something?" She shook her head. "I could never, like... stick somebody..."

Phil raised a hand, interrupting her. "Not so fast," he said. He held up the umbrella. "Actually, this is a stun gun and an umbrella. Hit the guy with the tip... Pull the trigger..."

He demonstrated... "And it'll deliver eighty thousand volts right where they're needed."

Phil touched the metal counter edge and there was a buzz and a long blue spark leaped out. Ellen jumped in surprise.

He offered it to her. "You try it," he said.

A little scared – but fascinated just the same – Ellen took the umbrella.

Phil showed her the small metal prong embedded in the handle. "Here's the trigger," he said. "Now, go."

Ellen touched the metal rim. More buzzing commenced and another big blue spark jumped out.

Ellen laughed. The sense of power it gave her was thrilling. "Oh, I love it," she said.

"And it's perfect for Florida," Phil said. "In case you haven't noticed it rains quite a bit here."

Ellen nodded. "I noticed."

Phil snapped the umbrella open, showing that it was perfectly functional for wet weather. Then he snapped it closed again. He picked up a clear plastic bag that contained an array of colorful umbrella pouches.

"And that's not all folks," Phil said, purposely sounding like a home-shopping network announcer. "For your convenience you get a variety of pouches to ensconce your umbrella in the most... well, you know... Most... "

Giggling, Ellen supplied, "Lethal fashions?"

"I like that," Phil said. "Lethal fashions. If we can steal that line from you for our advertising, I'll knock ten – no fifteen percent off

Allan Cole

the low, low purchase price. Plus throw in three – count them, three – lethal fashion pouch accessories."

Ellen couldn't stop laughing. "How can I resist?" she said.

She stabbed the brolly at the counter and once more unleashed a long blue spark that rippled and buzzed and turned the metal white hot.

Allan Cole

CHAPTER TWENTY-SIX

WHEN THE ALARM clock went off the next day, Ellen woke up with the umbrella clutched in a white-knuckle grip. She cut the alarm and sat up, still holding the stun brolly. She puzzled at it a minute, then remembered and smiled.

Ellen brandished it like a sword. "En Garde," she said.

She zapped the lamp, the blue spark arcing out. "touché," she laughed.

The front door buzzer went off and Ellen jumped. She looked at the brolly, still sleepy and confused, wondering what the hell? The door buzzed again and she got it. Quickly she pulled on a robe and went into the living room, still holding the umbrella.

She approached the door cautiously. "Who is it?"

"Sam," came the familiar voice.

Relieved, Ellen opened the door. Sam looked down at the umbrella and grinned.

"Weather man calling for rain in your living room?" he asked.

Ellen blushed. "No," she said. "See, this umbrella is actually-"

Sam was impatient and cut through. "Ruth said you called last night," he said. "Something wrong?"

"Not any longer," Ellen said. "I got it solved on my own. Sorry I was a bother."

"No bother," Sam said.

He started to turn away, then stopped. "You going to see your mom today?" he asked.

"Yes, I was," Ellen said. "Maybe if you're going my way…"

"Sorry," Sam said. "Any day but today, it'd be fine."

"Sure, Sam, sure," Ellen said.

She raised the umbrella again. "Wait until I show you my new toy," she said. "It's got-"

But once again Sam's impatience didn't let her finish. "I'll check it out later, okay?" he said. "Got to go."

And he was gone. Ellen stared after him a moment, then shrugged and shut the door.

She glanced at the clock on the wall, gave a little squeak – it was getting late – and rushed into the bedroom to change.

Ellen paced the room, while her mother watched an episode of "I Love Lucy," on her new TV set.

She was wearing a light sun dress of her own creation and sitting on the floor was a color-coordinated handbag. The umbrella handle stuck out of the bag within easy reach.

Ellen grimaced, thinking she was really being paranoid now, bringing the brolly with her when she visited her own mother.

But then she remembered Phil's advice: "Make it second nature to have it with you at all times," he'd said. "That way you won't have cause to be sorry later on. And don't worry about it looking weird. People carry umbrellas all the time in Florida. It rains a lot here."

Good advice, she thought. It didn't hurt that her advisor was such a good-looking guy. It helped make the lesson stick. Too bad she didn't know him better. There were an number of things she'd dearly love to tell somebody about. Not necessarily for the advice they'd offer – you can only solve your own problems, after all. But by talking things over with someone else, maybe she could make some sense of it all.

"I wish you were in there, Ma," she said, "so you could understand what I'm saying. Things are really building up, you know? I'm afraid they're going to explode and I'll wind up like before. Right under Harry's thumb."

"Harry bought me a new TV set," Mrs. Berman said.

"I know, Ma," Ellen said, frustrated as hell. "That's all you've been talking about."

She threw herself in a chair. "God, I wish you could speak up for me," she said. "Tell Harry to leave me alone… And that detective…" Ellen shivered. "I'm sure Harry wouldn't want that," she said. "He might not like me very much, but I am his sister."

Allan Cole

"I'm going for a boat ride today," Mrs. Berman said. "Harry's going to take me."

Ellen was surprised as hell. "Harry's coming here?" she said. "Twice in one week?"

"He comes every day," Mrs. Berman said.

"Sure, Ma," Ellen said, not believing a word. "And so does the Pope and Golda Meir."

"I wish Ellen could come with us," Mrs. Berman said. Tears welled up in her eyes. "I miss her so much."

Ellen's eyes teared in sympathy. She went to her mother and hugged her. "She misses you too, Ma," she said. "She really does."

Sam and Danny were ensconced in their usual spot under the tree when Ellen exited the nursing home and headed for the waiting cab.

Danny grinned. "Right on time," he said. "That's what I like best about the broad. Real dependable, you know?"

"A rare quality in a woman," Sam said.

When the cab left hopped out of the Mustang. "Get in back," he told Danny. "We're expecting company, remember?"

As he headed for the nursing home, Danny gave a weary sigh and climbed into the back seat.

"I hate it back here," he complained to the empty air. "What's the big deal? Shit, she's such a ditzy old broad she wouldn't know where we put her."

Allan Cole

CHAPTER TWENTY-SEVEN

ELLEN WAS BACK in her painting togs – spattered cutoffs and halter – and putting the finishing touches on the picture of Sam.

She stepped back to examine it, frowning. "I don't know," she said.

Her feelings about the painting and her intentions were no clearer now than when she'd started with the stick of charcoal.

The door bell buzzed. Ellen turned and she automatically started for the door. But then she came to an abrupt halt, as the new moves cut in. She opened her mouth to call out, but once again caution came to her rescue.

The door kept on buzzing, putting her into motion. Very carefully she crept up to the door and peered through the eyepiece.

She jumped a mile. "Shit," she hissed. It was that damned Sergeant Propp.

Propp banged on the door and Ellen reeled back, as if he'd struck her. "Ellen," he shouted. "Open up. I know you're in there."

Ellen raced into her bedroom. Propp kept up his hammering. A moment later she came running back out. But now she'd pulled on a shirt over her halter top and slipped on a pair of sandals.

More importantly, she had her stun umbrella – handle poking out of a beach bag stuffed with some quick necessities. Ellen moved swiftly to the living room window and as Propp buzzed the door bell again and hammered some more, she slid the window open and climbed out.

In the backyard, she quietly pulled the window shut, then sprinted across the lawn to the gate. There, she lifted the bar lock, pulled the gate open then raced out. And, boom! she collided with someone and let out a small shriek.

The other person did some shrieking of her own. It was Ruth. Her friend staggered back from the collision and Ellen had to grab her arm to keep Ruth from tumbling over.

"Oh, Ruth," Ellen said. "I'm so sorry."

Ruth laughed. "Just about peed my pants," she said. Then, eyeing Ellen's odd outfit and the beach bag – "Where are you goin' in such a hurry?"

Ellen glanced over her shoulder into the backyard. Nothing. So far, so good. "To tell the truth, Ruth," she said, "I was trying to avoid someone."

"Old boyfriend, huh?" Ruth said.

Ellen's flesh goose-pimpled at the thought. "Something like that," she said.

"I know how that is," Ruth said. "Some men turn out to be real pains in the ass, if you'll excuse my French. Won't go away when they're told to." She gave Ellen a sympathetic pat. "Want me to get Sam to have a word with him?" she asked.

Ellen gave a vehement shake of her head. "Oh, no, Ruthie," she said. "That wouldn't work with this guy at all. But I would take it as a real favor if I could maybe hang out at your place for a little while. Just until he goes away."

"I've got a better deal for you than that, honey," Ruth said. "Just so happens I was gonna come get you in a few minutes. Sam called and said a buddy of his is letting him use his boat. He said to come on down to the Cove and we could take a cruise and have a little picnic."

"I wouldn't want to impose," Ellen said. "You two have done enough for me as it is."

"Don't be silly," Ruth said. "He told me to fetch you and that I wasn't to take 'no' for an answer."

Ellen looked down at her paint-spattered outfit. Ruth saw the look and understood her concern. "They're just fine, hon," she said. "You don't have to go back to your place to change. Not with that bozo lurkin' around. This is gonna be real relaxed. You'll be sort of like our – what do you call it – Bohemian guest. Real artsy fartsy, if you'll pardon my French again."

She indicated a bright yellow Volkswagen parked in the driveway, with a large picnic basket in the back. "Come on," she said. "I've got the car all loaded."

136

Allan Cole

Ellen was happy to comply. The two women got into the car and Ruth backed it down the driveway to the street.

But just as the car straightened out and started to drive away, Sergeant Propp came running out of the apartment building. He spotted the Volkswagen with Ellen inside and sprinted to the curb where his dirty diaper brown Chevy Nova waited.

Propp jumped inside and headed off after the women.

At the Paradise Cove marina, Ruth found a parking place next to the boat slips. They got out and looked around at all the boats.

"I wonder which one it is?" Ruth said. "He said it was called the Freebooter."

Ellen pointed to one of the nicest yachts in the cove – with Freebooter painted across its bow. It was Harry's boat, but Ellen couldn't know that.

"Is that it?" Ellen said.

Ruth frowned. "It's much too grand," she said doubtfully.

At that moment Sam came out of the bridge. He spotted them and waved. "Hey, Ruthie," he shouted. "Over here, baby."

Ruth put a hand across her ample bosom. "Oh, my heart," she said.

Then she and Ellen hoisted the picnic basket out and hurried over to the yacht. They put the basket down on the deck and looked around.

"I didn't know you had fancy friends like this, Sam," Ruth said.

Sam laughed at her clumsy remark and Ruth blushed. "I didn't mean that how it came out, hon," she said. "Still-"

Sam gave her an affectionate whack on her shapely behind, cutting off the rest. "I move in classy circles these days, Ruth," he said.

He looked at Ellen, saying, "Seriously, though, my buddy got lucky getting into the market and smart getting the hell out. He's big bucks city, now."

Ellen looked around the yacht, impressed. "So, I see," she said.

137

Allan Cole

Sam indicated the luxurious main cabin, which could be seen through the big picture windows. "Why don't you ladies check out the amenities," he said, "while I get things moving?"

Ruth touched a hand to her bosom. "Amenities?" she said. Then laughed. "Oh, my."

The women started to go below.

"Oh, one thing, though," Sam said. "Stay out of the cabin next to the wetbar. My buddy's got some stuff in there he'd like to keep private."

As the women ducked into the main cabin, Ruth muttered, "Probably porn."

Ellen laughed. "As long as I can use the ladies' room," she said, "I don't care if he has Paris Hilton in there cavorting with one her beaus."

After watching the women go into the cabin, Sam trotted up the steps and went back into the bridge. Danny was there – on his knees, a mass of cables pulled from the control console.

He had two wires stripped bare and held them up for Sam to see. "This is a helluva lot easier than stealing cars," he said.

He touched the wires together and the big engines roared into life. Quickly, he twisted them together and wrapped a piece of duct tape around them. Then he adjusted the throttle until the engines steadied.

He gave Sam the thumbs up.

Sam hurried down the stairs to the main deck. He cast off the lines, then turned and cupped his hands to his mouth. "Hit it," he shouted.

And Danny smoothly pulled the boat away from the dock, his face alight with joy.

Sergeant Propp watched the Freebooter head out into the main channel.

This was getting damned interesting.

138

Allan Cole

Drowned Hopes

He had a cell phone glued to his ear. "Hey, Susie," Propp said. "This is Sergeant Propp. I need you to check a boat registration for me..."

Allan Cole

CHAPTER TWENTY-EIGHT

ELLEN AND RUTH lounged on soft leather couches, sipping wine and thoroughly enjoying themselves.

"I'm so relaxed," Ellen said, "I almost feel giddy. I can't believe that less than an hour ago I was sneaking out my apartment window."

"I had a boyfriend like that once," Ruth said. "A real stalker. It was before I met my last husband."

"How did you handle him?" Ellen said.

"I didn't," she said. "I got married and let my husband take of it. He was Cuban, you know."

"You mentioned that," Ellen said.

"So, he like cut the guy," Ruth said.

Ellen sat up straight. She made stabbing motions. "Like with…"

Ruth nodded. "Yeah, a knife," she said. "He didn't kill him or anything."

Ellen shook her head – No, of course not.

"My husband was a very civilized person," Ruth said.

Ellen nodded – Yes, of course he was.

"But the old boyfriend didn't come back anymore to bother me," Ruth said. "No more stalking." She giggled. "Men," she said. "Can't live with them. And you can't live with them."

For some reason – maybe from the feeling of sudden relief – Ellen found this hilarious. She laughed so hard she spilled her wine.

Ruth laughed with her, helping her mop up and refilling her glass.

She said, "Who was your guy?" Meaning, the guy who'd made a fool out of Ellen.

Still laughing, Ellen choked out the name: "Andre."

Ruth's eyes grew big with humor. "Andre?" she laughed. "Andre. Holy hell, woman, with a lover named Andre I just know for certain that you were taken to the penis cleaners. Don't lie to me. You know I'm telling the truth."

Rolling with laughter, Ellen just helplessly nodded. Ruth was right. So right. Boy, had she been taken to the penis cleaners.

At the at moment Sam entered the cabin. He looked over the scene with a big smile on his face, as if he were in on the joke, which of course he could never be.

Sam had his cell phone out and flipped open, as if he was about to call someone. "Comfortable, ladies?" he asked.

"Are you kidding, honey?" Ruth said, wiping her eyes, calming down. "We feel like queens."

"That's good," Sam said. "Because before we get too deep into this deal, there's something I want to discuss with Ellen. A little bit of business, then we can get on with our fun."

Ellen was puzzled. "What kind of business?" she asked.

"Hang on," Sam said. "Let me get my partner in here. He'll want to hear this."

He turned to the door. "Okay, Danny, boy," he said. "You can come on in."

Ellen's eyes widened when she heard that name. Her reaction was even more severe when a grinning Danny entered the cabin.

"What's he doing here?" Ellen demanded.

"That's what I want to discuss with you, Ellen," Sam said. "See, it's like this. Every since we met I've had a good feeling about you. A feeling that you were going to make me a whole lot of money."

He indicated Ruth, then Danny. "Enough to share with my friends.

Danny chuckled at this, but Ruth became furious at the turn of events.

"I don't want any part of your scheme, Sam Barr," she said. "I took you on in good faith that you were gonna change your ways. No more crooked stuff. No more hurtin' people."

Ruth clambered to her feet. "You'd better turn around right this minute and take us home, you hear?" she fumed.

Sam shook his head, looking sad. Then he gave her a push. Not a hard push – just enough to tip her back into the couch.

Allan Cole

"I'm disappointed that you feel that way, Ruthie," he said. "But that's okay. It just makes the shares of the pie bigger for me and Danny."

Ellen finally got her wits about her. Oddly, she didn't feel one tremor of fear. She was only really, really pissed.

"You must be crazy," she said. "I don't have a penny to my name. Except in trust. And my brother controls that."

"I know all about it, Ellen," Sam said. "And for awhile it had me stumped. I couldn't figure out how to get my hands on that trust money."

Sam went to the small cabin door next to the wet bar. "But then I found my answer," he said. "Here. Let me show you."

He opened the door.

Ellen gasped in horrible realization. For sitting there was her mother.

"Harry," Mrs. Berman whined. "Where's the TV? It's almost time for Perry Mason."

Sam whipped up the cell phone, aiming it at Mrs. Berman. "Smile, Mom," he said cheerily. "You're on Candid Camera."

And there was a click as he snapped her picture.

Allan Cole

CHAPTER TWENTY-NINE

HARRY WAS POUNDING his running machine again, shadow boxing as he trotted on the endless belt. On his desk, the intercom crackled into life.

His secretary, Linda, said, "Mr. Berman? There's an urgent call for you."

Harry was annoyed. "I asked not to be disturbed, Linda," he said. "This is my personal time. Our clients are just going to have to learn-"

Linda broke through what was obviously a familiar speech. "I'm sorry, sir," she said. "But it's a man about your mother."

This jolted Harry so hard he almost lost it on the machine. He had to hit the kill button to keep from falling.

Gasping, he said, "Put him through, Linda."

Immediately, the phone buzzed. Harry leaned over and tapped a button to activate the speaker. He got a towel and started swabbing off. "Harold Berman," he said. "How may I help you."

"Hey, Harry," Sam said, in his cheeriest voice. "Sam Barr here."

Harry was impatient. "What's this business about my mother, Mr. Barr?" he demanded.

"Got your cell phone handy?" Sam asked.

Harry snorted his impatience. "Answer my question."

"Hold your horses, Harry," Sam advised. "This'll only take a second."

Harry heard a low chuckle. "Man, you sure have packed this boat with trick gear, Harry," Sam said. "Satellite tracking, sonar, a computer station and even a by-god state of the art cell phone booster."

Harry frowned, puzzled. "My boat?" he said. "What are you talking about, Mr. Barr?"

Sam said, "Wait a minute…"

Drowned Hopes

Over on his desk, Harry heard his cell phone chime the Rocky theme.

There was a pause, then Sam said, "Now, go check your cell messages, Harry, my friend, and come on back and we'll have ourselves a nice little chat."

Harry hurried to his desk and grabbed the cell. Checked his messages. There was a new one, presumably from the guy who was bugging him about his mother.

He called it up, took one look at the picture on the tiny screen, nearly jumped out of his skin.

"Oh, my God," he said.

Harry rushed back to his workout station, glaring at the speaker phone as if it were his deadliest enemy.

"What the hell is this all about?" he thundered. "I want an explanation. And I want it fast. You've got my mother. You want something from me. So spell it out."

"I really do admire your style, Harry," Sam said. "I mean, we haven't even officially met and we're already on the same page."

Harry snorted. Looked down at the faxed Polaroid snap of his mother and growled, "Cut the crap and bottom line me, Barr."

Sam whistled in appreciation. "Bottom line me?" he said. "Wow, I have to remember that. Talk about a phrase that really cuts to the chase.

"Okay, so that's what I'm going to do, Harry. I'm gonna bottom line you. Here's the deal. I want you to fix this number into your mind: Five hundred thousand dollars. Got it? Five hundred thousand dollars."

Harry kept his cool. He would not be impressed, no matter what this asshole said. "Five hundred thousand dollars?" he repeated. "Why is that such a magic figure?"

The answer surprised the shit out of him. Reminding him of the old law school adage – Never ask a question you don't know the answer to.

Sam said, "Because that's how much is left in your sister's trust fund after you ripped her off for two and a half million."

Allan Cole

Drowned Hopes

Harry stared at the phone in total shock. Then he said, "See here, I'm an attorney. I have fiduciary responsibilities that I take seriously. Especially those obligations involving family members and family trusts. How dare you accuse me of such improprieties?"

He was about to go on, to really drive in his point. But then he realized the phone was dead.

Sam was not only gone, but he was not impressed. Harry got busy thinking of ways to turn that attitude around.

Sam was laughing when he cut the connection. Man, he was having a good old time.

Mrs. Berman had been moved next to Ellen, who had a protective arm around her. The old woman was oblivious. She had her "book of secrets" in her lap and was turning pages, muttering to herself.

Ellen had pulled herself together. She gave Sam a curious look. "How did you figure out what Harry was up to?" she asked.

Sam crossed the cabin to Mrs. Berman and Ellen. "Didn't your mom tell you about her book of secrets?" he asked.

Ellen frowned and said, "Well, sure, but-"

She stopped in mid-sentence as Sam leaned down and gently slipped the book from Mrs. Berman's grasp. She looked up at him, concerned, grasping empty air where the book had been.

"I just need to borrow this for a sec, Mom, okay?" Sam said, very gently.

Mrs. Berman smiled at him. "Sure, Harry," she said. "But don't forget to give it back."

"I won't, Mom," he said.

Sam removed some loose documents from the back and waved them at Ellen. "You should have listened to your mother," he said. Pleased with his own joke, Sam went on, "Isn't that the girl scout mantra? Listen to your mother."

Ellen didn't answer, so Sam went on, pushing the pages under her nose. "Your mom's got the whole deal spelled out right here," he said. "I guess before your mom went Looney Tunes, she hired a

Allan Cole

detective. So the whole rip off is spelled out in spades, kid. In spades."

He went to the fax machine, which sat on a desk next to the main communications unit. "I should fax these to your brother before I call him back," he said. "He'll want to make sure I've got proof of his evil ways."

Ellen was outraged. "Proof?" she said. "What does the son of a bitch need proof for? You're holding our mother hostage."

Sam fed the documents into the fax – smiling, not unmindful of the fact that Ellen was just as pissed at her brother as she was at him.

"No biggie," Sam said. "He's a businessman. He'll want to see all the cards he can."

Ruth finally stirred in her seat – a deck chair near the wet bar. She had a large drink in her hand and was obviously under the weather. "So, you're back to the old game, huh, Sam?" she said. "A crook robbin' crooks."

She turned to Ellen. "Sorry, kid, but that's what your brother is. And that's why Sam here latched onto him – and you."

Ellen shrugged. No apologies were necessary.

Ruth took a swig of her drink and turned back to Sam. "They're gonna put you back in jail, Sam," she said. "And this time you ain't – aren't – ever gonna get out. I'll damned well see to that."

Sam sighed. "I hope you're not thinking of doing something stupid, Ruthie, hon," he said. "We've been getting along pretty well, haven't we. Why not go with the flow? Jesus, we're talking about half a million dollars, here, baby."

Ruth made a derisive noise. She slugged back her drink and refilled the glass from a bottle beside her. "Yeah, and we'll see how long that lasts," she said. "Christ, my apartment building's worth almost that much and it is all legal and all. Shit, I thought you knew that when you got all cozy with me. I didn't mind. Gonna take advantage of the widow woman and I get some sweet lovin' in exchange."

She emptied her glass, filled it again. Her hand swaying, she toasted Sam.

Allan Cole

"So, here's to you, Sam Barr," she said. "You already had it made, you didn't even know it."

She upended her glass, gave out a belch, which she covered belatedly with a semi-dainty hand, then refilled her glass – staring defiantly at Sam.

"Now here's my bottom line, Sam my man," she said. "You were cheatin' when you were broke and needed me. What's it gonna be like when you've got some money in your jeans? So here it is – baby, I'm checkin' out. Want no more of you."

She sagged back in her seat, spent by her long, impassioned speech.

Sam gave a weary s shake of his head. "You just keep hitting the bottle, Ruth," he said. "You're making yourself real attractive, you know?"

Ruth muttered under her breath, turned her face away so she couldn't look at Sam and went back to her drink.

Ellen said, "What about Ma and me? Are you really going to let us go?"

Sam gave her a surprised look. "Sure, why wouldn't I?" he said.

Ellen asked, "Aren't you afraid I'll blab to the police?"

"You worry too much," Sam said. "I've got it all figured so that the fewest people necessary get hurt. Lot cleaner that way."

Sam stood up straight. "I'm good at organizing things," he said. "Even my shrink said so." He crossed the room to the intercom. "Take a look," he said. "Check, it out."

At the intercom, now, he pressed the button, buzzing the bridge. "Yo, Danny," he said. "Head for Paradise Cove."

"You got it," came Danny's voice. Then he giggled. "I mean, Aye, aye, Cap'n."

Sam laughed. He turned to Ellen and Ruth. "Isn't he a pistol?" he said.

Ellen didn't reply. She put her arm across her mother's shoulders, guarding her like a she-wolf protecting her cub.

Ruth just tipped a bottle into her glass. She was getting angrier and angrier.

Allan Cole

CHAPTER THIRTY

HARRY DIRECTED HIS driver to the dock where his boat was normally berthed. He grimaced when he saw the empty slip, then got out of the car, lugging a heavy briefcase.

He hadn't had time to change and was still dressed in his jogging outfit – which had been designed to show off his impressive build.

Harry looked around the harbor and didn't see his yacht. "The son of a bitch," he said under his breath.

Then there was a loud buzzing sound and he turned to see to spot the little outboard that belonged to the Freebooter heading his way.

Harry rapped on the limo window, which came down. "Take off, Joe," he told the driver. "I'll make my own way home."

"Yes, sir, Mr. Berman," the chauffeur said. And he reversed the hell out of there fast as he could, glad to get an unscheduled holiday.

Harry walked to the edge of the dock at the motorboat slid in. Danny peered up at him.

"Got the money?" Danny said.

Impatient because he had to deal with underlings, Harry snapped, "Of course I've got the money, you dumb son of a bitch. Why else would I-"

Then he broke off, realizing he really was dealing with a dumb son of a bitch. He said, "You are obviously not the brains of this outfit."

Danny glowered, pissed at the insult. He almost told him that if he – Danny - was so stupid, how come he was the day manager of a check cashing joint? But then he saw the hard set of Harry's jaw and the size of his shoulders and biceps and decided to shut up for the time being.

Harry jumped down into boat and took a seat. Danny continued his glowering. Fuck this muscle man cream puff, he was starting to think. How'd he like a gun shoved up his butt? Play asshole Russian roulette.

Harry said, "Jesus, let's get this over with, shall we?"

Danny curled a lip at the guy, just so he wouldn't think he was a wimp, and pushed off from the dock. Then he engaged the engine and sped away.

Not more than a few seconds passed before a car screeched up. A man leaped out and ran to the edge of the dock, looking out at the boat.

"Shit," he said.

It was Sergeant Propp. He looked around, frantic.

Then he spotted a young boating couple – man and wife – backing their spanking new Chevy pickup down a ramp.

On a trailer hitched behind their blue Silverado, was a 20-foot Wellcraft, also brand new. The young wife was driving the pickup, while her husband directed the trailer into the water. At just the right moment, the young man signaled his wife and she stopped. He did some quick things here and there and the Wellcraft slid neatly into the water.

Propp ran toward them. "Hold it right there," he shouted.

The woman and her husband turned to gawk as Propp raced up to the boat, splashing through the shallow water.

He dug out his badge and flashed it at the husband. "Police," he yelled. "I'm commandeering this boat."

The husband gaped at this insane man. "Hey," he cried. "You can't do that."

"The hell I can't," Propp said, knocking the guy into the water.

Quickly, he unhooked the line and pushed the boat deeper into the water. In a flash he was on board and starting the engine. Then he powered away at top speed, bounding over the waves.

The terrified couple watched him go, wondering what the hell had just happened to them.

149

Allan Cole

CHAPTER THIRTY-ONE

DANNY GUIDED THE boat up to the Freebooter. Harry reached out, grabbed the rail, and ran up the ladder. Despite the heavy briefcase under his arm, he made the maneuver look easy.

It was his damned yacht after all. And Harry prided himself in being always ready and always being in shape.

Sam Barr - big as a mountain with a grin like the half moon – was waiting for him.

Harry's stomach knotted. This was no body builder – the son of a bitch was just damned strong. But, Jesus Christ, so was he. And smart, too. Nobody, but nobody was both stronger and smarter than Harold Berman.

It was then that he saw the light of intelligence in Sam's eyes. Oddly, it made him feel better. This was somebody he could reason with. Somebody he could slicker with lawyer talk, backed up by his own hard muscle. Harry had no doubt in his mind that Sam was just smart enough to underestimate his opponent and overreach himself.

Sam waved at the small crowd gathered on the deck. It consisted of Mrs. Berman, ensconced in a deck chair, Ellen, who hovered nearby, her beach bag with its stun umbrella in easy reach, and Ruth who lounged in the doorway, taking frequent sips of booze and muttering to herself. This was one unhappy woman.

"Glad you could join our little party," Sam said. He indicated Mrs. Berman and Ellen. "Mom's doing okay, but Sis hasn't had such a good time," he said. "'Course, now that you're here, I'm sure things will liven up."

Mrs. Berman peered at Harry, a deep frown furrowing her brow. She turned to Sam. "Why did you invite him, Harry?" She snorted and settled back in her chair. "He doesn't look like our sort," she said.

Sam was vastly amused by this. Ellen shook her head in disgust. Then she leaned over to her mother, pointing at her brother. "That's the real, Harry, Ma," she said. She indicated Sam. "He's nothing but a common thug."

From her post by the door, Ruth toasted Ellen. "Common through and through," she said. And she swallowed some more booze.

Mrs. Berman, meanwhile, had found Ellen's remarks objectionably. "Don't try to fool me, young lady," she said. "I certainly know my own son."

She reached over and gave Sam's hand a squeeze. "Such a good boy, too," she said. "Buying me presents. Visiting me every day."

Ruth broke into laughter – border line hysterical. "Good boy. Ha," she said. "Shoot, he's no better than a whore in the streets. 'Cept he lives off women."

That really pissed Sam off. The woman was getting under his skin, now. "Shut up, Ruth," he said. "You don't know what you're talking about."

Ruth sneered at him. "Shut up yourself," she said. "I'm jus' truthin', that's all. You screwed me over. You screwed Ellen over and now you're screwing over that poor old woman."

She gave Sam a look of pure hatred. "Pimp," she said. "Whoremonger."

Sam took a step toward her, raising his hand. But Harry was growing impatient with all this bullshit quarreling.

He said to Sam, "Look, my friend. I'm a busy man. You're a busy man. You want to smack your woman around, have at it. I'd smack her myself, the way she's talking to you. But, please, have the courtesy to wait until we're finished with our business."

He offered the briefcase. "Take it and go," he said. "You can have the deck boat. Unlike the yacht, no one will question its ownership. A small, but handsome bonus for your efforts."

Good humor restored, Sam took the briefcase. He opened it, looked inside, then his head came back and he looked very, very pissed.

"What the hell is this?" he said.

Allan Cole

And he pulled out a ten pound gym weight And then a single, check-sized piece of paper. He looked at the paper, his face purpling with rage, then hurled the weight and the briefcase on the deck.

Ellen looked dismayed, correctly reading doom for all of them in Sam's expression. "What are you doing, Harry?" she said. "You're going to get our mother killed."

Harry paid her no attention whatsoever. He said to Sam, in very reasonable tones: "What you have there is a cashier's check – made out to me – for two hundred and fifty thousand dollars. All I have to do is countersign it and the check's in play. Good at any bank anywhere in the civilized world."

While Sam was taking this in, Danny blew high wide and handsome at this betrayal. A pistol suddenly appeared in fist and he leaped across the deck.

Shoved the gun up against Harry's goddamned head.

Danny said, "Think you're a smart ass, huh? Well, I'll show you a smart ass." And he got next to Harry, jamming the gun up against his head. He cranked the hammer back.

Harry kept his cool. Looking quite unconcerned. He said to Sam, "Is this how you negotiate?"

Sam couldn't believe what he was hearing. "You dumb mother fucker," he said. "You thought I was negotiating? What are you out of your fucking mind? What world have you been living in?"

He stuck his big face into Harry's. "I am a criminal, fuck head."

He indicated Danny. "We are both fucking criminals."

Ruth laughed bitterly. "Ain't that the truth," she said.

Sam shot her a dirty look. But before he could give Ruth a piece of his mind, Harry broke in. And he was very, very calm.

"Okay, so I don't have a great deal of experience with this exact sort of situation," he said. "But please, anybody born in America knows that everything is negotiable."

He indicated the check. "You are looking at half the money that you demanded right there in front of you. Two hundred and fifty thousand dollars. Now, I doubt whether you really considered what this whole deal would be worth when you started out."

152

Allan Cole

Harry gave Sam a shrewd look. "I think you just picked a figure – five hundred thousand dollars. That's what you saw in the books, am I right?"

Sam gave an inadvertent nod. That had been his thinking.

Harry took some encouragement at Sam's hesitation. He said, "Okay, so what I am saying is two hundred and fifty thousand dollars is an equitable settlement. A handsome sum. You can take it and go with no worry about police interference. Or, you can refuse my generous offer. Then wait until I collect the rest of the money and turn it into a cashier's check. Remembering, of course, that the longer this goes on, the more likely it is that something will go wrong."

Danny did not like all of the theoretical talk about this money goes to somebody and this money does not. He was about to explode with the supreme desire to bottom line old Harry.

"You're damn straight," Danny said. "Like being dead, kind of wrong."

But Sam sort of saw Harry's point. He waved Danny aside. "Let him go," he said.

"The asshole's tryin' to make a fool out of us, Sam," Danny protested.

Sam stayed firm. "I said, let him go."

Danny let Harry go. But reluctantly - keeping the gun on Harry as he backed off. Wanting to shoot him so bad he could taste it.

Sam said, "Okay, Harry, my boy, you wanted to negotiate. Get to it, then. My buddy here is getting damned impatient."

"What's to say?" Harry said. "I've already outlined my offer." He indicated the check. "Two hundred and fifty thousand dollars. Not a penny more." Sam pointed to Mrs. Berman. "One word," he said, "and Danny boy will blow her away."

"Damn straight," said Danny, getting really freaking tired of the whole stupid thing.

"Okay, so you kill my mother," Harry said. "But that won't get you more money. And it sure won't get me to counter-sign the check you've already got. Making it worthless."

Allan Cole

Drowned Hopes

Sam couldn't believe this guy's act. "You're betting that at some point I'm not going to lose my cool," he said.

He indicated Danny. "If you were dealing with just my friend Danny over there, he'd have already blown you and your mother and your sister away."

"Damn straight," Danny said again.

"That wouldn't be too intelligent," Harry said.

"But damned satisfying to Danny," Sam said.

"Nothing's more satisfying than money," Harry said.

"Do you really think that?" Sam said, starting to become amused. Getting relaxed. And not really giving a whole lot of shit about what happened next.

Sam decided that a dramatic gesture was needed. He walked over to Ruth, who looked up at him, alarmed.

"What are you doin', Sam?" she asked.

Sam ignored her. He said to Harry, "Allow me to demonstrate the criminal mind, Mr. Berman. This is how men like Danny and me cut to the final bottom line."

He suddenly grabbed Ruth by the scruff of the neck. She shrieked and her glass went flying, shattering on the deck.

Ruth shrieked, "Sam, don't."

Sam dragged her kicking across the deck.

Ellen freaked. "Stop it, Sam, please," she cried.

She jumped forward to help Ruth, but Sam pushed her away as if she were a child and she went skidding across the deck.

Sam said to an aghast Harry, "Check it out."

And he lifted Ruth up bodily and hurled her screaming into the sea.

Allan Cole

CHAPTER THIRTY-TWO

RUTH WENT UNDER for a long time, then came kicking up, coughing and sputtering, the boat moving slowly by her.

Danny woke up from his drug stupor big time. Laughing, he ran to the rail and watched Ruth swim for the yacht.

"Swim, Ruthie, swim," he cried.

The yacht's speed was minimal, so she caught up to it right away. She grabbed at the ladder, but Sam picked up a peevee pole and pushed her away.

Ruth screamed, "Sam. Sam."

Ellen rushed over and tried to pull the pole away. During the struggle, Ruth recovered enough to swim to the other side, grasping at anything she could get her fingers on. Sam batted Ellen away and she fell to the deck.

He looked down at Ruth, whose grip was slipping across the boat's smooth surface.

Sam held out the peevee pole for her. "Come on, Ruthie, baby," he said. "Come on, sweetheart."

Ruth turned toward the pole and struck desperately out for it.

Sam dangled it just beyond her reach. "Daddy was only teasing, sweet pie," he crooned. "Only teasing."

Ruth got a grip on the pole, putting a death grip on that sucker. Keeping herself from drowning.

And Sam laughed like he'd just sprung the biggest joke in the world and plunged the pole deep into the water, pushing Ruth under.

"Psyche," Sam shouted.

Danny liked that. And he shouted: "Oh, wow, psyche,"

Ruth came up again, gasping.

Danny said, "Do it again, Sam."

Sam did it again, catching Ruth by the neck with the pole's hook and pushing her under.

He let go, laughing with Danny as she came up, sputtering, mouth wide. "What a blow job that'd be, man." Danny said, really getting into it.

That made Sam mad. Ruth was his woman, after all.

He got a firm grip on the pole, hooked the tip into Ruth's blouse and bra, and pushed her under. As deep as he could.

"Enough," Sam said. "I'm bored."

He held it there for a very long time. He had to struggle a couple of times as Ruth fought. But he finally got the pole steady. And then a long stream of bubbles rose to the surface and the pole went lax.

Sam let go and turned to Harry. "See how it is?" he said.

Harry was stunned. He tried to speak, but nothing came out.

Sam immediately recovered his good mood. He rubbed his hands together. "I can't imagine that you didn't get my point," he said. "Smart man like you.'

Harry could do no more than nod.

Sam said, "Okay, then let's get the show back on the road."

He held up the check, pursed his lips and asked, "Where's the rest of it?"

Harry was way too battered by what had happened to deal with Sam sensibly. He said, numbly, "What are you talking about?" He indicated the piece of paper Sam held. "The check – that's all of it."

Sam laughed in his face. He knew when he had a guy cracked and ready.

"Don't try to con a con man," he said. "You can't tell me that a smart man like you would put yourself at the mercy of the likes of a mean-ass fellow like myself without some kind of a fallback."

Danny got what Sam was talking about. He poked Harry with his pistol. "Wanna get wet like old Ruthie?" he teased.

Even with this ultimatum, Harry still hesitated.

Ellen broke first. "For God's sake, Harry," she said. "Give him the damned money. As much as I hate your guts, I don't want to see you dead."

Grimly, Harry fished another cashier's check from his pocket and handed it over.

Allan Cole

Sam looked at it and his face lit up. "That's a lot better, Harry buddy, old boy," he said. "You should listen to your sister more often."

He reached into his pocket to get out the other check. "Got a pen?" he said, kidding, really in a good mood now.

Harry glumly shook his head.

Still going for his good mood, Sam said, "What about you, Ellen? Got a pen in that big damned bag of yours?"

He strode over and scooped up Ellen's beach bag. Ellen was practically coming out of her skin as he fished around.

He noticed the umbrella. "Still expecting rain, Ellen?" he said.

Ellen just shrugged, hoping to hell he didn't look a little closer.

Sam said, "Hey, here we go." And he pulled out a pen.

Dropped the beach bag and went to Harry. Shoved the pen into the lawyer's hand. Then he turned his back, leaning over to make a human writing surface. Harry just stood there, too scared not to comply, too humiliated to do what Sam wanted.

Sam said, "Get to it, Harry. My time's valuable too, you know?"

Harry hissed something under his breath, then signed. Sam laughed and craned his head to look over at Ellen. "Remember how the four grand tickled?" he said.

Ellen just stared at him.

Sam shrugged. "Just thought you'd like to know that half a million tickles more," he said.

When Harry was finished, Sam turned and plucked the checks from his fingers. He waved them at Danny. "Now, that's what I call a good day's work," he said. "Two hundred and fifty goddamned dollars for you. And two fifty for me. And Bob's your fucking uncle."

Danny frowned. "Who's Bob," he said.

Harry's spirits were returning. And with them, his nerve. "Jesus, what a dope," he said of Danny.

Sam sighed. "You just had to have the last word, didn't you?"

He stepped away to the corner and poured himself a drink. "Okay," he said. "Fine by me."

Allan Cole

Then he flexed his big muscles and strolled over to Harry, motioning for Danny to follow. "He thinks he's Jesus Christ," he said to Danny. "Let's see if he can walk on water, my friend."

Danny giggled and joined Sam.

Alarmed, Harry backed up, holding out his hands as if they could shield him.

"Hey," he said. "I thought we had a deal."

Allan Cole

CHAPTER THIRTY-THREE

SAM LOOKED OVER at Danny - a big grin on his face. "You remember this guy's action at Fist City?" he said.

Danny laughed. "Sure the fuck do."

Harry reacted to this, frightened. "You followed me to my gym?" he said.

Sam ignored him. "He acted like he was fucking Mike Tyson," he said to Danny. "Think he can keep it up?"

Danny moved toward him, raising his fists in a half-assed, street fighter way.

Harry was surprised and backed off, although he automatically raised his hands. "Hey," he said. "We had a deal."

Sam said, "Well, you know, my word's as good as my bond, Harry. Of course, I'm a criminal and hardly bondable, but don't let that influence you."

Harry kept backpedaling. Holding out his hands as if they could shield him. Sam joined Danny, pushing the attorney back and back.

Harry said, "Hold on. Maybe we can-" And he bumped into the rail.

Sam said, "I guess I just cancelled whatever deal you had in mind."

Desperate, Harry took a swing at Sam.

Sam slipped the punch easily and knocked Harry down with a blow so hard it took all the strength out of him.

Harry came up, grabbing at air, catching one of Sam's arms – but only because Barr let him.

Sam rocked him back and forth, thinking Harry's death grip was funny. "Help me out here, Danny," he said. "This guy's a heavy son of a bitch. All that damned muscle, you know?"

Laughing at the joke, Danny holstered his gun, then grabbed Harry by the other arm. With Sam helping, he swiveled Harry's big body around and got ready to run the attorney over the side.

"He and Ruth can have some fun together, " Danny shouted as they raced toward the rail.

But Ellen was up before them, brandishing her stun umbrella. "Please, Sam," she pleaded. "No."

She raced over, fumbling for the trigger with nervous fingers. But before she could get a steady grip, Sam gave her a shove and she fell back on the deck.

Mrs. Berman thought it was all a game. She clapped her hands and shouted, "Let's all go swimming."

Sam and Danny got Harry under the elbows and were about to give him the old heave, ho, when a voice cracked out: "Well, Well. What are you folks up to? No good, by the looks of things."

Jolted, the men turned to see Sergeant Propp standing there in a classic shooter's crouch, gun aimed straight at Sam. Just behind him, the Wellcraft bobbed up and down in the warm seas, tied by a light line to the Freebooter.

Propp said, "Now, you boys stay just like you are. I don't want to have to do anything hasty."

Ellen, lying sprawled on the deck, the umbrella clutched in her hand, couldn't believe her good fortune. "Thank God," she said.

"Never thought you'd be glad to see the likes of me, huh?" Propp laughed.

Ellen shook her head, grinning like a fool. But before she could say anything more, Propp came out of his crouch and advanced on Sam and Danny.

"You really should have been nicer to me Ellen," Propp said. "Now I don't give a shit what happens to you."

He wagged the gun at Sam. "Give," he said.

Sam shrugged and said, "Top pocket."

Propp nodded and carefully reached out with his left hand and dug the checks out of Sam's shirt pocket. He fumbled them apart with one hand and glanced at the figures. Then whistled in appreciation.

"Five hundred grand," he said. "Damn. I thought that's what I heard you guys talking about. But I figured it was too good to be true."

160

Allan Cole

He took a step back. "You can resume killing yourselves, boys," he said. He used his gun to indicate Harry, who was still being held up by Sam. "Over the side with that asshole first."

Propp motioned at Ellen and Mrs. Berman. "The broads next." Then he gave a wide grin. "Maybe we'll have a last drink together before I do you and your pal, there."

But Sam wasn't going that easily. He shouted, "Get him Danny."

At the same time, Sam dropped Harry on the deck and lunged forward, Danny only a half step behind him, drawing his gun and screaming at the top of his lungs:

"Fuck youuuu!"

Propp got off a shot, but it was too hurried - Danny's sudden scream had unnerved him. Sam powered into the cop, knocking him flat on his back. Propp tried to get up, but Danny fired, the bullet slamming Propp back down.

While this was going on, Harry saw his chance and charged into the melee, swinging his big fists as he bulled into Sam and Danny.

Sam was momentarily stunned by Harry's desperate charge, but Danny stepped to the side. He raised his gun to fire, but Propp managed to recover enough to get off a final shot.

The bullet hit Danny in the chest and he toppled to the deck, dead.

Propp tried to fire once more – aiming at Sam - but then all his strength left him and he fell back, shuddering his last breath.

Even so, Harry had been given just enough time to regain his senses. He squared off against Sam, head hunched between muscular shoulders, fists high, coming at Sam with a boxer's flat-footed shuffle.

"Now we'll see who's boss, you stupid son of a bitch," he said.

Sam looked him up and down and laughed. "Yeah, I guess we will," he said.

He advanced on Harry, sneering, mocking him by keeping his hands down at his side. Harry swung, but Sam easily slipped the punch and slapped Harry across the face.

161

Allan Cole

Harry's eyes widened as he realized that this wasn't going to be as simple as he thought. He charged into Sam, delivering a flurry of blows, but Sam danced around him, playing with him.

Then Sam stumbled over Propp's corpse and Harry leaped forward to deliver a pile driver blow. Sam ducked his head, taking the punch on his skull.

There was the sound of bones cracking. His fist broken, Harry shrieked.

Sam laughed and slapped his face again. "So, now who's boss, Mr. Lawyer man?" Sam said.

Then he slammed a fist into Harry's gut, doubling him over. He said, "Hey – quick lawyer joke. What's the difference between a lawyer and a tick?"

Harry moaned, trying to suck air into his tortured lungs.

Sam said, "The tick falls off you when you're dead." He laughed. "What's the matter, Harry?" he said. "Don't like lawyer jokes?"

Another hammer blow drove Harry to his knees. "You know," Sam said, "I've always wondered if you really could kick shit out of a man," Sam said. "And I aim to find out before this day is through."

He kicked Harry in the side, knocking him on his back to paw at the air helplessly. Sam kicked him again. And then again.

"Oh, God," Harry wept. "God."

"I like to see a man who knows when to pray," Sam said.

Then he said, "Another lawyer joke: Two law partners go to lunch. In the middle of lunch, one of the lawyers suddenly jumps up. 'Jesus,' he says, 'we forgot to lock the office safe.' His partner shrugs. 'What's to worry about?' he says. 'We're both here.'"

More laughter. Then Sam leaned down to examine Harry, who was writing in pain. "Shit, man," he said. "You need to get yourself a sense of humor."

And he kicked him again.

Allan Cole

CHAPTER THIRTY-FOUR

ELLEN WAS HORRIFIED at the terrible beating her brother was taking. But she had sense enough to realize this might be her last chance to save her mother and herself.

She snatched the umbrella up and grabbed Mrs. Berman by the elbow. "Come on, Ma," she whispered fiercely.

Mrs. Berman pulled back, very upset. "Why is Harry hurting that man?" she asked.

"Shh, Ma. Shh," Ellen said.

She coaxed her mother from the chair and the two women fled along the deck to the bow, where Ellen found Propp's boat tied up.

Ellen guided her mother to the ladder. "Down there, Ma. And hurry," she said.

Mrs. Berman obeyed, clambering over the side and going down the ladder.

Meanwhile, Ellen grabbed the rope and slowly pulled Propp's boat closer to the yacht.

Mrs. Berman started to step onto the deck of the Wellcraft, then hesitated. She looked up at Ellen, eyes wide with worry. "We have to help Harry," she said.

Two gunshots erupted from the stern of the yacht. Ellen jumped at the sound. Two more shots followed.

She looked down at her mom. "Harry's dead, Ma," she said as calmly as she could. "Some bad men killed him. Now we have to save ourselves… Okay?"

Mrs. Berman gave a negative shake of her head. This was all too much for her.

"Ma," Ellen cried. "Don't give up now. Please, Ma?"

Suddenly, Mrs. Berman's face cleared. To Ellen it seemed like a light dawning.

"I won't, Ellen," she said, calling her daughter by her name for the first time.

Despite their desperate situation, Ellen couldn't help be rocked by her mother's sudden recognition of her. Tears streamed down her face.

"Go on, Ma," she said. "Hurry, please."

Mrs. Berman dropped to the deck of the Wellcraft and scrambled out of the way. She looked back up at her daughter.

"Come on, Ellen," she said. "It's your turn now."

Ellen started climbing over the rail so she could follow her mother down the ladder. But there was a sudden noise of a heavy feet and Ellen looked up to see Sam poised on the flying deck above her.

"Weren't you even going to say goodbye, Ellen?" he said. "After all I've done for you?"

Then he jumped lightly down to Ellen's deck. She held up the umbrella toward him off. "Don't come any closer," Ellen warned him.

Sam looked at the umbrella and laughed. "What are you going to do with that thing?" he said. "Play Mary Poppins on my sweet white ass?"

He reached out a hand.

Immediately Ellen jabbed him. A long blue arc of electricity streaked out and Sam howled as he was knocked to the deck by 80,000 volts.

He sat up, gasping for breath. "Jesus," he said. "What was that?"

Sam jumped back onto his feet and pulled his gun from his waistband. Jabbed the barrel at the umbrella.

"You've been shopping for tricky stuff, haven't you, Ellen?" he said. He raised the pistol. "Too bad you didn't buy a gun instead."

Before he could fire, Ellen lunged forward again. This time she zapped the gun. Sam wrenched back. The pain was hot and awful.

"God damn," he shouted. And in his agony, he reflexively pulled the trigger.

And bang! The sound of the gun going off turned Ellen's ear drums into fiery bells. She flinched to the side, but the bullet had already gone by, plowing into fuel cans tied up against the bulkhead.

Allan Cole

Drowned Hopes

Gasoline poured out and ran down the deck. The smell of it frightened Ellen and she backed off.

Sam made a grab for her, but Ellen was quicker, letting him have it with her weapon. This time the jolt knocked the gun out of his hand.

She advanced on her enemy, the umbrella at the ready.

Sam backed up a few steps, splashing through the running gasoline. "Screw this," he said. "I'm getting the other gun."

He whirled and ran down the alleyway.

Ellen bolted for the railing. She started to clamber over, but before she could escape, Sam came racing back.

He spotted her and raised the gun to fire. "Nice knowing you, Ellen," he said.

But Ellen was quicker and she desperately stabbed the umbrella into a pool of gasoline on the deck.

A long blue arc leaped from the tip and the fuel exploded in Sam's face.

He screamed and fired wildly in every direction as he spun around and around. His whole body engulfed in flames.

Ellen turned and dived into the water. She surfaced, then struck out for Propp's boat. She grabbed the ladder and climbed up on deck. She rushed past her mother to the captain's chair. She grabbed the wheel and searched around for the starter.

"Do you know how to drive one of these things, Ellen?" Mrs. Berman asked.

"No, Ma," Ellen said.

Then she saw the key in the ignition and gave it a twist. The engine roared into life. She pulled on the throttle and instantly the boat lurched backward, slamming into the yacht.

"Damn," Ellen said.

She pushed the throttle forward.

The engine stalled.

Frantic, she hit the ignition switch.

Nothing.

Another attempt and this time the engine roared into life.

Allan Cole

But suddenly a burning figure leaped from the yacht and dove into the water.

It was Sam.

He surfaced, eyes crazy in his blackened face. Sam lunged forward, grabbing one of the lines trailing behind the boat.

He wrapped a length around his wrist then pulled himself toward the Wellcraft, hand over hand.

"Ellen," he said in a ghastly croak.

Ellen throttled forward and the boat surged away. But Sam clung to the line.

On the deck, the line was unraveling from a coil. Attached to the end of a coil was an anchor.

Sam's weight pulled the anchor across the deck and it started to go over the side.

Then it jammed against the rail and Sam began to use his incredible strength to pull himself closer and closer to the Wellcraft.

Ellen rushed to the anchor and struggled to free it. "Help me, Ma," she shouted.

Mrs. Berman ran to her daughter's side.

The two women fought with the anchor – Sam getting closer all the time.

Then it jerked free and splashed into the water.

Sam suddenly found himself treading water – and Ellen's boat was speeding away.

Then the anchor's weight started to pull him under.

He gulped water and fought like hell to stay afloat and untangle the line from his wrist.

His head went under – once, twice, three times.

Ellen looked back and saw him disappear from sight, never to rise again.

At that moment the Freebooter exploded into flames.

And suddenly Ellen found herself back at the wheel, guiding the Wellcraft through a hailstorm of fiery debris.

Then it was over and Ellen sagged in relief as she realized they were finally safe.

166

Allan Cole

Her mother hugged her. "I'm so glad to see you, Ellen," she said.

"Me too, Ma," Ellen said, laughing and crying at the same time.

Mrs. Berman glanced at her watch. "If we hurry we can catch Perry Mason," she said.

"I'm hurrying as fast as I can, Ma," Ellen said.

And she threw the throttle forward and the boat shot toward the blue rim of the Florida coast.

THE END

167

Allan Cole

DROWNED HOPES

THE SCREENPLAY

By Allan Cole

DROWNED HOPES

BY ALLAN COLE

FADE IN:

EXT. RUM RUNNER'S CLUB - NIGHT

Hot DANCE MUSIC singes the night as a YOUNG COUPLE exits a
trendy Florida nightclub. The GIRL is sexy as can be in her
micro-mini dance outfit. She does some impromptu bumps to the
music, driving her boyfriend nuts. He coaxes her into the
dark parking lot.

                    GIRL
               (sulky)
          I wanna dance some more!

                    BOYFRIEND
          Sure, baby. But let's rest in the
          car for awhile.

                    GIRL
          Resting? Ha!

But the kid persists and the girl lets herself be drawn
onward until they reach a flashy JEEP. The boyfriend gets the
door open and pulls the girl in after him. At the same time
his hands grope under that micro-mini. The girl is starting
to go for it, then her eyes widen in sudden fear as she sees:

A MUGGER

Looming over them. Grinning and waving a gun. The frightened
girl slaps at her oblivious boyfriend.

                    GIRL
          Stop! Stop!

                    THUG
               (to the boyfriend)
          You heard the bitch!

The boyfriend realizes what's going on and reacts - scared as
hell. He pushes the girl away.

                    BOYFRIEND
          No problem, man. No problem.

The thug fishes a trash bag out of his back pocket. Shoves it
into the kid's hands.

                    THUG
          Put it in there, shit for brains.
          And I mean everything!

                    GIRL
          Just don't hurt us.

They do what they're told. Stripping off jewelry and watches.
Getting out their wallets. Dumping them into the bag.

                    THUG
          Hurry up, assholes.

Just then - from behind the thug's back - a HAND shoots into
FRAME!

The hand clamps across the thug's mouth, cutting off his
squeal of surprise.

Then he's jerked backward by an enormous force. We hear two
heavy THUMPS and the thief's groans of pain.

Beat, beat. The hand comes away and the thug sighs and slowly
sags to his knees. Then he pitches forward on his face.

The girl and her boyfriend stare in shock as:

SAM BARR

Steps into the FRAME. Sam is as big as a mountain and crafty
as a fox. A breaker or heads and hearts. Few who meet him are
lucky enough to escape unscathed.

Barr leans down and plucks the gun from the mugger's fist.
Puts it in his pocket.

                    BOYFRIEND
          Thanks, man. I thought he was gonna
          kill us.

But the girl is still staring at the unmoving figure.

                    GIRL
          Is he... he... dead?

Sam kicks the mugger. No reaction. He chuckles.

                    SAM
          Guess I don't know my own strength.

The girl gives a little squeak. The boyfriend just stands
there, frozen in place.

Still chuckling, Sam fishes a handful of pills from his
pocket and pops them into his mouth. Chews. Then he indicates
the bag of loot in the boyfriend's hand.

                    SAM
               (continuing)
          I'll take that.

                         BOYFRIEND
                    (puzzled)
          What?

                    SAM
          The bag. Give it here.

                         GIRL
          You mean... you're... you're ...
          robbing us?

                    SAM
          Nope. I'm robbing the guy who was
          robbing you.
               (chuckles)
          You know - mugging the mugger.

He takes the bag of loot from the boyfriend. Goes to the
girl. She's too spooked to move. And her boyfriend sure isn't
going to say anything.

Sam sniffs her hair appreciatively, as if it were rare wine.

                    SAM
               (continuing; softly)
          Hmm. Nice.
               (beat)
          Maybe I'll give you a call a little
          later on.

The girl doesn't say a word as he strokes her face. She
shudders but she stands very straight and still, scared of
what might happen. Sam leans in and kisses her on the lips.

                    SAM
               (continuing; voice low)
          Yeah, I just might do that.

Then he turns and strides off into the night. The girl scrubs
furiously at her lips.

                         BOYFRIEND
          Shit! We gotta call the cops.

                         GIRL
          Are you crazy? He's got our
          wallets. Our addresses.
               (beat)
          Let's get out of here before he
          comes back!

Immediately, the boyfriend comes unstuck and the two leap into the Jeep. He panics and the Jeep jerks backward, bumping over the mugger's body.

                    GIRL
                 (continuing)
           Shit, shit, shit!

Then he gets it straightened out and they peel away!

EXT. SPANISH OAKS DRIVE - TRACKING LIMO - DAY

A sleek limo moves through a blue collar neighborhood. It's slow-going - dozens of PEOPLE are out getting ready for a street party: There's banners, a bandstand, food booths, etc. KIDS run in and out of the scene, shouting and getting generally underfoot. Music and sporting events blare from half-a-dozen car radios and boomboxes.

People move out of the way when the limo driver taps the horn, staring as the car goes by, trying to peer through the darkened windows to see who is inside.

At the end of the street is an older apartment house, painted in faded Florida colors. The place seems forbidding. Especially when we see:

SAM BARR

Sitting on the front steps. He's chewing on pills and slugging down orange juice. Barr wears cutoffs and a muscle shirt. This guy makes Arnie look like a hundred pound weakling. You could break rocks on his biceps.

He looks up with sudden interest as the limo pulls in front of the apartment house. A uniformed CHAUFFEUR steps from the limo and goes to the rear door. The whole neighborhood watches as he opens the door and:

AN ELEGANT WOMAN - ELLEN BERMAN

Climbs out of the car. She pauses, looking around. Ellen's an attractive woman in her late thirties or early forties. She looks as out of place in this neighborhood as the limo.

                    CHAUFFEUR
           I'll get your things, Mrs. Berman.

He pops the trunk and unloads a few pieces of luggage. He also lifts out several tubes used to transport paintings; an easel; Paint-spattered boxes and containers; rolls of colorful material. All and all a very weird assortment of possessions for a place like this.

While he unloads the stuff, the front door of the apartment building opens and RUTH CASTRO comes out. Ruth is attractive, in a slatternly sort of way. She goes to Ellen.

> RUTH
> Hi. I'm Ruth Castro. You must be my new tenant.

> ELLEN
> (shakes her hand)
> Pleased to meet you, Mrs. Castro.

> RUTH
> Just call me Ruth. My husband was Cuban. But he's dead now.

Ellen doesn't quite know how to take this. But manages to bury her reaction. Ruth looks at the chauffeur. Indicates the stuff on the lawn.

> RUTH
> (continuing)
> Bottom floor, front.

> CHAUFFEUR
> (snotty as hell)
> My job ends at the sidewalk.

> ELLEN
> (anxious to avoid a scene)
> That's okay. I can get it.

But just then Sam walks into the Frame. He goes to the driver, grips his shoulder with one vise-like hand and picks up a suitcase with the other.

> SAM
> The lady said bottom floor, front.

The driver winces in severe pain.

> RUTH
> Apartment Six.

Sam squeezes harder, almost bringing the guy to his knees.

> SAM
> Got that?

> CHAUFFEUR
> (nodding vigorously)
> Yea-yea-yeah!

Sam lets go and the driver grabs luggage and starts hauling ass. Ellen smiles at Sam in gratitude.

                         ELLEN
              Thank you, Mister - uh...

Looks at Ruth. Who quickly steps into the breach.

                         RUTH
              This big hunk of lovin' is Sam
              Barr.
                   (beat)
              Sam, this is Ellen Berman. Your new
              neighbor.

Barr eyes Ellen with appreciation.

                         SAM
              My pleasure.

He pops some more pills, brushes off his hand. Holds it out.
Ellen nervously takes it.

                         ELLEN
                   (a little awkward)
              How do you do?

Barr releases her hand. Fishes out some more pills, then
washes them down with orange juice. Ellen eyes the pills, a
little shocked. Barr notices and chuckles.

                         SAM
              Have to get my daily dose of
              aminos.

Ellen looks puzzled. Sam flexes a huge bicep.

                         SAM
                   (continuing)
              Like vitamins. They help with my
              workouts.

Ellen gets it. Blushes.

                         ELLEN
              Oh. Yes... Workouts.

Sam nods pleasantly, then strolls back to the steps - Ellen's
curious eyes following him. Ruth clears her throat and
Ellen's eyes snap back.

                         RUTH
              About the rent...

                         ELLEN
                   (slight panic)
              But I mailed it to you. First and
              last, plus a deposit.
                   (MORE)

                    ELLEN (cont'd)
          It was a money order for one
          thousand, five- hundred-

                    RUTH
               (breaking in)
          Never got it.

                    ELLEN
          But it was a money order!
               (digs in her purse)
          I have the receipt for it somewhere
          in here.

Ruth gives her a shrewd look. She can see that panic city is
starting to set in. For some reason, this pleases her.

                    RUTH
               (soothing)
          Calm down, Ellen. I can call you
          Ellen, can't I?

                    ELLEN
          Of course, but...

She's still frantically digging in her purse. Ruth stops her.

                    RUTH
          Never mind. Today's mail didn't
          come yet. The guy's always late on
          Saturday. It'll get cleared up
          then.
               (beat)
          Come on. I'll show you your new
          place.

As they approach the front porch, Sam nods at Ellen
pleasantly. Ruth opens the front door and motions for Ellen
to go first.

                    RUTH
               (continuing; whispering)
          Hands off. He's mine.

                    ELLEN
               (startled)
          Oh! Sure. Sure.

As she goes inside Sam eyes her figure with gleaming eyes.

                    SAM
          Nice.

INT. ELLEN'S APARTMENT - DAY

Ellen and Ruth step aside as the chauffeur dumps the last of
the stuff and bulls past them.

                    RUTH
         Be it ever so humble...

She waves her hand at the living room. It's nice enough, in a
Motel Sixish sort of way. ND furniture. Matching pictures on
the wall. Ellen looks around. Poker faced.

                    ELLEN
         Very nice, thank you. I'm sure I'll
         be quite comfortable here.

                    RUTH
              (grinning)
         Used to a whole lot better, huh?

                    ELLEN
              (embarrassed)
         No, honestly. It really is very
         nice. I'll have it looking like
         Ellen's Place in no time.

                    RUTH
         That's a relief. I was worried
         you'd hate it.
              (beat)
         Tell the truth, I've never done a
         rental like this. Sight unseen on
         both sides. Everything by long
         distance phone and overseas mail.
              (beat)
         Jamaica, right?

                    ELLEN
         Right.

                    RUTH
         I didn't know you from Adam. Still
         don't.
              (laughs)
         On the other hand, I'm not
         acquainted with Adam, either.

She looks at the easel and painting gear heaped by the
window.

                    RUTH
              (continuing)
         You some kind of artist?

                    ELLEN
              (shyly)
         I like to think that I am.
              (beat)
         I had a gallery in Jamaica. It was
         just getting popular when I had to,
         uh, you know - leave.

                    RUTH
Had to split in a hurry, did you?

                    ELLEN
          (embarrassed)
It was just a... you know...
business misunderstanding.

                    RUTH
I hear you. Didn't mean to pry.
Hells, bells. There's nothing Ruth
Castro doesn't know about business
misunderstandings. Been on my own
since my husband died and I tell
you, it's shameful how ready people
are to cheat a woman alone.
          (beat)
You really have to watch yourself,
you know?

                    ELLEN
          (warming to her)
Absolutely! I never realized...
until... well... recently... what
some people are capable of. I
suppose I was naive.

Ruth eyes her speculatively.

                    RUTH
That was quite a car you showed up
in. The neighbors have never seen
anything like it. Me neither, as a
matter of fact.

                    ELLEN
I hope I didn't give them the wrong
impression. My brother arranged for
the car to pick me up at the
airport.

                    RUTH
By arranged, you mean he's payin'
for it.

                    ELLEN
          (laughing)
He'd better! I don't have that kind
of money. Especially after... well,
you know... Jamaica.

                    RUTH
The business misunderstanding?

                    ELLEN
Yes. It was, umm—

MUSIC blares OS, interrupting her.

                    RUTH
          There's a street party tonight.
          Cinco de something that the Latinos
          celebrate every year. Check it out,
          if you want. Meet some of the
          neighbors.

                    ELLEN
          Thanks. I'll do that.

Ruth starts to leave. Then stops in the doorway.

                    RUTH
          About Sam. He'll probably come on
          to you. You know how men are?

                    ELLEN
              (smiles)
          I should just slap his face and
          send him home, right?

                    RUTH
              (suddenly serious)
          Oh, honey! You don't want to slap a
          man like Sam Barr. Not ever!

And she leaves. Ellen stares after her, emotion building up
inside. Her hands start to shake. Then she forces calm.

                    ELLEN
          Come on, girl! Get a grip!

She turns. Looks around the living room. The ugly picture
over the couch catches her eye. She makes some sort of
decision and lifts it off its hanger and puts it on the
floor.

She gets one of the tubes, pops off the end and pulls out a
large poster. Unrolls it, revealing a fabulous tropical
montage swirling with fiery colors. It's advertising a
gallery opening. But advertisement or not, one glance at the
poster and there's no doubt that Ellen is a talented artist.

The poster reads: CATCH A FIRE AT ELLEN's WORLD.

She starts pinning the poster to the wall with thumbtacks,
humming the Jimmy Cliff song: "You can get it if you really
want... You can get it if you really want..."

EXT. SPANISH OAKS DRIVE - NIGHT

The party's going full blast. Barricades set up at either end
of the street. Colorful lights. Smoky barbecues.

Kids and - people making merry. On the bandstand, a GARAGE
BAND tunes up.

Sam Barr mans a grill, flipping huge burgers and swigging
from a bottle of juice. A PRETTY GIRL in a thong bikini
nuzzles up to him. He whispers in her ear. The girl giggles
and shakes her head. He whispers again. More head shaking.

Finally he sets the flipper down, takes her by the elbow and
escorts her to a little alleyway between the apartment
building and the next house.

They disappear into it just as Ruth emerges. She looks around
the street, searching for Sam.

                    RUTH
               (calling out)
          Sam? Sam?

No answer. Then she spots the untended burgers, frowns and
hurries over to the grill and starts turning them.

                    RUTH
               (continuing)
          Damn him.

INT. ELLEN'S APARTMENT - NIGHT

The place has been transformed. Her artwork on the walls.
Bolts of colorful cloth cover the furniture. Her easel placed
by a picture window that overlooks the backyard. OS we can
hear the shower running and Ellen humming to herself.

INT. ELLEN'S BATHROOM - NIGHT

Ellen's in the shower still humming that tune. She cuts the
water, grabs a towel and emerges, the towel wrapped around
her. At the mirror she rubs the steam off and studies herself
a moment. Then shakes her finger at the image.

                    ELLEN
          We're getting a whole new start,
          right, girl?

A sudden OS THUMP against the outside wall startles her.
Ellen turns to look. But sees nothing. Another THUMP. Then
another. Ellen goes to the bathroom window. Cracks it open.
The thumps come louder and clearer.

                    ELLEN
               (continuing)
          Hello? Who's out there?

The thumps continue.

                    ELLEN
              (continuing; furious)
        Get away from there, you hear me?
              (beat)
        I'll tell your mother.

Someone laughs. Ellen backs out of the bathroom, the towel
pulled tight around her.

EXT. APARTMENT HOUSE - NIGHT

Ruth is at the grill, serving burgers to people when Ellen
exits the building and hurries over to her. She's clearly
upset and ready to complain. But before she can speak:

                    RUTH
              (snapping)
        Have you seen my Sam?

Ellen's taken aback by her tone.

                    ELLEN
        No.

                    RUTH
        He didn't come knocking at your
        door, asking if maybe you needed
        something?

                    ELLEN
        Certainly not. As matter of fact, I
        was just taking a shower, when-

OS laughter interrupts her. She and Ruth turn to see Sam and
the girl emerging from the alleyway. They both spot Ruth
staring daggers at them. Sam holds up several large avocados.
The girl makes herself scarce. Sam strolls over to the grill.

                    SAM
        Little Kimberly there wanted to see
        your avocado tree.

                    RUTH
              (angry)
        Avocados, huh?

                    SAM
        Sure, baby. How else can we make
        guacamole?

Sam chuckles. He skillfully juggles the avocados, then hands
them to Ellen with a flourish.

                    SAM
              (continuing; winking)
         You know how to make guacamole,
         don't you, Ellen?

                    ELLEN
              (nervous laugh)
         I'm afraid I missed that issue of
         Martha Stewart Magazine.

                    SAM
         Is that so?
              (yawns and stretches)
         I think I'll go take a little nap.

He leans forward and kisses Ruth on the cheek. Then turns and
strolls off. Ruth stares after him - she's furious. Ellen
tries to pretend she didn't notice anything.

Then Ruth sighs and gives a little laugh. Goes back to
flipping burgers.

                    RUTH
         I shouldn't get so mad at him. He's
         like a little boy. Wants everything
         he sees.
              (beat)
         It's those bitches like Kimberly
         who are to blame. Wagging their
         asses at him all the time. What's
         he gonna do? He's a man, isn't he?

Ellen doesn't say anything. Glances at the avocados in her
hand and shivers - yuk. She gets rid of them.

                    ELLEN
         How long have you and Sam been
         going together?

                    RUTH
         Six months.
              (beat)
         Ever since he got out of prison.

Ellen tries to bury her shocked reaction.

                    ELLEN
         Prison?

                    RUTH
         Sure. Where'd you think he got
         those hunky muscles?

Ellen doesn't know what to say.

                         RUTH
                  (continuing; grinning)
            I know what you're thinking. You're
            wondering what he was in for.

                         ELLEN
            Well, I have to confess that I'm
            curious.

                         RUTH
            He was a bank robber.
                  (beat)
            Not a common thug, but a real class
            act, you know?

                         ELLEN
            Uh... well... Sure.

                         RUTH
            He's not into that line of work
            anymore. Besides making all those
            nice muscles, he got himself two
            years worth of college credit while
            he was in prison. Soon as he gets
            enough money saved, he's going to
            get his degree. You watch and see.
            Sam is a determined man. He's going
            places, that's for sure.

                         ELLEN
            Very admirable.

                         RUTH
            He's gonna get his degree in
            psychology. Then open a clinic to
            help troubled kids.

                         ELLEN
            What kind of work does Sam do now?

                         RUTH
            Little of this and a little of
            that. You know... self employed.
                  (beat)
            He does very well, believe me.

Over Ruth's shoulder we can see the curtains part in Ellen's
living room. Someone is watching the women.

INT. ELLEN'S APARTMENT - NIGHT

It's Sam! He chuckles, then turns away, letting the curtains
fall back into place. He strolls over to the poster hanging
over the couch. Studies it.

                    SAM
        Not bad.

He moves around the room, picking up things and examining
them. Humming a little tune to himself. Sam moves to the
bathroom. Enters.

INT. ELLEN'S BATHROOM - NIGHT

Sam spots the open window, goes to it and sticks his head
out, looking this way and that. He's got a big smile on his
face when he pulls his head back in.

                    SAM
        Naughty boy.

He goes to the medicine cabinet. Pops it open, picks up each
item he finds one by one. Even the toothbrush and toothpaste.
Shakes his head.

                    SAM
                (continuing)
        Ellen, Ellen. What do you do about
        birth control, woman?

He exits the bathroom and goes into:

INT. ELLEN'S BEDROOM - NIGHT

He switches on the light. Several of Ellen's tropical
paintings hang here and there. And there is a colorful bolt
of cloth thrown over the bed.

Sam goes to the bureau, opens a small jewelry case and paws
through Ellen's jewelry. He examines each item with an
expert's eye. He sighs. Nothing of value here. Shuts the
case, then starts checking out each bureau drawer.

He finds her underwear drawer, fingers the material.

                    SAM
        Better and better.

He digs under the underwear and comes up with something.
Holds it up to the light. It's a diaphragm case.

                    SAM
                (continuing)
        There's my girl.

He opens the case. Examines the contents, then replaces them.
And tucks the case back where it belongs.

There's the OS SOUND of a door opening and somebody coming
into the apartment. Sam quickly cuts the light. He flips a
knife out. The long blade gleams in the light streaming
through the open bedroom door. Sam moves closer to the door.
Through the crack, he can see Ellen moving around the room, a
cell phone at her ear.

INT. ELLEN'S LIVING ROOM - NIGHT

Ellen paces, puffing angrily on a cigarette. She reacts as
she and we hear the faint VOICE of an answering machine.

                    ELLEN
          Pick up the damned phone, Harry.
          It's Ellen. Your sister!
                    (no response)
          Damn you, Harry. Answer the stupid
          phone. You know why I'm calling. I
          need my money right now! No more
          excuses.

INT. ELLEN'S BEDROOM - NIGHT

Sam listens with increasing interest.

INT. ELLEN'S LIVING ROOM - NIGHT

Ellen stubs out the cigarette.

                    ELLEN
          Jesus Christ, Harry. You've got me
          living in some dump with an ex-con
          and his god damned gun moll
          girlfriend!
                    (beat)
          You hear me, Harry? You better pick
          up the phone. I won't stand for
          this one minute-

Ellen runs of steam and stops midsentence. She snaps the
phone shut and dumps it on the couch. She lights another
cigarette and starts pacing again. Smoking and pacing. She
stops in front of the painting. Frowns. Reaches out to touch
it as if it had been interfered with. Shakes her head.

                    ELLEN
                  (continuing)
          What am I going to do?

She puts out the cigarette. Starts to get another, but the
pack is empty. She crumples it and goes to the bedroom.
Pushes the half-closed door open and walks in.

INT. ELLEN'S BEDROOM - NIGHT

Ellen snaps on the light. No one there. Ellen crosses to the
bureau, opens a drawer and gets out another pack. Suddenly
she stops. Something about the jewelry box catches her
attention. Frowning, she opens it and fingers the contents.
Satisfied, she closes the box.

Then her hand goes to her underwear drawer. More frowns. As
if she senses something. She opens the drawer, moves things
around. Then shakes her head. Sighing she shuts the drawer.

Ellen turns to leave. Then notices that the closet door is
open. And we're wondering - is there where Sam is hiding?

She crosses to the closet. And for a minute we're scared to
death she's going to look inside. Instead, she slams the
door.

                    ELLEN
          Harry is such an asshole!

And she hurries out of the room, snapping off the light as
she goes. We can hear her cross the living room, open the
front door, then exit the apartment.

Beat, beat. Then the closet door slowly opens and Sam steps
out, the knife in his hand. He chuckles, flips the knife
shut. And exits the room.

EXT. SPANISH OAKS DRIVE - NIGHT

Ellen strolls along the street, trying to forget her
troubles. But as she moves away from the apartment building:

CHEATER ANGLE

A SHADOWY FIGURE steps out from behind a parked van. The
Figure waits until she's well ahead, then follows her.

The block party is going full blast now. The BAND is playing
Spanish rock. People dancing. Kids playing and shooting off
fireworks.

Lovers duck into the shadow of the trees to embrace. Soon
Ellen visibly relaxes, a smile on her face.

The mysterious figure - always seen from CHEATER ANGLES -
stalks her through all this, watching as she laughs at the
antics of children. Or stops at the bandstand.

Finally, she nears the barricades at the end of the block.
It's much darker here.

There's the OS MUSIC of an ice cream truck. Ellen steps out of the way as two kids burst out of the darkness, ice cream cones in their hands.

>   ELLEN
>   Yum, that looks good.

One of the kids - a little girl - points beyond the barricade.

>   LITTLE GIRL
>   He's right down there. Better hurry
>   if you want some.

The kids run off. Ellen laughs, then steps past the barricade. She could use a little sweet stuff to cheer her. Beat, beat, and the Shadowy Figure follows.

ON THE ICE CREAM TRUCK

Where the ICE CREAM MAN, dressed in the traditional white uniform, serves a few kids. Ellen comes up.

>   ELLEN
>   Do they still make Eskimo pies?

>   ICE CREAM MAN
>   (laughing)
>   Sure, lady. Here you go.

He digs an Eskimo pie out of the freezer and hands it over. She gives him money.

>   ICE CREAM MAN
>   (continuing)
>   Enjoy.

He hops in the truck and drives off, music playing. Ellen watches him go. She unwraps the ice cream. Takes a big bite.

>   ELLEN
>   Ambrosia thy name is Eskimo Pie.

She starts back toward the barricade. But as she passes a thick clump of bushes:

THE SHADOWY FIGURE

Leaps out and grabs her from behind! Ellen struggles and tries to scream. But her attacker is too strong and muffles her screams with a gloved hand. He drags her back into the bushes. Ellen kicks and kicks, but it's no use.

IN THE UNDERBRUSH

Ellen's attacker forces her down. She rakes his face with her nails, drawing blood. Pissed, the guy rears back to punch her.

Suddenly, a muscular hand shoots into the FRAME. Grabs the attacker by the offending arm and jerks him to his feet.

There are several loud THUMPS and then the man is just hanging there, dazed.

ON ELLEN

As she looks up from the ground and sees Sam Barr, the would-be rapist dangling from his big fist. Sam punches the man. Blood spurts from his face.

                    SAM
          Goddamn freak!

ANOTHER ANGLE

Sam punches him again. Then drops him. Gives him a kick. The man groans. Sam's knife comes out and he grabs the guy by the hair and pulls his head back.

                    ELLEN
               (shouting)
          Sam, don't!

Surprised, Sam lets the guy go. Immediately, he scrambles away and sprints down the street. Sam stares after him.

                    SAM
          Nothing I hate more than a pervert.

Then he looks over at Ellen. She's trying to straighten her clothes, but they are pretty messed up. Sam's wearing an Hawaiian shirt. He strips the shirt off and hands it over. She pulls it on - it's so big she could wear it as a dress.

                    ELLEN
          I don't know how I can...

She breaks off and starts to weep. Sam kneels beside her, but Ellen waves him away. Gets herself under control.

                    ELLEN
               (continuing)
          I'll be all right.

                    SAM
          Sure you will.
          (beat)
          Look, I'm sorry about this. It's
          really not a bad neighborhood. Nice
          people. I guess the party drew the
          creep onto our turf.

Ellen climbs to her feet. Determined to get her act together.

                    ELLEN
          I'm sure they are all absolutely
          wonderful people!

Sam offers her his arm. She takes it and they start to walk
back toward the block party. The music and crowd sounds
getting louder as they go. Ellen gives a shaky little laugh.

                    ELLEN
          (continuing)
          I really owe you an apology.

                    SAM
          For what?

                    ELLEN
          When we met I made a snap judgment.
          I was wrong.

                    SAM
          (chuckling)
          Ruth probably helped you along with
          that snap judgment. Told you about
          my ill-spent youth, right? And you
          were wondering what you'd gotten
          yourself into. Moving next door to
          an ex-con.

                    ELLEN
          (grimaces)
          Something like that.

                    SAM
          It's not a bad way to think. Very
          few ex-cons remain "exes" for long.
          I could tell you stories that
          would... well, it's no time to talk
          about Sam Barr's theories on the
          criminal justice system.

                    ELLEN
          For a minute there I thought you
          were going to kill that man.

                    SAM
               (shrugging)
          For a minute there, so did I.

                    ELLEN
          I wanted you to, I'm ashamed to
          say.
               (nervous laugh)
          But only for that theoretical
          minute.

                    SAM
          Nothing to be ashamed of.
          Theoretical, or otherwise.

They have reached the apartment house again. Ruth reacts when
she's sees that Ellen is wearing Sam's shirt

                    RUTH
               (super suspicious)
          What's going on here?

                    SAM
          Ellen just met some asshole on the
          way to the ice cream truck. Nearly
          got herself raped, is what is going
          on.

Ruth relents. She goes to Ellen, very concerned.

                    RUTH
          Are you okay, honey?

She pulls her toward the house.

                    RUTH
               (continuing)
          Let's get rid of those things and
          put on something fresh. And then
          we'll get you a nice, strong drink.

Soothed by Ruth's mothering, Ellen lets her take command.

                    ELLEN
          Thanks, Ruth.

Then she stops, remembering something.

                    ELLEN
               (continuing)
          Did the money come?

                    RUTH
               (frowning)
          What money?

                         ELLEN
          The money order. For the rent.

                         RUTH
                       (all smiles)
          Oh, sure it did. See. I told you.
          Nothing to worry about at all.

And she leads Ellen into the house. Sam staring thoughtfully
after them.

INT. ELLEN'S APARTMENT - DAY

It's the next day. Ellen, an artist's brush loaded with paint
in hand, stands before the big picture window. She's staring
out at an enormous tree that is ablaze with colorful
blossoms. She touches the brush to the glass and sketches a
faint outline of the tree on the window.

She suddenly breaks away, and turns to her easel where a
blank canvas is already in place. She hesitates, staring at
the blank canvas. She seems a little fearful at first. Then a
determined look transforms her face and her body language.

                         ELLEN
          So, let's start already, Ellen!

And she starts to paint.

A SERIES OF DISSOLVES

As the picture takes form. Ellen painting quickly and
expertly. Finally:

ANGLE ON THE PAINTING

It seems complete. A fabulous portrait of tropical life.

ANOTHER ANGLE

But Ellen doesn't seem satisfied. Her hand keeps going to an
empty place beside the tree.

                         ELLEN
          What, damn you? What are you trying
          to tell me?

Her cell phone rings, jarring her. Disgusted, she hurls the
brush down and grabs up the phone.

                    ELLEN
                 (continuing)
           Yes?

Her eyes widen in surprise.

                    ELLEN
                 (continuing; flat)
           Oh, it's you, Harry.

Listens some more, suspicion on her face.

                    ELLEN
                 (continuing)
           I don't need lunch at your club,
           Harry. I need my money.
                 (more listening)
           Don't start with me. Just do the
           right thing for a change.
                 (more listening; she
                  sighs)
           Okay, Harry. You win. As always.
           I'll see you at one o'clock. And
           never mind the stupid limo. I'll
           get there myself, if you don't
           mind.

She cuts off. Then she stands there very still, emotions
boiling within. She closes her eyes, holding the cell phone
to her breast like a child. Breathes in and out, getting
herself under control. Then she looks at the drawing. Sudden
hatred flares.

                    ELLEN
                 (continuing)
           What shit!

And she grabs a brush loaded with red paint and slashes a
large smear across the painting.

EXT. ELLEN'S APARTMENT - DAY

An old Mustang convertible is parked outside. Hood up, music
blaring from the radio. Sam is working on the engine. The
front door of the building bangs open and he sees Ellen stalk
out. His eyes light up. She's wearing a light summer dress,
heels, etc. Very sexy.

Just then a taxi pulls up and Ellen hurries over to it and
gets in. Immediately, Sam slams the hood down, leaps into his
car and takes off after the cab.

EXT. BEACH HIGHWAY - DAY

Ellen's cab cruises along A1A. It's a lovely South Florida day and the beach is full of nubile people at play. Sam follows, keeping well back.

EXT. COUNTRY CLUB DRIVE - DAY

The cab turns into a road that leads through tropical landscape to an exclusive Boca Raton country club. They stop at the GUARD SHACK, where a guard checks a list, then motions the cab inside.

ON THE MUSTANG

Sam pulls up and watches the cab vanish through the trees.

INT. COUNTRY CLUB - DAY

A MAITRE-DE escorts Ellen across a posh dining room with windows that look out on the INTERCOASTAL. Yachts and sailboats cruise the sparkling waters. But the fabulous view is lost on Ellen. She comes to a full stop as she sees:

ANGLE ON RACHEL BERMAN

Posed at the table like she's waiting for her close-up. About Ellen's age, she's got trophy wife written all over her. Expensively - and tastefully - dressed, coifed and jeweled. She spots Ellen, gives her a superior smile and raises a glass of white wine in a welcoming toast.

                    RACHEL
          It's good to see you again, Ellen.

Ellen comes unstuck and stalks over. She looks down at the table, notes the place settings.

                    ELLEN
               (flat)
          It's only set for two, Rachel.

Rachel sips her wine and nods.

                    RACHEL
          Yes... well, unfortunately Harry's
          on his way to Hawaii. Important
          business, you know. But he does
          send his regrets.

                    ELLEN
                (stunned)
            Hawaii? But... But... I just talked
            to him on the phone.

                    RACHEL
                (embarrassed shrug)
            He called from the airport.

                    ELLEN
                (furious)
            This is just so much bullshit! He
            can't even be bothered to have it
            out with his own sister. Instead he
            sends his wife. What a coward.
                (beat)
            I'm out of here, Rachel. Tell Harry
            that Ellen said to go screw
            himself!

But before she can storm away, Rachel holds up an envelope.

                    RACHEL
            Please, Ellen. I know this is
            awkward. But Harry did give me a
            check for you.

Ellen looks at the envelope. Then at Rachel, whose facade of
superiority has cracked. Ellen can tell that she really feels
bad about the situation.

                    ELLEN
            This is so humiliating, Rachel.

                    RACHEL
            I know. Harry can be infuriating
            sometimes. Come on, sit. There's
            things to discuss.

                    ELLEN
                (wary)
            What things?

                    RACHEL
            Well, your mother to start with.

Ellen's eyes widen.

                    ELLEN
            My mother! Is there something-

                    RACHEL
                (breaking in)
            Nothing urgent. But we have to
            talk. Please, Ellen. Sit.

Resigned, Ellen sits.

EXT. COUNTRY CLUB - DAY

Sam's parked across from the club entrance, chilling while he
waits for Ellen to emerge. A loud BACKFIRE gets his attention
and he turns to see a CITY BUS pull up. The doors open and
men and women pour out. Mostly black and Hispanic, they're
all country club employees.

But then, from out of a clump of tropical bushes, an immense
redneck CRACKER emerges. Wearing a Hawaiian shirt, Panama hat
and a generally mean attitude. He motions to the people.

                    SAM
          What's this?

Immediately, the workers go to him and one by one they hand
the Cracker money, then hurry off to work.

                    SAM
               (continuing)
          Smart!

One WORKER in a waiter's uniform tries to push by. Shaking
his head at the Cracker and telling him no deal. There's a
quick flurry of thumps and the waiter is knocked on his ass.

                    SAM
               (continuing)
          Not so smart.

Sam gets out of the Mustang and moseys over to the Cracker
just as the waiter hands over money and is sent on his way
with a kick in the butt. The Cracker sees Sam and turns,
glaring at him.

                    CRACKER
               (growling)
          What the hell you want, boy?

                    SAM
               (chuckling)
          Everything you've got, pal.

He reaches out a hand, snapping his fingers for the Cracker
to give. Instead the man explodes into motion, hurling an
enormous fist at Sam.

Sam slips gracefully to the side, grabs the man's hand and
slams down on the forearm with his own big fist.

There's a loud CRACK and the Cracker falls to his knees,
screaming in agony!

                         SAM
                     (continuing)
                 Jesus, what a baby!

He rips the shirt off and stuffs it in the guy's mouth,
muffling the screams. He pats him down, pulling out wads of
money and shoving the bills in his own pocket.

Whistling, Sam strolls away, leaving the Cracker kneeling
there. A black SECURITY GUARD comes running out of the
entrance. The guard sees the Cracker and stops. A big grin
appears on his face. He gives Sam a questioning look.

                         SAM
                 (continuing; shrugging)
                 Drunk, I guess.

And he sticks two bills into the Guard's pocket. The man's
grin gets bigger.

                         GUARD
                 That's my guess too.

INT. COUNTRY CLUB - DAY

Ellen toys with a salad, while Rachel eats with dainty gusto.

                         RACHEL
                 Everyone's still talking about you
                 in New York, Ellen. You've always
                 been so much more adventurous than
                 the rest of us. I simply don't know
                 how you managed the courage to run
                 off with that handsome beach boy.
                 All of us were dying with envy.

                         ELLEN
                 He wasn't a beach boy. He was an
                 attorney. A Jamaican attorney.

                         RACHEL
                 But he was... well, black, wasn't
                 he?

Ellen's anger gets the better of her.

                         ELLEN
                 As the ace of spades. Any other
                 details you want to know? Shirt
                 size? Penis size?

Rachel raises a hand.

                    RACHEL
          Please, Ellen. I didn't mean
          anything. It was just stupid
          nervous talk.

                    ELLEN
               (relenting)
          I'm not in the greatest shape,
          myself, Rachel. Sorry I blew up.
               (beat)
          To be honest, I'm pretty
          embarrassed. My Jamaica adventure
          went to hell. Along with the man of
          my so called dreams. My gallery, my
          paintings, my commissions - poof!
          Up in smoke.

                    RACHEL
          Harry said there was trouble with
          the authorities.

                    ELLEN
          Authorities! Please! They are
          thieves, it's as simple as that. I
          didn't know that I was basically
          living there under the protection
          of Andre.

                    RACHEL
          ... The man of your so called
          dreams?

                    ELLEN
          Well, yes. But I shouldn't give you
          the idea it was his fault. We broke
          up. He took a position in France.
          And the moment he was gone, the
          wolves moved in on me. They took
          everything I owned, then barred me
          from the country on some trumped up
          excuse.

                    RACHEL
          But, now you're back home, right?
          You can start over again. A new
          leaf, as they say.

                    ELLEN
          As they say.

She looks pointedly at the envelope next to Rachel's elbow.

                    ELLEN
               (continuing)
          Not to be crass, Rachel. But new
          leaves are expensive, you know?

Rachel nods, then picks up the envelope. Hands her the
envelope, but holds onto one corner as Ellen tries to take
it.

                    RACHEL
          But there are certain conditions,
          Ellen.
               (beat)
          Harry's conditions.

And she lets the envelope go. Ellen opens it, takes out a
check and examines the total. She reacts, pissed.

                    ELLEN
          What the hell is this? It's not
          even half!

                    RACHEL
          I know, I know. And I told Harry
          not to do this. Or, at least not
          force me to be the bearer of bad
          tidings.
               (sighs)
          But you know how he is.

                    ELLEN
          Cut to the chase, Rachel. What's
          Harry's pound of flesh? What do I
          have to do to get what's rightfully
          mine?

Rachel hesitates. She clearly finds this uncomfortable. Then:

                    RACHEL
          He wants you to assume more
          responsibility for your mother.

                    ELLEN
          My mother? He doesn't have to pay
          me to help my mother.
               (beat)
          That's why I came to Florida,
          instead of going back to New York.
          So I could be near her.

Suddenly, Ellen loses it. She slams her hand down on the
table! Glasses topple over. Water spills. People look.

                    ELLEN
               (continuing)
          What the hell is wrong with Harry?
          She's his mother too! And he can't
          talk to me about her face to face!

                    RACHEL
               (soothing)
          I know, Ellen. I know.

                    ELLEN
          No you don't know. He turned our
          father against me. And when father
          died, he did everything he could to
          control me. Forbid me to divorce
          Jim.
               (beat)
          Is that out of the Middle Ages or
          what? A brother ordering his sister
          to remain in a marriage with an
          absolute bastard.
               (mimics man's voice)
          Don't be so hasty, Ellen. Jim's an
          important client.

                    ELLEN
               (continuing; normal voice)
          Not only that, he brainwashed our
          father and made him put anything
          that was mine into a trust. A trust
          that Harry controls.
               (beat)
          If I... If I...

The anger suddenly goes out of her and she sags back.

                    ELLEN
               (continuing)
          Never mind, Rachel. I'm so tired I
          could cry. Just get over it. What
          does Harry want?

In the renewed calm, a waiter rushes over to repair the table
settings. And people go back to eating. Rachel takes a deep
breath, then dives in.

                    RACHEL
          Your mother is getting worse,
          Ellen. I hate to put it this way,
          but she's not with us anymore.
               (beat)
          I found a nice home for her, right
          here in Boca Raton. She's getting
          good care... excellent care...
          they're really very professional.
          But, somebody has to be there as
          often as possible because even
          professional people may let things
          slip if the family isn't around.
               (beat)
          I've been going over once a week.
          That's really not enough. But I
          don't have time to do more.

                    ELLEN
          What about Harry? How often does he
          go?

                    RACHEL
          Well, he, uh... Well.. You know how
          uncomfortable he is around sick
          people and he, uh...

                    ELLEN
               (breaking in)
          Never mind, Rachel. I get the
          picture.
               (beat)
          And of course I'll go see her.
          Every single day if I can. But I
          was going to do that anyway. Why is
          Harry trying to make me feel like
          an unfeeling daughter by bribing
          me. If that's even possible - the
          money's mine, after all.
               (beat)
          Why is he doing this, Rachel?

Rachel shrugs helplessly. Ellen takes pity and pats her hand.

                    ELLEN
               (continuing)
          That's not fair of me. I know why.
          Because he wants to drag me down to
          his level.

Ellen suddenly stands. She slips the envelope in her purse.

                    ELLEN
               (continuing)
          I'd better go, Rachel. Or I am
          going to lose it so badly that
          they'll send for the police.

She leans over and gives Rachel a quick peck on the cheek.

                    ELLEN
               (continuing)
          Thanks for lunch. And for your
          empathy. Harry doesn't know what a
          prize he has in you.

And she turns and stalks away, poor Rachel staring after her.

EXT. COUNTRY CLUB - DAY

Sam's back in his Mustang, waiting. A CAB slowly exits the
club and he spots Ellen. Quickly, he starts the car. He waits
a beat for the cab to get well ahead, then follows.

EXT. FLORIDA ATLANTIC BANK - DAY

The cab stops in front of the bank. Ellen gets out, pays the
driver and goes into the bank. The moment the door closes
behind her, Sam glides the Mustang into a parking place.

INT. FLORIDA ATLANTIC BANK - DAY

Ellen's at the NEW ACCOUNTS desk. A snooty lady BANK OFFICER
looks up as she approaches. Waves her into a seat.

                    BANK OFFICER
          How may I help you?

                    ELLEN
          I'd like to open a savings account,
          please.

She hands over Harry's check. The Bank Officer studies it.

                    BANK OFFICER
               (frowning)
          This is a personal check.

                    ELLEN
          Yes, it's from my brother - Harold
          Berman. He has an account here. So
          there shouldn't be any-

                    BANK OFFICER
               (interrupting)
          May I see some ID, please?

A little taken aback, Ellen digs in her purse.

                    ELLEN
          Certainly. Right here.
               (hands over documents)
          Here's my passport. Driver's
          license. My social security card.

                    BANK OFFICER
          Social Security isn't valid ID.

                    ELLEN
          Oh. Fine, then. You've got my
          passport and driver's license. I'm
          sure they'll do.

                    BANK OFFICER
               (studies license)
          This is a Jamaican license.

                    ELLEN
              (a bit exasperated)
          But the passport is American. You
          can use that, can't you?
              (beat)
          You see, I just arrived in the
          States after closing down my
          business in Jamaica and-

                    BANK OFFICER
          I'll be right back.

She rises, taking Ellen's documents with her. Ellen's looks
worried. What's wrong with this bank?

EXT. CAFE - DAY

Sam lounges in an outdoor cafe just across from the bank.
He's reading a paper and watching the entrance. A MIDDLE AGED
COUPLE strolls by. Sam's sharp eyes note that the WOMAN'S
purse is open, her wallet revealed. Just then a clean cut
YOUNG MAN exits the cafe and bumps into the woman.

                    YOUNG MAN
          I'm sorry. How clumsy of me.

As he speaks Sam sees his fingers dip into the purse. At the
same time a SECOND YOUNG MAN passes close by and the wallet
is handed off, with no one but Sam the wiser.

                    MIDDLE AGED WOMAN
          That's quite all right, young man.
          No harm done.

The Young Man smiles and strolls away.

                    MIDDLE AGED WOMAN
              (continuing)
          Such a polite young man. So rare
          these days.

The couple moves onward. But Sam isn't watching them any
longer. His eyes are on the Young Man, who has crossed the
street and is ducking into an alley next to the bank. Two
beats later the Second Young Man walks casually toward the
alley, then slips inside when he thinks he's unobserved.

                    SAM
          Lucky day.

INT. FLORIDA ATLANTIC BANK - DAY

Ellen's still at the desk, cooling her heels. The Bank
Officer returns and is even colder than before.

                    BANK OFFICER
          I'm sorry, Ms. Berman, but with
          your credit record I'm afraid we'll
          have to reject your request for an
          account.

                    ELLEN
               (surprised)
          What's wrong with my credit?

The Bank Officer slides a document across the desk.

                    BANK OFFICER
          If you want to see your credit
          report, you'll have to fill out
          this request form. Processing
          usually takes ten working days.

Ellen pushes the form back. She's had it with these people.

                    ELLEN
          Just cash the check, please, and
          I'll get out of your hair.

                    BANK OFFICER
          Very well. But I'll have to call
          your brother to verify the
          transaction.

                    ELLEN
               (alarmed)
          But he's in Hawaii. On business.

                    BANK OFFICER
          How unfortunate for you.
               (beat)
          Perhaps when he returns. Hmm?

                    ELLEN
               (frustrated)
          But I need this now!

The Bank Officer wants shut of her.

                    BANK OFFICER
          Why don't you try our main branch?
          Perhaps they can help. It's on
          North West 13th Street and Glades.

Ellen gets to her feet.

                    ELLEN
               (sarcastic)
          Thank you so much for all your
          help.

                    BANK OFFICER
                 (equal sarcasm)
            Service with a smile. That's our
            motto.

Ellen would like to rip this bitch's lungs out. Instead, she
turns and walks as calmly as she can for the front door.

EXT. ALLEY - DAY

Sam has the two pickpockets spread eagled against the wall.
From the blood on their faces and clothes, we know that both
young men have taken a beating. Sam has a fistful of bills
and credit cards.

                    SAM
            Not bad. Not bad at all.

He pockets the loot. Then slaps one of the men across the
back of the head.

                    SAM
                 (continuing)
            Where's the rest?

                    YOUNG MAN
            That's all there is.

Sam punches him in the kidney. The Young Man groans in pain
and nearly falls. But Sam steadies him against the wall.

                    SAM
            If I have to hit you again you'll
            be pissing blood for a month. So
            don't bullshit a bullshitter. I
            know how guys like you operate.
            Where's your stash?

                    SECOND YOUNG MAN
                 (scared spitless)
            Jesus, Al! Tell him!

                    YOUNG MAN
            Look in the trash bin.

Sam turns to a nearby dumpster. Lifts the lid.

                    YOUNG MAN
                 (continuing)
            There's a Burdines bag right on
            top.

Sam spots the department store bag, pulls it out and looks
inside. A big smile spreads across his face.

                    SAM
          I could tell you two were hard
          workers, but this is impressive. It
          really is.
                    (beat)
          Okay. You can go now.

Immediately, the two pickpockets spin around and sprint
toward the mouth of the alley. Sam grins at them, enjoying
this. But then:

ACROSS THE STREET

Ellen exits the bank. And she's moving fast. She lifts a hand
to signal and a cab pulls up.

BACK TO SAM

Reacting, then breaking into a run. The two pickpockets think
he's after them. They squeal in terror and run even harder.

EXT. THE MUSTANG - DAY

Sam vaults into the convertible and starts to pull out. Up
ahead Ellen's cab speeds through a yellow light. But before
Sam can follow a bus pulls in front, blocking his car. Sam
sounds the horn, but it's no good. He slams the car into
reverse and rams the car behind him. A space opens up.

Sam stomps the pedal and backs through the narrow opening at
top speed, nearly hitting another car. Shouted curses and
blaring horns. Sam just flips them the finger and speeds off,
nearly colliding with several other vehicles. Then he's out
of there, squealing down the street and through the red
light.

Almost immediately, he spots Ellen's cab and slows down.

EXT. VARIOUS BANK LOCATIONS - DAY

Ellen hits several other banks, but to no avail. Each time
she exits, Sam can see that she's getting more and more
discouraged. Until finally:

EXT. BANK BRANCH - DAY

Sam's parked next to an AUTO SUPPLY STORE a few doors down
from yet one more bank branch. He thoughtfully chews on a
handful of pills, washing them down with OJ. You can
practically see the wheels turning in his head.

Then he glances at the auto supply shop. Big grin as the
lightbulb goes on. He exits the car and goes into the shop.

INT. BANK BRANCH - DAY

Ellen is squaring off with yet another bank officer - a
smiley-faced suit who looks like he's too young to smoke,
much less manage a bank.

                    ELLEN
          I've only been out of the country
          for two years. Could things have
          changed that much? Why are you
          denying me access to my own money.

The kid banker gives her an annoying smile.

                    KID BANKER
          Technically, it isn't your money
          until we cash the check. Until that
          time it still belongs to...
               (glances at a card)
          ...Mr. Harold Berman.

                    ELLEN
          My brother.

                    KID BANKER
               (smiling)
          So you say.

Ellen jumps too her feet.

                    ELLEN
               (shouting)
          This is too much! How dare you
          judge me? You aren't even old
          enough to be away from your mother!
          Hell, I could be your mother. Have
          you no respect? Have you no
          sympathy? My God, where are you
          people from? Rude-ville USA?

ANGLE

A BANK GUARD is at Ellen's shoulder. An older man, he seems
more on Ellen's side than the bank's.

                    BANK GUARD
          Excuse me, ma'am?

Ellen whirls on him.

                    ELLEN
          What's this? Have you come to
          arrest me? Well, go right ahead.
          Why spare me this last indignity?

                    BANK GUARD
                    (super polite)
          No, ma'am. Nobody's gonna arrest
          you. But, you see I have to keep it
          peaceful here. That's my job. And
          if you don't leave, well...
                    (he shrugs)
          Please don't force me to make a
          fool out of both of us, ma'am.

Ellen sags in defeat.

                    ELLEN
          Okay. I'll go.

But she turns on the kid banker for a parting shot.

                    ELLEN
                    (continuing)
          Look at this face!
                    (points at her face)
          Look at this finger!
                    (gives him the finger)
          I promise you, the day you die,
          this face and this finger are going
          to be the last things you remember!

The kid banker turns white. Ellen stalks away, the bank guard
at her side.

                    BANK GUARD
                    (low voice)
          That was some curse!

                    ELLEN
          Learned in Jamaica from a voodoo
          queen.

EXT. BANK BRANCH - DAY

But as Ellen exits the bank the anger - and with it her
spirits - collapse. All she wants to do is crawl into some
hole and feel sorry for herself. She looks up and down the
street for a cab, but doesn't see one. She fishes out her
cell phone and speed dials. But from the look on her face,
you can tell there's something wrong. She smacks the phone on
her thigh.

                    ELLEN
          Damn, damn, damn.

Listens again. Still no good. At that moment a HORN beeps and as Ellen looks up, Sam pulls up in his Mustang.

                    SAM
          Hi, neighbor. Need a lift?

Ellen reacts - what the hell is Sam doing here? As if guessing what she's thinking, Sam holds up a large bag. The label reads: GLENN'S AUTO PARTS.

                    SAM
                (continuing)
          Had to pick up a new distributor.

He indicates the auto parts store down the street. Ellen's suspicions vanish.

                    SAM
                (continuing)
          That's my favorite store.

                    ELLEN
                (sudden smile)
          I'd love a ride home. I've spent a
          small fortune on cabs and all my
          patience on banks today.

Sam leans over and opens the passenger-side door and Ellen gets in. They drive off.

EXT. MUSTANG - TRACKING - DAY

Sam guides the car down the street. Ellen leans back, letting the breeze blow over her.

                    ELLEN
          God, that feels so good. I don't
          know what it is about banks, but
          you always feel dirty when you
          leave them.

                    SAM
                (laughing)
          Nothing filthier than money. Think
          about all the places the stuff's
          been and the places it's gonna go
          before it meets its Maker in the
          big Federal Reserve Incinerator In
          The Sky.

                    ELLEN
                (teasing)
          Are you speaking as an expert?
                (then realizes what she
                 said)
                    (MORE)

                    ELLEN (cont'd)
          Oops. I'm sorry. I shouldn't have
          said that. I've met so many rude
          people today, that I guess some of
          it has rubbed off.

                    SAM
          No big deal. Actually, I thought it
          was pretty funny. I mean, who knows
          more about banks than the people
          who rob them, right?

                    ELLEN
               (suddenly grim)
          Well, I know some perfect
          candidates for robbing. It'd serve
          them right, by God!

Sam glances at her. Consummate con man actor that he is,
concern is written all over his face.

                    SAM
          They've been giving you a bad time?

                    ELLEN
          That's certainly an understatement.
               (pats her purse)
          I've got a perfectly good check.
          It's from my brother, for goodness
          sakes, and he's richer than King
          Midas, so you just know it's good.
               (turns to Sam)
          They won't let me deposit it. And
          they won't even let me cash it.

                    SAM
          Let me guess - credit problems?

                    ELLEN
               (bitter laugh)
          You'd better believe it. I don't
          know what's happening, but somehow
          my credit rating has gone to hell
          over night.
               (beat)
          Like somebody's stalking me on the
          computer.

Then it suddenly occurs to her. She smacks the dashboard!

                    ELLEN
               (continuing)
          Harry!
               (another bang on the dash)
          What a bastard!

                    SAM
          Harry's your brother?

                         ELLEN
                    (astonished)
          You're good. How'd you guess that?

                         SAM
          I got to be a pretty decent judge
          of human nature in prison.

                         ELLEN
          That's right. You're studying to be
          a psychologist.

                         SAM
                    (shrugging)
          Never mind that just now. What
          about the check? How are you gonna
          get your money?

Ellen slumps back in the seat. Tears well up.

                         ELLEN
          God knows.
                    (beat)
          Everybody seems so... so against me
          lately.

                         SAM
                    (soothing)
          It just feels that way because
          you're new to town and haven't made
          any friends yet.

                         ELLEN
          I guess...

Sam's eyes widen - reacting as if the thought has suddenly
struck him. He snaps his fingers.

                         SAM
          Hey, I know. My buddy Craig manages
          one of those check cashing joints.
          And boy, does he owe me big time.
          Maybe he can help.

                         ELLEN
                    (doubtful)
          It's a pretty big check. And a
          private party one at that.

                         SAM
          All Craig can do is say no.
                    (wolfish grin)
          And Sam Barr is not a guy you say
          "no" to lightly.

INT. CHECK CASHING STORE - DAY

Sam and Ellen enter a typical check cashing joint. It's crowded as hell, with several lines of PEOPLE snaking back from barred cashier windows. Tacked all along the walls are dozens of signs advertising the various services. Everything from check cashing to paying utility bills to wiring money.

Ellen looks super intimidated. She's just spotted the fees the place charges for check cashing. Sam notices her look.

                    SAM
          What's wrong, Ellen?

                    ELLEN
          They charge so much money.

                    SAM
               (sarcastic laughter)
          Welcome to the Poor Man's First
          National Bank. After your boss
          screws you, we get in a poke of our
          own.
               (beat)
          Don't worry about it. Like I said,
          Craig owes me.

                    ELLEN
               (lowers her voice)
          But the check's for four thousand
          dollars, Sam!
               (indicates one of the
                signs)
          That's a five hundred dollar
          commission he'd be giving up.

                    SAM
          Leave it to me.

And he heads for the cashier windows, passing all the lined up people. There are various ad-libbed objections, but Sam just has to give them one look and the objections die.

AT THE CASHIER'S WINDOW

Where a bored clerk - LAURA - is counting out money to the FIRST MAN IN LINE. Sam elbows his way in.

                    SAM
          I need to get in here, pal.
               (to Laura)
          Yo, Laura. Get Craig for me.

                         FIRST MAN IN LINE
                    (angry)
               Hey! The hell you doin', man?

He reaches out to push Sam away. Sam just smiles and grabs
the man's fist. He pulls it below counter level and squeezes.

                         FIRST MAN IN LINE
                    (continuing)
               Jesus! Stop! Stop!

Sam lets go. And without another word, the man moves aside.
Sam turns back to Laura, who is staring at him in awe. He
snaps his fingers and she jumps.

                         SAM
               Craig! Remember?

                         LAURA
               Sure, Sam. Right away.

Sam turns to his victim, motioning him aside.

                         SAM
               Comin' through.

The man moves aside, fast!

                         FIRST MAN IN LINE
               Sure, man. Sure.

Sam strolls toward an iron door on the other side of the
room. Each line of people parting, like he was Moses ambling
across the Red Sea.

ON ELLEN

Watching Sam move across the room to the door. Frowning,
wondering what the hell is going on.

When Sam reaches the door, he bangs on it with a heavy fist.
A moment later it opens a crack and Ellen can see a rough-
looking character with a pony tail. It's CRAIG.

A discussion ensues. Sam doing most of the talking. Craig
shakes his head. Unhappy. Finally, Craig shuts the door and
Sam turns away and walks back to Ellen.

                         ELLEN
               I knew it! Too much money to take a
               chance on, right?

                    SAM
              (chuckling)
          You gotta have more faith in your
          new friends, Ellen.
              (beat)
          He'll cash it, no problem.

Ellen reacts, relieved. She digs out the envelope.

                    ELLEN
          Oh, my God! You're a miracle
          worker, Sam.

                    SAM
          Hang on. There's only one little
          catch. A hurdle we have to clear.

                    ELLEN
          You mean he's going to charge me
          five hundred dollars after all?
          Well at this point, I'm so grateful
          to just-

                    SAM
              (interrupting)
          Wait up. You've got to let a guy
          finish. It isn't going to cost any
          five hundred dollars. Fifty, maybe.
          Seventy five at the most.
              (beat)
          The thing is, he needs an hour to
          clear the check through his own
          sources, know what I mean?

                    ELLEN
              (shakes her head)
          No, I don't.

                    SAM
          You have to trust him to hold the
          check. For about an hour. No more.

                    ELLEN
              (very hesitant)
          I don't know...

                    SAM
          You're right to be suspicious.
          Hell, there's about a dozen con
          games that are spun on this very
          same situation.
              (beat)
          But Craig isn't conning us.

                    ELLEN
          Still...

                    SAM
          Okay, tell you what. If Craig
          screws around I promise that I will
          personally bust down that door and
          beat him to within an inch of his
          life.
                    (a big charming smile)
          How's that for a guarantee?

A long uncomfortable pause, as Ellen considers.

                    SAM
               (continuing; shrugging)
          No problem. I understand. I can
          drive you around to some more banks
          if you like.

This decides it. Reluctantly, Ellen hands him the check.

                    SAM
               (continuing)
          You have to endorse it.

Ellen looks at him for a long beat, then sighs, fishing a pen
from her purse and endorses the check. Another hesitation,
then she gives Sam the check.

                    SAM
               (continuing)
          You won't be sorry.

EXT. PARADISE COVE - DAY

Ellen and Sam stroll past the little tourist shops and beachy
bars Paradise Cove is known for.

                    ELLEN
               (rueful)
          I'm getting quite an education
          today. A regular crash course in
          the school of hard knocks.

                    SAM
          It's not so hard from my point of
          view. Of course, like the man said,
          I've been down so long everything
          looks up to me.
                    (beat)
          But then I wasn't brought up rich.

                    ELLEN
          We weren't rich. But we were
          certainly well off.

                    SAM
What happened?

                    ELLEN
I fell in love with an
inappropriate person. And I was
declared unclean by my entire
family. They thought I was crazy. I
guess, maybe I was. I left my
husband. A very important, very
rich New York investment broker. My
father and brother considered it a
personal betrayal.
          (beat)

                    ELLEN
          (continuing)
So they ganged up on me. Had me
declared insane and put in an
asylum. I lost my gallery. All my
paintings. My reputation. My...
everything.

Sam studies her with great interest through all this.

                    ELLEN
          (continuing)
Then my father died, which is how I
got out of the asylum.
          (bitter laugh)
I was so happy when he died. A
terrible thing for a daughter to
say about her own father.

                    SAM
I know all about screwed up
fathers, so don't feel like the
Lone Ranger. The the main thing is
that you got your freedom.

                    ELLEN
          (nodding)
I got my freedom. And I flew off to
Jamaica to be with my knight in
shining armor. I got another
gallery going. I was quite
successful until my knight's armor
developed a bad case of rust.
          (another laugh)
Anyway, I'm not sure who left who.
But the upshot was that when Andre
and I split up, the authorities
descended on me and...

Her voice trails off. She shakes her head.

                          SAM
          I get the picture.
               (beat)
          How do you live?

                          ELLEN
          I have a trust fund from my father.
          Unfortunately, my brother controls
          the trust fund.
               (sighs)
          Which made me so pissed off that I
          didn't touch the money for ages. I
          made my own way with my art.

                          SAM
          But then Jamaica hit the fan?

                          ELLEN
               (shrugs)
          Yeah.
               (beat)
          Anyway, when I tried to get my
          money my brother finally got his
          clutches on me again. Practically
          making me beg for what's rightfully
          mine. Then doling it out, penny by
          penny.

                          SAM
          No one else in your family to take
          your side?

                          ELLEN
               (shakes her head)
          My mother used to speak up for me.
          But she was pretty beaten down by
          my father. And now she's... Well,
          sick. Like in Alzheimer's sick.

Sam stops in front of a bar - the Rum Runner's Club we saw in
the first scene. Checks his watch.

                          SAM
          Let's get a drink.

And he escorts her inside.

INT. RUM RUNNER'S CLUB - DAY

A definite party place at night, the Rum Runner is fairly
quiet during the day. Sam and Ellen sit at the bar, which
looks out on the colorful waterfront.

The bartender - PHIL - brings a glass of white wine for Ellen
and an OJ for Sam.

Phil is a tall, handsome man in his early fifties. He moves
away to give them privacy, but as Sam spins his web Phil
keeps glancing over at Ellen, concerned.

> SAM
> I'll give Craig a call and see
> what's up.
> (pats his pocket)
> Damn! Left my phone at home.
> (hold out a hand)
> Let me use yours.

> ELLEN
> (embarrassed)
> That's another thing. They cut off
> my service for nonpayment.
> (shakes her head)
> But what I'm really worried about
> is getting a phone at home. They'll
> probably give me the same run
> around the bank did. And I need to
> keep in close touch with my mom's
> nursing home.

Sam grins one of his con man grins and digs into his pocket
and fishes out a thick wad of prepaid phone cards.

> SAM
> Let me introduce you to the Poor
> Man's phone service.
> (hands her a card)
> They're prepaid. Get 'em at any
> drugstore, whatever. Never have to
> worry about the bill, because when
> the card runs out, so do you.
> (beat)
> Used to be folks who couldn't
> afford it used pay phones. Now
> they're either impossible to find,
> or when you do find them, they cost
> an arm and a leg.

Ellen looks at the thick wad of cards in his hand.

> ELLEN
> Why do you buy so many at a time?

> SAM
> (laughing)
> Buy? You must be kidding.
> (shrugs)
> But you never mind that. Let's just
> say that I have my ways.

> ELLEN
> (nervous laugh)
> Well, I guess it's better than
> robbing banks.

                    SAM
          Actually, I never really robbed
          that many. Oh, that's what I was
          busted for. And I tell people
          that's what I did. Bank robbing is
          considered one of the classier
          crimes. Like jewel thieves and cat
          burglars. But the truth is, that
          was only my third bank.
                    (beat)
          I was helping a friend who ended up
          being not such a good friend.

                    ELLEN
                    (with feeling)
          I know how that goes.
                    (beat)
          So... if it wasn't banks...

Sam nods, getting her drift.

                    SAM
          I robbed other crooks.

                    ELLEN
                    (puzzled)
          Come again?

                    SAM
          I specialized in taking out strong
          arm men, pick pockets, muggers, con
          man, even armed robbers. I got
          pretty good spotting them. I'd
          follow them until they did the
          deed. Then I'd liberate the money
          they'd just stolen from honest
          citizens.
                    (beat)
          Of course, I realize now I was only
          rationalizing. And that by putting
          a middle man, so to speak, between
          the innocent victim and me, I was
          trying to distance myself from
          moral responsibility.
                    (laughs)
          My prison shrink said I was a
          sociopath's sociopath. Which I
          always thought was a pretty good
          line.

                    ELLEN
                    (in awe)
          But... wasn't that... you know...
          dangerous?

                    SAM
          They usually give it up pretty
          quick when I explain how it is.

And he holds up a fist that looks like a sledge hammer. Ellen
shudders and Sam realizes maybe he's gone too far.

                    SAM
                  (continuing)
          But I'm not the same man, Ellen.
          I've not only had extensive
          therapy, but I plan to become a
          psychologist myself. My dream is to
          open a clinic for ex-cons to help
          them stay straight and build a good
          life for themselves.
                  (chuckles)
          Who better to cure a thief than a
          man who was one?

This gets a laugh from Ellen.

                    ELLEN
          That's a very admirable goal. Ruth
          must be proud of you.

                    SAM
          Ruth? Oh... uh... sure. Ruth's been
          very supportive.

Then he holds up a hand to catch the bartender's attention.

                    SAM
                  (continuing)
          Yo, Phil. Two more of the same.
                  (turns to Ellen)
          Hold the fort while I use the
          gent's room. And I'll check with
          Craig to see where we're at.

As he heads for the rest room Phil fetches another round.
Ellen smiles at him politely and takes a sip of her wine.

                    ELLEN
          You pour a decent house wine.

                    PHIL
          Oh, that's not the house wine. The
          house wine is what we get when I
          drain the sink. This is the good
          stuff. It comes from Chile in
          steamed out gasoline cans.

Ellen laughs. Toasts Phil and takes a sip.

                    ELLEN
          Thank God for the people of Chile.

From the way Phil eyes her you can tell he likes her laugh
and how she handles herself. He looks like he wants to tell
her something, but is holding back. Finally, he goes for it.
But not before testing the waters.

                    PHIL
          Are you and Sam coming back for the
          dance party tonight? We've got a
          pretty hot group booked.

Ellen hastens to correct Phil's error.

                    ELLEN
          Oh, no. I'm not with Sam.
               (beat)
          I mean, I'm here with him now. But
          just as a friend. He's helping me
          with something.
               (beat)
          If he goes dancing, I'm sure it'll
          be Ruth he brings along.

Phil looks at her speculatively. Nods.

                    PHIL
          That's right... Ruth.
               (beat)
          I suppose you're new to the area.

                    ELLEN
          I just moved into Ruth's place
          yesterday. Sam and I are neighbors.

                    PHIL
          So you and...uh... Sam... just...
          uh... met, right?

                    ELLEN
          What of it?

Phil starts to say something but Sam comes out of the rest
room. He moves away.

                    PHIL
               (low voice)
          You seem like a nice lady. So be
          careful, huh?

Ellen reacts, but before she can reply Sam is at her side.

                    SAM
          Craig came through!

Ellen claps her hands in glee.

>   ELLEN
>   That's wonderful news!

>   SAM
>   Let's go. He's waiting for us.

As he hurries Ellen away Phil stares after them, sadly
shaking his head.

EXT. CHECK CASHING STORE - DAY

Sam comes out of the store waving a thick manila envelope at
Ellen, who is waiting in the car. He tosses it to her and
vaults into his seat and speeds away.

Excited, Ellen digs out a handful of bills. She waves it
about and let's out of whoop of glee.

>   ELLEN
>   Screw you, Harry!

INT. MUSTANG - DAY

She clutches the fat envelope to her breast.

>   ELLEN
>   My brother's going to have a fit
>   when he realizes that I've gotten
>   around him.
>   (beat)
>   I'll bet he told the bank people to
>   give me a hard time. But now I've
>   beaten him at his own game.
>   (turns to Sam)
>   How I can ever repay you.

>   SAM
>   (all smiles)
>   Don't try. Like the man said, pay
>   ahead, not back. Help somebody else
>   in trouble someday.

>   ELLEN
>   (nodding)
>   I like that. Pay ahead, not back.
>   (beat)
>   Listen. If it's not too much
>   trouble, could you drop me off at
>   my mother's place? I was dreading
>   seeing her before because I was
>   already so depressed.
>   (beat)
>   (MORE)

> ELLEN (cont'd)
> But now - hell, I can take
> anything!

> SAM
> Can't keep a good woman down,
> right?

> ELLEN
> (with feeling)
> Right!

EXT. NURSING HOME - DAY

Sam pulls up in front of a pleasant-looking South Florida
nursing home. Ellen gets out.

> SAM
> Want me to wait?

> ELLEN
> No, no. Thanks, but I don't know
> how long I'll be.

> SAM
> (nodding)
> Later.

ANGLE ON SAM

As he drives off he checks the mirror, watching Ellen enter
the nursing home. Soon as she's gone he comes to a stop.

ANOTHER ANGLE

Sam does a U-turn then tucks his car beneath a large tree
where he can see the entrance, but nobody can see him. He
pops some pills and chews. Turns on the radio. A Beatles song
comes on: "Lady Madonna." He hums along with the music,
tapping time on the dash. After a few bars he suddenly grins
and starts singing along:

> SAM
> ... Wonder how you manage to make
> ends meet. Who finds the money?
> When you pay the rent? Did you
> think that money was... hea-ven
> sent?

INT. MRS. BERMAN'S ROOM - ANGLE ON TV - DAY

A Perry Mason episode is on the tube. The volume is very loud
- blasting out the show's opening THEME MUSIC.

ANOTHER ANGLE

We're in a small comfortable room. MRS. BERMAN - the picture of health at seventy five - sits primly in a chair in front of the TV. She's dressed as if she's about to go shopping. There's even a purse looped over one arm.

The door opens and a nurse - BETTY - escorts Ellen in. Ellen sees her mother and goes to her. It's an awkward moment.

                    ELLEN
               (hesitant)
          Hello, Ma!

She tries to kiss her - blocking the view. Immediately, Mrs. Berman pushes her away and cranes around to see the TV.

                    MRS. BERMAN
          That's nice, dear.

Ellen looks up at the nurse, bewildered. Betty smiles.

                    BETTY
          Your mom loves Perry Mason. Watches
          it faithfully every day at this
          time.

                    ELLEN
               (shaky laugh)
          She can remember when a TV show's
          on, but not her own daughter.

                    BETTY
          You'll break your heart if you take
          it personally, Ellen. It's plaque
          on the brain instead of the teeth.
          Nothing more.

                    ELLEN
               (sighs)
          I know.
               (beat)
          I'll just sit here and keep her
          company.

                    BETTY
          She likes company. Even though she
          doesn't always know who anyone is,
          the mere presence of people perks
          her up. And sometimes she surprises
          you and remembers certain people.
          Your sister-in- law, for instance.

                    ELLEN
                 (Flat)
            Rachel.

                    BETTY
            Yes, Rachel.
                 (starts to close the door)
            Just ring if you need me.

Ellen nods. After the door closes, she pulls another chair
over next to her mother and sits. A commercial comes on and
Mrs. Berman cuts the sound with her remote. Still, she keeps
her eyes on the tube, not Ellen.

                    MRS. BERMAN
            Rachel doesn't like the
            commercials. But I don't mind.
            Sometimes you see something you
            need. Then I turn the sound up.

                    ELLEN
            It's me, Ma... Ellen... Your
            daughter.

                    MRS. BERMAN
            Ellen went away to Jamaica. Harry
            says she's not coming back.

                    ELLEN
            But, I'm here, Ma. Right here.

                    MRS. BERMAN
            I keep thinking that maybe Harry's
            wrong. Or just being spiteful.
                 (sighs)
            I miss Ellen.
                 (beat)
            She's my daughter, you know.

Tears stream down Ellen's face. She nods.

                    ELLEN
            Yes... I know.

Mrs. Berman gets up.

                    MRS. BERMAN
            Do you want to see my book of
            secrets?

                    ELLEN
            I'd love to, Ma.

Mrs. Berman opens a bureau drawer and draws out a photo
album. Clippings and loose photos stick out the sides. She
resumes her seat and spreads the book open on her lap.

                    MRS. BERMAN
                 (pointing)
          This is Ellen.

It's a picture of Ellen when she was younger.

                    MRS. BERMAN
                 (continuing)
          It's before she went crazy.
                 (beat)
          I didn't think she was crazy. But
          Frank and Harry said she was.

                    ELLEN
                 (soft voice)
          Oh, Ma!

Mrs. Berman turns the page.

                    ELLEN
                 (continuing; pointing)
          Here's Frank.

An older man, quite handsome.

                    ELLEN
                 (continuing; little voice)
          Daddy.

                    MRS. BERMAN
                 (more page turning)
          And Harry.
                 (beat)
          That's when he was captain of the
          Yale boxing team.

A picture of a muscular young man in boxing togs, fists
raised in the classic pose of a pugilist. She turns to a
graduation picture of the same young man.

                    MRS. BERMAN
                 (continuing)
          That's when he graduated.
                 (proud smile)
          Top of his class, you know.

                    ELLEN
                 (soft voice)
          I know.

Mrs. Berman shuts the book. Indicates the TV where Perry
Mason is boring in on a suspect on the witness stand.

                    MRS. BERMAN
          Perry's going to get him, now.
                 (beat)
                    (MORE)

> MRS. BERMAN (cont'd)
> Then I have to take my nap.
> (beat)
> If you come back, I'll show you
> some more secrets. And maybe...
> I'll show you the biggest secret of
> all.

Ellen gets the hint. She leans over and kisses her mother on
the cheek. Mrs. Berman pulls her head away - not rudely. But
she clearly doesn't want to be touched.

> MRS. BERMAN
> (continuing)
> If you see Ellen... tell her to
> come and visit me, will you?

> ELLEN
> (practically choking)
> Sure, Ma. I'll tell Ellen.

And she leaves. Mrs. Berman clicks the remote and the Perry
Mason theme song booms out of the set.

EXT. NURSING HOME - ANGLE ON MUSTANG - DAY

Sam looks up from a dog track racing form as a cab pulls in
front of the nursing home. The horn HONKS and Ellen comes
running out. She climbs in and the cabbie drives away.

Sam waits until the taxi is out of sight, then climbs out of
the Mustang. Whistling "Lady Madonna," he walks to the front
entrance and goes inside.

INT. ELLEN'S APARTMENT - NIGHT

Dressed in paint-spattered cutoffs and halter top, Ellen
paces, glass of wine in hand. She goes to the refrigerator,
opens it and looks in. There's nothing in there but a bottle
of wine and a head of lettuce. She fetches out the wine,
refreshes her glass, then breaks off some lettuce.

Nibbling lettuce and sipping wine she resumes pacing, with
frequent looks at the easel sitting by the window. A large
blank canvas glares back at her like an accusing eye.

> ELLEN
> (to the canvas)
> Shut up!

Back to pacing. She turns on the radio. A Jimmy Cliff song
comes on: "You Can Get It If You Really Want." Ellen reacts,
grinning as if greeting an old friend. She hums along sipping
wine and swaying to the music.

> ELLEN
> (continuing; singing)
> You can get it if you really, want.
> You can get it... really get it...

Ellen starts dancing. Singing along with Jimmy. Spinning around and around... Really getting into it. The song ends and she bumps into the easel. Ellen steadies it.

> ELLEN
> (continuing; to the easel)
> We really have to stop meeting like
> this.

Then her mood changes. She stares at the easel, long and hard. As if willing it to reveal some inner secret.

> ELLEN
> (continuing; exasperated)
> Why do I always have to do all the
> work?
> (beat)
> Aren't you going to even give me
> one little hint? Just one, hmm? For
> old times sake?

There is no reply. Ellen's temper flares.

> ELLEN
> (continuing)
> When are you going to be satisfied?
> I give and give, but you're never
> happy. My husband. My family. My
> lover. I don't have anything left,
> damn you!
> (beat)
> What more do you want? Do you want
> to turn me into a drunk? Ellen the
> god damned crazy drunk?

She hurls the glass to the floor, shattering it.

> ELLEN
> (continuing)
> Well, I refuse, damn you. Do you
> hear that? I - Ellen Berman - will
> not allow you to destroy me!

She grabs up a piece of charcoal and starts drawing with a fury. In the background, the radio starts playing Cliff's "The Harder They Fall."

A SERIES OF DISSOLVES

As the song keeps playing and the picture emerges. Until
finally we see:

ANGLE ON CANVAS

It's a picture of Sam Barr. Not the charming con man mask
that Ellen has seen. But someone powerfully evil!

ON ELLEN

As she stops drawing. She reacts to what she sees, stepping
back from the picture as if it's going to attack her.

                         ELLEN
               Jesus, Ellen! What the hell's in
               your head, girl?

Confused, she starts to move away. There's the sound of
BROKEN GLASS and Ellen reacts in pain. She looks down and
sees that she's stepped on the remains of the wine glass. One
of her bare feet is bleeding on the rug.

                         ELLEN
                      (continuing)
               Shit! Ruth's rug! She'll kill me.

She hops awkwardly to the kitchen, tears off a thick handful
of paper towels and wraps them around her foot. Then she
grabs the bottle of wine from the fridge and another glass
and hops into the bedroom.

                                        DISSOLVE TO:

INT. ELLEN'S BEDROOM - NIGHT

Perched on the bed, first aid kit by her side and her foot
bandaged properly now. She grimaces at the bloody wad of
paper towels and dumps it into a wastebasket next to the bed.
She returns the kit to its home in the bedstand drawer -
revealing the envelope of money as she does.

Ellen removes the envelope and pulls out a sheaf of money -
as if checking to see if it's still there. Sighing and
shaking her head, she puts it back.

                         ELLEN
               It's not right, Harry.

She replaces the envelope and grabs her cell phone. Starts to
punch numbers, then stops, grinning ruefully.

She gets out the phone card Sam gave her and resumes punching numbers. Ellen listens as the phone rings, then:

> ELLEN
> (continuing; into phone)
> It's your sister, Harry. With one more message for your fucking answering machine. And you know what that message is? Listen real close, Harry. Put your ear right up next to the machine so you don't miss a word.
> (beat)
> Okay, here it is. From me to you, big shot!

Ellen gives the phone a big fat raspberry. Giggling, she snaps the phone shut. Then leans back into the pillows and takes a large hit off her wine.

> ELLEN
> (continuing)
> What a life.

> DISSOLVE TO:

INT. ELLEN'S BEDROOM - NIGHT

Ellen's asleep, dimly illuminated by moonlight streaming through the window. There's an OS CRUNCH of broken glass and she stirs. Another CRUNCH and her eyes snap open. We and she can hear the FAINT SOUNDS of someone in the living room. Ellen stays very still as the FOOTSTEPS come nearer.

A DARK FIGURE slips into the bedroom. Then a PENCIL FLASHLIGHT snaps on, the beam sweeping slowly over the room. As the light passes over Ellen's face she closes her eyes. The light goes to the bedstand, where it finds the money envelope in the open drawer.

The dark figure comes closer, leaning over the bedstand. A hand closes over the money envelope. But then:

> ELLEN
> Explodes out of bed!

> ELLEN
> (shouting)
> That's mine!

She grabs the envelope. There's a furious tug-of-war. The intruder cracks Ellen across the head with one hand, while holding on to the envelope with the other.

But Ellen's a tiger. She won't give up. She kicks and screams and rakes the intruder with her nails.

Then her hand encounters the wine bottle and closes over it.
She smashes the intruder across the head. The bottle
explodes, sending glass everywhere.

The intruder staggers back, still holding onto the envelope.
Dragging Ellen out of the bed.

                    INTRUDER
                  (shouting)
            Bitch!

And he slams a fist into her head, knocking her away.
Immediately, he spins about and flees the bedroom. Ellen
leaps up and runs after him.

                    ELLEN
            You can't have it! It's mine!

INT. ELLEN'S APARTMENT - NIGHT

She pursues the intruder into the living room. But he gets to
the door first, flinging it open and rushing outside.
Slamming it into her face. Ellen goes down again. But she
scrabbles to her feet, sobbing and yanking at the door. It
comes open and she rushes into:

INT. HALLWAY - NIGHT

The intruder runs out the front door. Ellen slips and falls,
then is up again. Continuing her pursuit. But as she reaches
the front door she hears the ROAR of a MOTORCYCLE ENGINE.
Ellen jerks the door open and runs into the night.

EXT. ELLEN'S APARTMENT BUILDING - NIGHT

Ellen comes to a stop when she sees a motorcycle speeding
down the street. She whirls and runs back inside.

INT. HALLWAY - ANGLE ON DOOR - NIGHT

Ellen hammers on the door.

                    ELLEN
            Ruth! Help, Ruth!

The door comes open and we see Ruth standing there in her
nightclothes. Behind her is Sam. Both react when they see
Ellen's bruised face and fright wig hair.

                    ELLEN
                  (continuing)
            I was robbed.
                  (MORE)

                         ELLEN (cont'd)
                    (points down the hall)
          He... he... took all my money,
          Ruth! Every damned cent.

Sam pushes forward.

                         SAM
          Where is the son of a bitch?

                         ELLEN
                    (shaking her head)
          Already gone!

                         RUTH
          Come on in, honey!

And she and Sam pull Ellen inside.

INT. RUTH'S APARTMENT - NIGHT

Rather garish - like the owner's unit in a trailer park. When
Ellen enters she runs immediately to the phone. Sam stops
her.

                         SAM
          Who you calling?

                         ELLEN
          The police.
                    (impatient)
          Didn't you hear me? I was robbed.

                         SAM
          Hold on a second, Ellen. The cops
          won't do shit. Let's think things
          out on our own.

Ellen shakes her head, no. And takes a firm grip on the
phone.

                         ELLEN
          I'm calling the damned police.
          That's what they're for.

Ruth goes to her and puts a comforting arm around her.

                         RUTH
          You go right ahead, honey.
                    (turn to Sam)
          Better make yourself scarce.

Sam nods, goes into the bedroom and returns with his clothes.

                         ELLEN
                    (confused)
          Why's he leaving?

                    SAM
          With my record, it's best to avoid
          all contact with the police.

And he's out the door. Ellen lifts the receiver and dials
911.

                    ELLEN
                 (into phone)
          I want to report a robbery...

INT. ELLEN'S APARTMENT - NIGHT

A robe wrapped around her, Ellen huddles on the couch near
the painting of Sam. She's still pretty shook up. A detective
- SGT. PROPP - is parked on a chair across from her, notebook
in hand. He's middle-aged. Crooked at the smirk on his face.

                    SGT. PROPP
          Okay... he fled on a motorcycle...
          Now, let's back up a minute.

He indicates the broken glass on the rug.

                    SGT. PROPP
                 (continuing)
          The first time you were aware of
          the perp was when you heard him
          step in the glass, right?

                    ELLEN
                 (nodding)
          See how it was ground in by his big
          fat foot.

                    SGT. PROPP
          Yeah. But what I want to know is
          how the glass got there in the
          first place.

                    ELLEN
          Oh... uh... A wine glass that I
          broke earlier. I was, uh... tired.
          And decided to clean it up
          tomorrow.

                    SGT. PROPP
          You always leave things like that
          until tomorrow?

                    ELLEN
                 (puzzled)
          No... But this time I did.

                    SGT. PROPP
          Drinking a little, were you?

                    ELLEN
          Sure. I was drawing... Making an
          under-painting and sipping wine. So
          what?

                    SGT. PROPP
               (shrugs)
          Just trying to get the picture.
               (points at easel)
          Speaking of which... Is that what
          you were working on?

                    ELLEN
          Yes. But what does that-

                    SGT. PROPP
          Who's the guy?

                    ELLEN
          A friend.

                    SGT. PROPP
          I guess you make friends pretty
          fast, Ellen.
               (checks his notes)
          You arrived in town day before
          yesterday, right?

                    ELLEN
          Right.

                    SGT. PROPP
          From Jamaica?

                    ELLEN
          Sure. Jamaica.
               (beat)
          Listen, Sergeant Propp, I don't
          know what you're after, but-

                    SGT. PROPP
          Your friend looks kind of familiar.

                    ELLEN
          He's a neighbor. The owner's
          fiance. He helped me get situated.

                    SGT. PROPP
          Is that right? Situated, huh?

                    ELLEN
               (getting frosty)
          What are you implying, Sgt. Propp?

                    SGT. PROPP
          Just sorting through the details.

                    ELLEN
          Well, I'll have you know that when
          I went to Ruth's for help Mister
          Barr was right there with her. He
          could not have been involved in the
          theft. I saw the motorcyclist flee
          not two minutes before.

                    SGT. PROPP
                    (jots notes)
          Mister Barr, huh?
                    (beat)
          Sam Barr, by any chance?

Remembering Sam's worries, Ellen becomes concerned.

                    ELLEN
          Please don't bother the poor man,
          sergeant. He's been a great help to
          me. And so has Ruth.

Propp shuts his notebook and gets to his feet.

                    SGT. PROPP
          You ought to be careful who you you
          get your help from, Ellen.
                    (beat)
          Well, I'll just stroll on down the
          hall and see what your friends have
          to say for themselves.

Ellen doesn't reply. Propp gives her a long look, as if
mentally stripping her, then grins and lets himself out.
Ellen shudders. This is not what she expected from the cops.

INT. RUTH'S APARTMENT - DAY

The next morning. Ruth and Ellen look like they've been up
all night. There's the OS SOUND of a key turning in a lock.
Ruth jumps up and runs across the room. Ellen rises, but
hangs back - looking a little shame-faced.

                    RUTH
          Thank God! There's Sam now.

The door comes open and Sam walks in. Unshaven, bleary-eyed
and in none too good a mood. Ruth tries to hug him but he
pushes her away.

                    SAM
          Aw, Jesus, Ruth. I smell like a
          pig!
                    (MORE)

                    SAM (cont'd)
          (beat)
     Damned cop shops get filthier by
     the day.

                    ELLEN
     I'm so sorry, Sam. I didn't know-

                    SAM
     Nothin' to be sorry about, Ellen.
     You're the victim, here, not me. So
     they kept me all night. Least they
     didn't lay into me too much.

He finds himself a chair and sits. Ruth, meanwhile, is
fetching him a tall glass of OJ.

                    ELLEN
          (shocked)
     They... they... beat you?

Sam shrugs and drinks the juice down in one long swallow.

                    SAM
     Just a rap on the skull bones every
     now and then to let me know they
     were serious.

                    ELLEN
     That's terrible!

                    SAM
     No big deal.
          (beat)
     The main thing is, what about your
     money? They're too busy circling
     around their own rectums to find
     it.

                    ELLEN
          (sounding helpless)
     What can I do?

                    SAM
     Hell, we don't need Sherlock
     Holmes. Just a little common sense.
          (beat)
     I mean, who knew about the money?
     Did you tell anybody at the nursing
     home? Or the cab driver on the way
     back here?

                    ELLEN
     Certainly not.

                    SAM
     So the only people who knew were
     me, Ruth, and...

                         ELLEN
                    (getting it)
               Craig!

                         SAM
               Bingo!
                    (beat)
               Okay, I can get your money back but
               you have to go along with what I
               say.

                         ELLEN
               You're not going to hurt him, are
               you?

                         SAM
               Nah! Just scare the bejesus out of
               him.

                         ELLEN
               Fine! He sure scared more than that
               out of me.

EXT. CHECK CASHING STORE - DAY

It's quittin' time. Craig flips the sign on the door from
open to closed, then exits and locks up. He touches the
bandage on his head and winces. Then he jumps as:

                         SAM'S OS VOICE
               Looks like she really clocked you a
               good one, Craig.

ANOTHER ANGLE

Craig whirls to find Sam standing there. Over his shoulder he
sees Ellen standing at the mouth of an alley. Craig barely
has time to react before Sam sledgehammers a fist into his
gut, driving the air out of him like a curb-shot tire.

Sam grabs Craig by his collar and cake-walks him swiftly
toward the alley. Several PASSERSBY look at them in alarm.

                         SAM
               Bleeding ulcer.

He keeps going, leaving the passersby gawking in his wake.

IN THE ALLEY

Ellen hops behind the wheel of the Mustang. Sam forces Craig
inside and piles in next to him.

                         SAM
          Go!

Ellen goes, burning rubber all the way.

EXT. RURAL ROAD - DAY

The Mustang cruises along a rural highway. There's nothing
around for miles, except maybe gators. Up ahead a dirt road
leads off into tropical underbrush.

                    SAM'S VOICE
          Here we go.

Ellen makes the turn.

EXT. CANAL BANK - DAY

Ellen stops the car beside a slow, wide canal. Sam pops the
door and drags Craig out with him. Ellen starts to object to
the treatment, but a quick look from Sam silences her.

                         CRAIG
          For crissakes, Sam. I told the lady
          I was sorry!

Sam ignores him. He goes to the trunk, opens it and hoists
out two hefty cement blocks. Then a long heavy chain. Craig
stares at them warily.

                         CRAIG
                    (continuing)
          What're you doin', man?

Sam gestures at the canal.

                         SAM
          Some crackers told me that these
          canals can get forty, fifty feet
          deep.
                    (beat)
          Think they're lyin', Craig?

Craig licks his lips and slowly shakes his head.

                         SAM
                    (continuing)
          Well, I'm not too sure. Nobody
          likes to twist the truth more than
          a Florida cracker. It's his nature,
          you know?

Craig is silent. Ellen looks from one man to the other.
Wondering what Sam is up to.

                    SAM
               (continuing)
          I say we find out for ourselves.

He starts looping the chain around Craig's neck.

                    CRAIG
               (freaking)
          This isn't necessary, man. I told
          you - I blew the money at the dog
          track.

                    SAM
          Yeah, that's what you said.

He takes a lock from his pocket. Craig starts to struggle,
but Sam gives him a slap across the face.

                    SAM
               (continuing)
          Hold still.

Craig obeys and Sam slips the chain through the cement
blocks. Ellen is pale as a ghost. Despite Sam's promise to
not hurt Craig, she's afraid things might go to far.

                    ELLEN
               (blurting)
          Sam! Please!

Sam gives her a warning look and once again she shuts up.

                    CRAIG
          Listen to her, Sam. You don't want
          to do this. I mean, how am I going
          to pay her back if I'm... you
          know... in the canal?

                    SAM
               (mock surprise)
          Pay her back? Why, you never
          mentioned anything like that. This
          could shed a whole different light
          on things. A whole different light.
               (looks at Ellen)
          What would you rather have, Ellen?
          Money, or satisfaction?

                    ELLEN
          Satisfaction doesn't pay the rent.

                    SAM
               (nodding)
          How true.
               (to Craig)
                    (MORE)

                    SAM (cont'd)
          Do you hear what she said, Craig?
          Satisfaction doesn't pay the rent.

                    CRAIG
               (eager as all hell)
          I can get the four thousand up by
          the first of the month. Okay?

                    SAM
               (looking disappointed)
          Why, that's almost four weeks away,
          Craig. What's the lady going to do
          meanwhile?

He suddenly reaches out and slaps Craig across the face
again.

                    SAM
               (continuing)
          You took her last dime, you son of
          a bitch!

Craig cowers but Sam is suddenly calm again.

                    SAM
               (continuing)
          What I want to know, Craig, old
          buddy, is how much you can give
          this lady today. And I don't give a
          damn what you have to do to get it.

                    CRAIG
          I don't know, Sam. I-

                    SAM
               (growling)
          How much?

Sam raises his hand.

                    CRAIG
          Five hundred dollars! I can get her
          five hundred dollars. Today, man.
          Today!

Sam suddenly smiles and pats Craig on the back.

                    SAM
          See how easy that was?
               (beat)
          Now, what about next week?

                    CRAIG
               (jolted)
          What?

Sam sighs with exaggerated exasperation.

                    CRAIG
               (continuing; quickly)
          Five hundred more.

                    SAM
               (rolls his hand)
          And so on... and so on.

                    CRAIG
          Jesus, man! Okay - I'll give her
          five hundred a week until she's
          paid off.

                    SAM
               (shakes his head)
          Bullshit. The five hundred is the
          vig. The interest. She gets five
          hundred a week for four weeks. And
          on the fourth week you also pay her
          the four thousand you stole from
          her.
               (beat)
          Got it?

He raises hand to hit Craig - who cringes even more.

                    CRAIG
               (crying)
          Yeah, man! I got it!

Sam steps back, well satisfied. Ellen looks at him in
amazement.

                    SAM
          Start walkin', Craig. It's only
          about five miles back to town.
               (checks his watch)
          And you can come on over my house
          about... oh... eight thirty. And
          you bring that five hundred
          dollars, you hear?

                    CRAIG
               (bobbing his head)   .
          I hear.

Craig spins around and starts trotting toward the road. Sam
turns back to an astonished Ellen.

                    SAM
          So now you're a big time loan
          shark, Ellen. Got four thousand out
          on the street earning five bills a
          week.

                    ELLEN
                 (nervous smile)
          That's me - Public Enemy Number
          One.

INT. MRS. BERMAN'S ROOM - ANGLE ON TV - DAY

Perry Mason again, complete with theme music. But the sound
and the picture are fuzzy. Suddenly it goes blank.

                    MRS. BERMAN'S OS VOICE
          Oh, dear! Not again.

ANGLE

As Ellen goes to the set.

                    ELLEN
          Let me try, Ma.

Mrs. Berman watches anxiously from her favorite chair while
Ellen fiddles with the TV, but it's not much use.

                    ELLEN
                 (continuing)
          I think you need a new TV, Ma.

                    MRS. BERMAN
          Harry's buying me one.

                    ELLEN
                 (big surprise)
          You talked to Harry?

                    MRS. BERMAN
                 (nodding)
          Sure, I talked to Harry. He's my
          son, isn't he? He's not like Ellen.
          She never calls, or writes, or
          comes to visit me.

                    ELLEN
                 (exasperated)
          I'm Ellen, Ma. And I'm right here.

                    MRS. BERMAN
          Would you like to see more of my
          secrets?

                    ELLEN
                 (sighing)
          That'd be nice, Ma.

She fetches the scrap book from the bureau and sits beside
her mother, pretending great interest while the old woman
slowly turns the pages.

EXT. NURSING HOME - ANGLE ON MUSTANG - DAY

Sam's parked under a tree, watching the entrance. Craig sits
next to him. He touches his banged up head and face.

                    CRAIG
          First the broad, then you.
                    (beat)
          Christ, couldn't you have gone
          easier on me?

                    SAM
                    (shrugging)
          Had to look real.

Craig rubs his head again, wincing. Then he grins.

                    CRAIG
          Pretty cool move, man, using the
          bitch's own money to salt the mine.

Sam just grunts. He's not interested in small talk. Then his
eyes widen as he sees Ellen exit the nursing home. She walks
swiftly to a waiting cab, gets in and drives off.

                    SAM
          Show time, folks.

The two men get out of the car and go to the trunk. Sam opens
it then motions to Craig.

                    SAM
                    (continuing)
          Get the TV.

Craig nods and lifts out a large box containing a TV.

                    SAM
                    (continuing)
          Come on!

He hurries toward the home, Craig staggering after him with
the big box in his arms.

INT. MRS. BERMAN'S ROOM - DAY

Ellen's mother sits sadly in her chair, staring at the blank
TV screen. The nurse - Betty - opens the door. The towering
figure of Sam right behind her.

                    BETTY
          Look who's here, Mrs. Berman!

Mrs. Berman spots Sam and beams with delight. She throws her
arms open.

                    MRS. BERMAN
          Harry!

Sam bounds into the room, charm turned on full blast.

                    SAM
          Hi ya', Mom.

He gives Mrs. Berman a big kiss and a hug.

                    SAM
               (continuing)
          How's my girl, huh? When are we
          gonna blow this joint and go
          dancing?

Mrs. Berman laughs and gives him a playful slap on the arm.

                    MRS. BERMAN
          Oh, Harry. You're so fresh!

Betty smiles at the nice scene.

                    BETTY
          You sure have been popular lately,
          Mrs. Berman. Two visitors - and it
          isn't even time for lunch yet.

Sam gives Mrs. Berman yet another hug.

                    SAM
          Of course, she's popular! A regular
          heartbreaker, that's my Mom.
               (beat)
          Hey, wait until you see what I got
          you.

Mrs. Berman is all smiles.

                    MRS. BERMAN
          The TV?

                    SAM
          Just like I promised.

He waves to Craig who is out in the hallway.

                    SAM
               (continuing)
          Bring it on in, Craig.

Betty makes herself scarce while Craig brings in the TV box.

> SAM
> (continuing)
> Let's get it open.

Mrs. Berman watches with rapt attention as Sam fishes a switchblade out of his pocket and cuts the box open. He motions to Craig.

> SAM
> (continuing)
> Get lost.

Craig beats feet, and fast.

> SAM
> (continuing)
> Now wait till you see what we got here, Mom. A real super duper deal

And he lifts out a portable TV/VCR combination.

> SAM
> (continuing)
> Ta da!

Quickly, he removes the old set and puts the new one on its stand. Plugs it in, turns it on and bingo! An episode of Mayberry RFD fades into view. Immediately, she's transfixed.

Sam steps away from the set, watching her watch TV. Then he flicks the TV off.

> MRS. BERMAN
> But, Harry. Perry Mason's coming on soon.

> SAM
> In a minute, Mom. We have to do something else, first. Then you can watch all you want.

Mrs. Berman gives a wise nod.

> MRS. BERMAN
> You want to see my book of secrets again, right?

> SAM
> What a mind reader you are, Mom!

Sam fetches the book and sits down beside Mrs. Berman.

                         SAM
                    (continuing)
          But this time I want to concentrate
          on Harry. Never mind everybody
          else, just Harry.

                         MRS. BERMAN
                    (looks confused)
          But you're Harry.

                         SAM
          Sure I am.

He leans over and gives her another big kiss and a hug.

                         SAM
                    (continuing)
          I just want to relive the old
          times, Mom. The good times I had
          with you.

Mrs. Berman gives him a look of pure love.

                         MRS. BERMAN
          You could always get anything you
          wanted from me, Harry.

She starts flipping pages.

INT. ELLEN'S APARTMENT - DAY

Ellen's working on the picture of Sam. Except now she's moved
on to the painting itself, daubing the oils on thick as if
creating a clay sculpture. In color Sam looks even more
foreboding than before.

She steps back to study the painting.

                         ELLEN
                    (softly)
          Where are you going with this,
          Ellen?
                    (beat)
          And why does he look so mean?

Ellen picks up her brush again, but before she can continue,
there's a KNOCK at the door. Ellen groans with impatience.

                         RUTH'S OS VOICE
          It's Ruth, Ellen.

Ellen puts the brush down and starts for the door. A sudden
thought makes her stop, then go back to the painting and turn
it so Ruth can't see it.

                    ELLEN
          She wouldn't get it.
               (beat)
          Hell, I don't get it.

She hurries to the door and opens it. Ruth cranes her neck,
trying to look over Ellen's shoulder.

                    RUTH
          I thought I heard you talking to
          someone.

                    ELLEN
               (small laugh)
          Nobody here but us crazy people.
               (beat)
          Don't tell anybody, but I
          frequently talk to my paintings.

Ruth forces a smile.

                    RUTH
          I thought Sam might be here.

                    ELLEN
               (surprised)
          I haven't seen Sam since yesterday.

Ruth isn't quite satisfied, but doesn't press the point.

                    RUTH
               (indicating the painting)
          What're you painting?

Ellen hesitates, realizing that the green-eyed monster has
got a hold of Ruth.

                    ELLEN
          Nothing I want to brag about. I
          swear, I'm about to paint over the
          thing and start on something else.
               (beat)
          But, please. Come on in.

                    RUTH
               (shakes her head)
          You have somebody asking for you
          outside.

                    ELLEN
               (puzzled)
          For me?

                    RUTH
          Yeah, it's that limo guy again.
          Lazy jerk.
                    (MORE)

                    RUTH (cont'd)
          Couldn't fetch you himself. Instead
          he honked until I came out to see
          what all the fuss was about.

                    ELLEN
                  (exasperated)
          I'm sorry, Ruth. I'll go see what
          he wants.

She heads out the door.

EXT. ELLEN'S APARTMENT BUILDING - DAY

The Town Car is parked in front, the chauffeur lounging
against it. Ellen goes to him, a little pissed.

                    ELLEN
          What's with all the honking? Are
          you trying to get me evicted?

The chauffeur ignores her complaint.

                    CHAUFFEUR
          Your brother wants you.

Ellen reacts, insulted.

                    ELLEN
          What is this? Has Harry joined the
          Mafia or something?

The chauffeur shrugs.

                    CHAUFFEUR
          I'll tell him that you refused to
          come.

Ellen starts to give the chauffeur a real piece of her mind.
Then she calms herself. Indicates her painting outfit.

                    ELLEN
          You'll have to wait until I change.

                    CHAUFFEUR
          Whatever.

Barely keeping her temper in check, Ellen spins around and
stalks away.

INT. LAW OFFICE - ANGLE ON HARRY - DAY

HARRY is a powerful looking man in his forties and when we
come in he's jogging on a running machine. He wears a form-
fitting runner's outfit that shows off his muscular build.
He's listening to music on his headphones.

                    ELLEN'S OS VOICE
                      (annoyed)
            Turn the damn thing off, Harry.

ANOTHER ANGLE

And we see Ellen sitting in a client's chair, impatiently
waiting for Harry to finish. Harry raises a finger,
signalling that he'll be done momentarily.

Ellen sighs and looks around the room. Besides the usual law
books, one wall is devoted to pictures of Harry in various
athletic pursuits. Running, biking, tennis, etc. There's even
a blown up picture of the younger Harry that we saw before in
the boxer's pose.

Besides the running machine, there's other exercise equipment
scattered around the spacious office - a weight rack, folded
up exercise machines, a crunch board, etc. In the corner,
there's even a speed bag. Ellen rolls her eyes at all this.

Harry switches off the machine and dismounts, pulling the
headphones off.

                        HARRY
            Got my five miles in
              (strikes a pose)
            Pretty good for forty two, huh?

He picks up some barbells and starts doing biceps exercises.

                        ELLEN
            Nice to see you still think so well
            of yourself, Harry.

                        HARRY
              (sarcastic laugh)
            Still a bitch. You'll never change,
            will you?

                        ELLEN
            I don't know, Harry. You've tried
            everything else to change me. Up to
            and including throwing me into a
            loony bin.
              (beat)
            What great crime did I commit this
            time, Oh Lord And Master Of
            Morality?

                        HARRY
            A certain detective came to visit
            me... A Sergeant Propp.

                    ELLEN
               (reacts)
          I don't know why he bothered you.
          It was my robbery.

                    HARRY
          He was only following orders,
          Ellen. I've asked the local
          authorities to keep an eye on you.
               (beat)
          The Chief and I golf together with
          some regularity.

While he talks, Harry drops the weights and goes to an
exercise machine - one of Chuck Norris' Total Gyms. He drops
it down. Stretches out on the board and starts working the
cables, pulling himself up and down the board.

                    ELLEN
          Listen, Harry. I'm not going to get
          into it with you. I was robbed.
          Which can happen to anybody these
          days.

                    HARRY
          I know, Ellen. But why is it that
          everything always seems to be
          happening to you. I swear to God,
          if I heard that your nude body was
          pulled out of some rural lake I
          won't be surprised one bit.

                    ELLEN
          Well, until that happy day, Harry,
          what is it you exactly want to know
          about the robbery? I'd be glad to
          fill you in on the thrilling
          details, even though it really is
          none of your damned business.

                    HARRY
          I'm afraid it is my business,
          sister, dear. As the executor of
          our father's estate and overseer of
          your trust, I have certain
          fiduciary duties. Which include
          being what you believe is nothing
          more than a snoop.

                    ELLEN
               (bitter laugh)
          Peeping Tom is more like it, Harry.

                    HARRY
          Let's get to the point. I have a
          busy afternoon ahead.
               (beat)
                    (MORE)

                    HARRY (cont'd)
          Apparently you've carelessly lost
          the money I gave you. And I wanted
          to make plain that I will think
          carefully about the amount I
          disperse when the next payment
          comes due.

                    ELLEN
          Bullshit, Harry! You shorted me on
          the one and only check I managed to
          squeeze out of you. And every time
          I ask for what is rightfully mine,
          you always come up with some
          ridiculous excuse.
                    (beat)
          Sometimes I wonder if you're trying
          to cover something up.
                    (beat)
          Been dipping into the fiduciary
          till, have we Harry? Hmm?

Harry reacts. He immediately stops working the cables and
sits up straight.

                    HARRY
          That's just like you, Ellen. You
          blow it - and you blow it big time -
          and immediately look around for
          someone else to blame.

Ellen tires of the game.

                    ELLEN
          Let's not fight. The stolen money
          is no longer an issue. My friends
          found the man responsible and I'm
          being paid back.

Harry gets off the machine and goes to the speed bag. Starts
punching.

                    HARRY
          Did you notify the police? That's
          the proper course of action.

                    ELLEN
                    (scoffing)
          You mean Sergeant Propp? Give me a
          break, Harry. He was ready to
          arrest me for stealing the money
          from myself.

                    HARRY
          I don't like what I'm hearing,
          Ellen. And I'm telling you right
          now that I do not approve of the
          course of action you chose.

                  ELLEN
      Well, there are certain things I
      don't approve of, Harry, that are
      far more important than my robbery,
      or your efforts to humiliate me.
          (beat)
      I'm speaking of our mother.

Harry stops punching. Turns to Ellen.

                  HARRY
      What about her? I've placed her in
      the best facility available. And
      have provided her with the very
      best medical care. You can't
      believe the astronomical bills-

                  ELLEN
      Shut up, Harry! You don't pay the
      bills, so just shut up! You know
      very well that the money comes from
      mother's inheritance from father.
      Don't pretend otherwise.

                  HARRY
      This conversation has gone far
      enough, Ellen. I'm putting you on
      warning right now. I'm very
      influential in Palm Beach County.
      And if you get out of line I'll...
      Well, let's just say you'll rue the
      day that you crossed me.

Ellen gets to her feet.

                  ELLEN
      Just remember, do right by our
      mother, or you might be the one who
      ends up doing a little rueing for a
      change.

And she boils out of the room. Harry shrugs and starts
punching the speed bag again. But then an INTERCOM BUZZ
interrupts him. Toweling himself off, he goes to his desk.

                  HARRY
         (into intercom)
      Yeah, Linda?

               WOMAN'S INTERCOM VOICE
      It's Fistcity time, Harry.

A big smile erupts on Harry's face.

                    HARRY
         Thank God, Linda. After dealing
         with my sister I need a good bout.

EXT. LAW OFFICE - ANGLE ON LIMO - DAY

Harry slides into the back seat and the car pulls away. Beat,
beat and Sam's Mustang slides into view! Sam at the wheel,
Craig riding shotgun. Immediately Sam takes up position
behind the limo and follows.

EXT. FISTCITY - DAY

A large, flashy gym/entertainment center for well-to-do
sports world wannabes.

                    CRAIG'S OS VOICE
         What's this shit - workouts for
         candy asses?

ANGLE ON MUSTANG

As Sam and Craig drive slowly past the place. Sam reacts as
he sees:

ANOTHER ANGLE

Harry's limo parked out front. The Chauffeur lounging against
it, reading a newspaper.

                    SAM
         There's our boy. For a minute I
         thought we'd lost him.

He pulls into a parking lot and the two hop out and hurry
back toward the gym.

INT. FISTCITY - DAY

Sam and Craig stroll through the joint, which offers every
sports activity from racket ball and wall climbing to
billiards and boxing. There's even a full bar where you can
get a vitamin charged power drink with a single malt scotch
back. Craig's impressed, but tries to cover with a sneer.

                    CRAIG
         If this is how the other half
         lives, they can keep their half.

                    SAM
          I don't know. Sure beats the hell
          out of the prison exercise yard.

INT. BOXING RING - ANGLE ON HARRY - DAY

Harry and another FIGHTER are going at it in the ring.
Bouncing around, shooting punches and ducking and dodging.
Although Harry's opponent is slightly bigger, Harry is in
good form, socking the guy at will.

ANOTHER ANGLE

Sam and Craig lounge near the doorway of the boxing center,
watching the fight.

                    CRAIG
          Think that's him? Hard to tell with
          the head gear.

                    SAM
              (nodding)
          It's him. His mom's got a picture
          of him in the same getup.

In the ring, Harry hits his opponent with a nice combination,
and the guy goes back into the ropes.

                    CRAIG
              (admiring)
          Not bad!

But the guy in the ring isn't going down that easily. He
explodes back at Harry, driving him across the ring with a
flurry of blows. The way Harry's legs are wobbling it looks
like he's about to go down.

Then, all of a sudden Harry drives a powerful left into the
guy's groin. As his opponent doubles over with pain, Harry
slams a right into the back of his head. And his opponent is
down for good.

                    CRAIG
              (continuing)
          Shit! You see that? The guy cheats!

                    SAM
              (wolfish grin)
          Shoot, for awhile there I thought
          he was a bulked up wimp. I mean,
          what's up with that Yale Boxing
          Team business?

                    CRAIG
          Now we know.

                    SAM
               (eying Harry)
          Uh, huh.

INT. ELLEN'S APARTMENT - ANGLE ON SAM'S PICTURE - NIGHT

The painting is nearly complete. And Sam is more brooding and
evil than ever. Not one trace of the charm we've seen him put
on can be found.

OS we heard the SOUND of a Reggae song - "Put Da Lime In De
Coconut" - and Ellen singing along with the tune.

                    ELLEN'S OS VOICE
               (singing)
          She put da lime in da coconut\ She
          drank dem both up\ She put da...

Then over the music we hear CLICKING SOUNDS.

ANGLE ON THE DOOR

The sounds are coming from the lock - as if someone is
fiddling with the tumblers. Then a LOUDER CLICK as the lock
snaps open. The knob turns and the door slowly opens.

                    ELLEN'S OS VOICE
               (still singing)
          ... She called the doctor woke 'em
          up and said - DOCTOR!/ Ain't there
          nothing I can take/ DOCTOR!/ To
          relive this belly ache..."

CHEATER ANGLE

Of a shadowy figure entering the room. Shutting the door
softly behind him. The figure moves to the painting of Sam
and pauses there a moment to study it. Then he moves on to
the bathroom door, which is open a crack. Peers in.

THROUGH THE GAP

We can see Ellen in her tub, soaking away her cares. Glass of
wine in hand and singing along to the song. Oblivious to the
watcher at her door.

TRACKING WITH INTRUDER

Staying with CHEATER ANGLES we follow him into the bedroom
where a thorough search commences. Drawers ripped out from
the bureau and dumped on the floor. Clothes dragged from the
closet. A bedside lamp topples over with a loud crash!

INT. ELLEN'S BATHROOM - NIGHT

As Ellen hears the noises and reacts. Her hand goes to the
radio to turn the sound down, but she stops when she realizes
the intruder will notice the absence of music.

Cautiously, she rises from the tub, pulling on her robe. She
creeps to the door and listens. Now she and we can clearly
hear someone moving around her bedroom.

Very quietly, Ellen shuts the door. Locks it. Hurries to the
window. She opens it and upends a wastebasket for a stool.
She climbs up on the wastebasket and starts to crawl out the
window. But then:

The bathroom door crashes open! Ellen shouts for help and
tries to throw herself through the window. But the intruder
grabs her from behind and drags her back inside.

Ellen screams! But the scream is cut off by a large hand.
Then the intruder drags her into the bedroom and hurls her on
the bed. Ellen rolls off and is on her feet like a fighter.
She grabs the lamp off the floor for a bludgeon.

                    MAN'S OS VOICE
          Hold it right there!

ANGLE

As we - and Ellen - see Sergeant Propp standing there! Ellen
reacts in total shock. Drawing back as if she's going to
throw the lamp. Propp raises a hand.

                    SGT. PROPP
          Jesus, I'm not here to rape
          anybody.

Ellen looks around her destroyed room, then back at Propp.
Her fear has turned to fury.

                    ELLEN
          Just what are you here for,
          Sergeant?

                    SGT. PROPP
                (shrugs)
            Your brother wanted the place
            checked out. So I tossed it.

Ellen doesn't react. Nothing Harry does surprises her.

                    ELLEN
            Taking a big chance, weren't you?
            No warrant. No cause for one.

                    SGT. PROPP
                (shrugging)
            Oh, if I wanted cause, I could make
            one. Just as if I wanted
            evidence...

He reaches in his pocket and pulls out a baggy filled with a
white powder.

                    SGT. PROPP
                (continuing)
            ... I could manufacture it.

Ellen raises an eyebrow.

                    ELLEN
            Is that your intention?

Sergeant Propp gives her a nasty grin.

                    SGT. PROPP
            Maybe later. Or maybe I'll come
            back when you get this mess cleaned
            up and we can make some other
            arrangements.
                (beat)
            Private arrangements.

Ellen's temper blows! She hurls the lamp and it smashes into
Propp. He staggers back, hand going to his face.

                    SGT. PROPP
                (continuing)
            What the fuck! You crazy?

He examines his hand. There's blood on it and more blood is
dribbling from a wound on his cheek. Ellen grabs another lamp
and rears back to throw. Immediately, Propp pulls his gun.
Aims it at Ellen.

                    SGT. PROPP
                (continuing)
            Put it down you dumb bitch before I
            blow you away!

Slowly, Ellen recovers. She drops the lamp.

                    SGT. PROPP
                  (continuing)
          Okay, I'm leaving now. But I'll be
          back - that I guarantee. And you'd
          better start thinking what you've
          got that I want, bitch. And you
          better make me want it real bad. Or
          I'll put you in a world of hurt.
          Hear me? A world of hurt!

Propp exits the room. We hear heavy footsteps, then the front
door slamming. Ellen draws in a long shuddering breath. She's
two beats from dissolving into tears. Then she swipes her
eyes with an angry hand.

                    ELLEN
          This time you don't break, Ellen!

EXT. YACHT HARBOR - ANGLE ON CABIN WINDOW - NIGHT

Through the main cabin window we see Harry cavorting with a
very lovely half-naked woman who is definitely not his wife.
Raucous music plays on his stereo. Harry and the girl pause
in their love-making and knock back a couple of shooters.
With fat lines of coke vacuumed up for backs.

                    CRAIG'S OS VOICE
          I take it back. The other half does
          just fine, man.

ANGLE

And we find Sam and Craig standing on a dock next to Harry's
yacht. Swirling letters on the side announce its name:
FREEBOOTER. Both men are thoroughly enjoying the show in
Harry's stateroom.

                    SAM
          I like his style, you know? A "take
          no prisoners" kind of guy.
                  (turns to Craig)
          Let's do this. Enough screwing
          around. I'm ready.

They go back down the dock where Sam's Mustang is parked.

                    CRAIG
          You got any of that money left we
          took off the bitch? My old lady's
          all over my ass for the rent money,
          man.

                    SAM
          No can do. I paid out another five
          bills to Ellen today. We'd best
          keep the rest for expenses on this
          gig.

                    CRAIG
          Expenses? What expenses?

Sam gives Craig a smack across the back of his head.

                    SAM
          Don't push it. I'm stressed out
          enough as it is with all I've got
          on my mind.

INT. PALM BEACH AIRPORT - NIGHT

Ellen's at a bank of phones near the AIR FRANCE ticket desks.
There's a small suitcase on the floor next to her and a large
purse slung over one shoulder. She's on the phone, waiting.
Then she reacts as someone answers.

                    ELLEN
          Hello, Andre? It's me... Ellen.
               (listens, then glances at
               her watch)
          I'm sorry. I thought it'd be
          morning there.
               (nervous laugh)
          I mean, like eight o'clock morning.
          Not four o'clock morning.
               (listens, then)
          Well, I'm calling because I was
          thinking of visiting Paris. But the
          airfare doesn't leave much left
          over for a hotel room. And I
          thought maybe-
               (stops - cutoff by Andre)
          Yeah, it is kind of sudden, I know.
               (her voice goes higher)
          But it's important that I get out
          of here, Andre! I mean like right
          this very minute!

ANGLE

A few yards away - at the end of the phone bank - a young
THUG looks Ellen's way. He watches her as the conversation
continues and we can tell that he sees opportunity knocking.

                    ELLEN
               (continuing)
          Anyway...
               (MORE)

                    ELLEN (cont'd)
          I was hoping that since we parted
          friends - more or less - that maybe
          you could put me up for a little
          while. No strings attached. You'd
          just be helping an out an old
          friend.

                    ELLEN
               (continuing; listens,
                registers disappointment)
          Oh, I see.
               (beat)
          You're getting married.
               (beat)
          And yes, I certainly understand how
          my presence might make things
          awkward. But maybe one of your
          friends in Paris could-
               (another cutoff, nods her
                head as he talks)
          No, no. Don't trouble yourself,
          Andre. No hard feelings. And hey...
          Congratulations!

She hangs up.

                    ELLEN
               (continuing; under her
                breath)
          Bastard!

The young Thug is very much interested in her reaction. He
watches her take several deep breaths to calm herself.

Ellen picks up the phone, feeds the prepaid card into the
slot. Punches buttons. Waits for the pickup, then:

                    ELLEN
               (continuing)
          Ruth? This is Ellen. Is Sam there?
               (listens - more
                disappointment)
          That's okay. I just wanted to ask
          his advice about something.
               (listens, then:)
          No, there's no message. Sorry to
          bother you, Ruth. Good night.

Ellen hangs up. Stands there a beat, eyes shut, thinking. The
Thug is still watching her. Getting more and more curious.
Then he turns his face away as her eyes come open.

She looks around the airport at all the international airline
signs. Ellen bites her lip in frustration - she could be
anyplace else in the world in a matter of hours.

Then she checks inside the big purse. Pulls out a manila
envelope like the one Craig's money came in.

Reaches inside and pulls out a thin bundle of bills. Shakes
her head - she's way short - and shoves the money back
inside.

                    ELLEN
           (continuing; rueful smile)
         So much for a life as an
         international fugitive.

She picks up her suitcase and walks toward the exit. Beat,
beat... and the young Thug falls in place behind her.

EXT. PALM BEACH AIRPORT - NIGHT

Swaying on high heels, Ellen walks across the road to the
taxi island. There are only a few people there and not a cab
in sight. She puts her suitcase down to wait. But then:

ANGLE

The young Thug crashes onto the scene! He speeds past her -
grabbing her purse as he goes!

                    ELLEN
              (shouting)
         Hey!

She hangs onto the purse for dear life. But it's no use. The
thug rips it from her grasp, knocking her to the ground. He
races across the street to the parking garage.

Ellen appeals to the bystanders - several of whom are healthy
young men.

                    ELLEN
              (continuing)
         Stop him! He got my purse.

They ostentatiously ignore her. Immediately, Ellen leaps to
her feet, scoops up her shoes and sprints across the road
after the man.

Several cars and an airport bus nearly hit her, but she
dodges them and accompanied by SCREECHING BRAKES, HONKING
HORNS and SHOUTED CURSES, she makes it across. Then she runs
into the parking structure after the thug.

INT. PARKING STRUCTURE - NIGHT

Amazingly, she's gained on the young Thug. She spots him
running along an aisle.

>   ELLEN
>   (shouting)
>   Stop, damn you!

The Thug glances over his shoulder, reacting in amazement
that Ellen has followed him. He puts on a burst of speed...
but so does Ellen.

ANGLE

The young Thug skids around a corner and races up a ramp
leading to the roof. Ellen doggedly charges onward.

ANOTHER ANGLE

The Thug is panting like an old dog. Looks over his shoulder
and sees Ellen closing in on him.

>   THUG
>   Shit!

EXT. PARKING STRUCTURE ROOF - NIGHT

Gasping for air, the Thug reaches the roof. Pauses to look
around - lots of cars, but no people. Glances back at Ellen,
nodding in satisfaction when he sees she's still there. He
turns around to face her. Motions for her to keep coming.

>   THUG
>   Come on, you dumb bitch!

But instead of being intimidated, Ellen steams forward.

>   ELLEN
>   Don't you bitch me!

And she powers into the guy, swinging her high heels like
tomahawks. Pounding him furiously. Blood spattering
everywhere.

The thug is caught by surprise and goes back, cowering to
protect himself.

>   THUG
>   Goddamn! You're gonna kill me!

But Ellen shows no mercy and slashes away at him with those
deadly heels.

>   ELLEN
>   (screaming)
>   Fuck you! Fuck you! Fuck you!

Finally, the thug flings the purse at her and hauls ass out
of there. Ellen starts after him, then stops. Recovers her
purse. Then, overcome by sudden weariness, she nearly falls.
She forces herself upright, fighting to catch her breath.

ANGLE

A group of TOURISTS exit the elevator. They see Ellen and
react. One of the MEN comes over to her.

                    MAN
          Can I help you, lady?

Ellen gives him a withering look.

                    ELLEN
          Piss on your help.

Shocked, the man moves back to his friends.

                    ELLEN
          (continuing; to the group)
          Piss on all of your help.

They hurry off, trying to get away from this crazy lady.
Ellen gets to her feet.

                    ELLEN
          (continuing; at the top of
           her lungs)
          That's right. Run! Run for your
          lives. Ellen Berman just woke up.
          And she's not going to be anybody's
          victim ever again. You hear me?
          Never fucking again!

INT. CAB - NIGHT

A despondent Ellen is slumped in the back seat of a cab
heading out of the airport. Looking out the window at the
passing scene. Suddenly she reacts as she sees:

ANGLE ON BILLBOARD

The billboard shows a young woman with a gun, crouched,
pistol aimed, as if she's about to blow somebody away. The
sign reads: STOP BEING A VICTIM! BE-SECURE!

RETURN TO SCENE

Ellen taps the driver's shoulder.

                    ELLEN
          What's that sign all about?
              (points out the window)
          "Be-Secure?"

                    CABBIE
          It's sort of a fancy gunstore. Over
          where you live - in Deerfield.
              (beat)
          They cater to paranoid people -
          like me.

He pops the glove compartment and indicates a nasty looking
gun inside.

                    CABBIE
              (continuing)
          It's all about protection these
          days, you know? If AIDs don't get
          you, the muggers will.

                    ELLEN
              (shudders)
          I could never shoot anyone.

                    CABBIE
          Well, you might not say that if the
          right - or maybe I should say,
          wrong - circumstances came along.
          Of course, they have other stuff at
          Be-Secure's besides guns. Stuff
          that'll knock your average bad guy
          on his ass, but not damage him
          permanently, if you get my drift.

                    ELLEN
              (musing)
          Maybe I'll go by there tomorrow.

                    CABBIE
          I can drop you there now, if you
          want. They're open until midnight.
          You'd be surprised how many people
          get freaked out at night and find
          themselves wanting some protection
          fast.

                    ELLEN
          No. I wouldn't be surprised at all.
              (beat)
          Take me there. Please.

EXT. BE-SECURE GUN STORE - NIGHT

Ellen exits the cab and enters the upscale store.

INT. BE-SECURE GUN STORE - NIGHT

The place is fairly empty. Ellen looks around, bewildered by
all the weapons in their racks and behind armored glass.
She's also intimidated by the implied in-your-face violence
they represent. She starts to turn and go back out the door
but then she hears:

                    PHIL'S VOICE
          Excuse me, ma'am. But don't I know
          you?

ANGLE

She turns back, surprised when she sees Phil the bartender.

                    ELLEN
          Oh... Well, yes. We met at Rum
          Runner's.
                    (nervous laugh)
          Well, not exactly met. We weren't
          formally introduced.

Grinning, Phil extends his hand.

                    PHIL
          I'm Phil Collins. Bartender by day,
          part owner of Be-Secure's by night.

Ellen takes his hand.

                    ELLEN
          Ellen Berman. Painter by day and I
          can't think of anything clever to
          say about night.

The two laugh. Phil subtly starts guiding her around the
store. Moving past the many displays.

                    PHIL
          You looked like you were about to
          leave our fine establishment. Are
          we doing something wrong?

                    ELLEN
          Well... to be honest, I was kind of
          intimidated. I came here on the
          spur of the moment, but then when I
          started looking...

Her voice trails off and she shakes her head.

                    PHIL
          Suddenly you were looking at racks
          of guns and wondering if the
          problem you have requires such
          drastic action.

Ellen's impressed by his analysis.

                    ELLEN
          You seem to be an excellent student
          of human behavior. Years of
          experience behind the bar, I
          presume?

                    PHIL
              (shakes his head)
          Not that many years.
              (beat)
          Actually I spent most of my adult
          life in the military. Retired a few
          years ago and bought into this
          place with an old Army buddy. I
          took the Rum Runner's job to bring
          in cash until this place starts
          paying off.
              (laughs)
          Whenever that is!

He gives Ellen a look of concern.

                    PHIL
              (continuing)
          Don't mean to butt into your
          business, but does this sudden
          impulse to visit a gun shop have
          anything to do with Sam Barr?

                    ELLEN
              (a little surprised)
          Why, no! Not at all.
              (beat)
          Oh, that's right. When I saw you
          last you were trying to warn me
          about Sam.

                    PHIL
              (turns grim)
          That was not my place. I know that
          and I'm sorry. It's just that you
          seem to be such a nice lady. A real
          lady - in the old fashioned sense.
          And Sam has... well...

                    ELLEN
          I know he's an ex-con. He didn't
          hide that from me.

> PHIL
> Listen, I shouldn't have said
> anything. It's just that... Well,
> look... Let me be honest with you.
> Sam doesn't know me from the man in
> the moon. But he used to date my
> sister. She wrote to me about it
> when I was stationed in Germany.
> (beat)
> Anyway, he didn't do well by my
> Trish, you know? She's been in and
> out of rehab and off and on the
> streets ever since.

A long silence as Ellen takes this in.

> ELLEN
> I'm sorry to hear that. I truly am.
> But - in my case I first met Sam
> when he saved me from a rapist.
> (beat)
> He pulled the creep off me and beat
> him within an inch of his life. And
> I'm not ashamed to admit that I
> enjoyed every blow he struck in my
> behalf.

Now it's Phil's turn to take the long pause. Finally:

> PHIL
> 'Nough said.
> (beat)
> Maybe we can agree to disagree
> about Sam Barr and go on from
> there.
> (sticks out his hand)
> Shake?

Laughing Ellen takes his hand again.

> ELLEN
> Shake.

Phil stops before a display of non-explosive weapons - stun guns, mace, etc.

> PHIL
> Now, to return to your reasons for
> visiting Be-Secure.

> ELLEN
> (quickly)
> I'd rather not talk about it. The
> reasons, I mean.

                    PHIL
          I understand. But I'm assuming that
          they are perfectly good and
          legitimate reasons, correct?

                    ELLEN
          Correct. But I also don't want to
          kill anybody, you know?

                    PHIL
               (laughing)
          No killing. Got it!
               (beat)
          How about simply knocking this
          problem of yours on his ass? And
          making him stay there for a good
          deal of time.

                    ELLEN
          Just what the doctor ordered.

Phil turns to show her the display.

                    PHIL
          Mace. Stun guns. Collapsible
          batons...

He demonstrates the baton, snapping it open. Ellen frowns,
and shakes her head.

                    ELLEN
          I don't know.

Phil snaps his fingers.

                    PHIL
          I've got it.

He pulls what appears to be an umbrella from a basket
display.

                    ELLEN
               (puzzled)
          An umbrella? What, is there a sword
          hidden inside, or something?
               (shakes her head)
          I could never-

                    PHIL
               (interrupting her)
          Not so fast.
               (holds it up)
          Actually, this is a stun gun AND an
          umbrella. Hit the guy with the
          tip...
               (shows her)
                    (MORE)

                    PHIL (cont'd)
          ... Pull the trigger...
               (demonstrates)
          And it'll deliver eighty thousand
          volts right where they're needed.

Touches the metal counter edge and there's a buzz and a long
blue spark leaps out. Ellen jumps. Phil offers it to her.

                    PHIL
               (continuing)
          You try it.

A little scared - but fascinated just the same - she takes
the umbrella.

                    PHIL
               (continuing;
                demonstrating)
          Here's the trigger.
               (beat)
          Now. Go!

And Ellen touches the metal rim. More buzzing and another big
blue spark. Ellen laughs.

                    ELLEN
          Oh, I love it!

Phil picks up a clear plastic bag, with an array of colorful
umbrella pouches.

                    PHIL
          And, that's not all folks. For your
          fashion convenience you get a
          variety of pouches to hold the
          umbrella.

                    ELLEN
               (giggling)
          Lethal fashions!

                    PHIL
          Have I got a sale, then?

                    ELLEN
               (still laughing)
          How could I possibly refuse?

She stabs the brolly at the counter and once more unleashes a
long blue spark that buzzes like mad. MATCH SOUND TO:

INT. ELLEN'S BEDROOM - DAY

The buzzing of Ellen's alarm clock. It's the next day and
she's curled up in bed, the umbrella clutched in a death
grip.

She comes awake, cuts the alarm, then sits up - the stun brolly still in her hand. She holds it up, sleepy and puzzled, then remembers. A wide smile. She brandishes the brolly.

                    ELLEN
          You go, Grrll!

Just then her door buzzer goes off in the front room. Ellen jumps as if stung. Another buzz. Quickly she pulls on a robe and goes into the living room, still holding the brolly.

INT. ELLEN'S LIVING ROOM - DAY

She approaches the door cautiously, holding the brolly in front of her, ready to lunge.

                    ELLEN
              (calling out)
          Who is it?

                    SAM'S OS VOICE
          Sam.

Relieved, Ellen opens the door. Sam looks down at the umbrella and grins.

                    SAM
          Weather man calling for rain in
          your living room?

Ellen reacts, then remembers the brolly.

                    ELLEN
              (a little embarrassed)
          No. See this is actually-

                    SAM
              (cutting through)
          Ruth said you called last night.
          Something wrong?

                    ELLEN
          No, no. I got it solved on my own.
          Sorry I was a bother.

                    SAM
          No bother at all.
              (starts to turn away,
               then:)
          You going to see your mom today?

                    ELLEN
          Yes I am. Maybe if you're going my
          way...

                        SAM
          Sorry. Any other day, but today,
          it'd be fine.

                        ELLEN
          Sure, Sam. Sure.

She raises the umbrella again.

                        ELLEN
                    (continuing)
          Wait until you see my new toy. It's
          got-

                        SAM
          I'll check it out later, okay? Got
          to go.

And he's gone. Ellen stares after him a beat, then shrugs and
shuts the door.

INT. MRS. BERMAN'S ROOM - DAY

Ellen paces the room while her mother watches an episode of
"I Love Lucy." She's wearing a billowy sun dress and on the
floor is a color-coordinated handbag. The brolly handle
sticks out of the bag.

Ellen is clearly upset and in desperate to talk to someone.

                        ELLEN
          I wish you were in there, Ma, so
          you could understand what I'm
          saying. Things are really building
          up, you know? I'm afraid they're
          going to explode and I'll wind up
          like before. Right under Harry's
          thumb.

                        MRS. BERMAN
          Harry bought me a new TV.

                        ELLEN
          I know, Ma. That's all you've been
          talking about.
                    (beat)
          God, I wish you could speak up for
          me. Tell Harry to leave me alone.
          And that detective...
                    (she shudders)
          I know Harry wouldn't want that. He
          might not like me very much, but I
          am his sister.

                    MRS. BERMAN
          I'm going for a boat ride today.
          Harry's going to take me.

This surprises the hell out of Ellen.

                    ELLEN
          Harry's coming here? Twice in one
          week?

                    MRS. BERMAN
          He comes every day.

                    ELLEN
              (disbelieving)
          Sure, Ma. And so does the Pope and
          Golda Meir.

                    MRS. BERMAN
          I wish Ellen could come with us.
              (tears well in her eyes)
          I miss her so much.

Ellen's eyes tear in sympathy. She goes to her mother and
hugs her.

                    ELLEN
          She misses you too, Ma. She really
          does.

EXT. NURSING HOME - ANGLE ON MUSTANG - DAY

Sam and Craig - in their usual spot under the tree - watch as
Ellen exits the nursing home and heads for the waiting cab.

                    CRAIG
              (grinning)
          Right on time.
              (beat)
          That's what I like about that
          broad. Real dependable, you know?

                    SAM
          A rare quality in a woman.

He hops out of the car.

                    SAM
              (continuing)
          Get in the back. We're expecting
          company, remember?

And as he heads for the nursing home Craig sighs and climbs
into the back seat.

INT. ELLEN'S APARTMENT - DAY

Ellen's back in her painting togs - spattered cutoffs and
halter - and putting the finishing touches on the painting of
Sam. She steps back to examine it, frowning.

                    ELLEN
          I don't know...

And the door bell buzzes. She turns and automatically starts
for the door then comes to an abrupt halt. She opens her
mouth, as if to call out, but once again caution comes to her
rescue. The door buzzes again putting her into motion.

Very carefully she creeps up to the door and peers through
the eyepiece.

THROUGH THE EYEPIECE

It's Sergeant Propp!

RETURN TO SCENE

Ellen reacts, scared.

                    ELLEN
                 (whispering)
          Shit!

Propp bangs on the door with his fist.

                    SGT. PROPP
          Ellen! I know you're in there!

Ellen races into her bedroom. More door pounding. A beat
later Ellen comes racing back out. She's pulled on a shirt
and slipped into a pair of sandals. More importantly, she's
got her stun umbrella - handle poking out of a beach bag.

She moves swiftly to the living room window and as Propp
buzzes the door bell and knocks some more, she slips it open
and climbs out.

EXT. BACKYARD - DAY

Ellen quietly pulls the window shut, then sprints across the
backyard to the gate.

At the gate, she lifts the bar lock, pulls the gate open and
races out. And, Boom! She collides with someone, letting out
a little eek.

ANOTHER ANGLE

The other person is Ruth! She staggers back and Ellen stops
her from tumbling over.

                    ELLEN
      Oh, Ruth! I'm so sorry!

                    RUTH
        (laughing)
      I just about peed my pants.
        (beat)
      Where you goin' in such a hurry?

Ellen glances over her shoulder. Nothing. Turns back.

                    ELLEN
      To tell the truth, I was trying to
      avoid someone.

                    RUTH
      Old boyfriend, huh?

                    ELLEN
        (shudders)
      Something like that.

                    RUTH
      I know how that is. Some men turn
      out to be real pains in the behind.
      Won't go away when they're told to.
        (beat)
      Want me to get Sam to have a word
      with him?

                    ELLEN
        (vehement shake of the
        head)
      Oh, no! That wouldn't work at all.
      But I would take it as a real favor
      if I could maybe hang out at your
      place for a little while. Just
      until he goes away.

                    RUTH
      I've got a better deal for you.
      Just so happens I was comin' to get
      you in a few minutes. Sam called
      and said a buddy of his is letting
      him use his boat. He said to come
      on down to the Cove and we could
      take a cruise and have a little
      picnic.

                    ELLEN
          I don't want to impose. You two
          have done enough for me as it is.

                    RUTH
          Don't be silly. He told me to fetch
          you and that I wasn't to take "no"
          for an answer.

Ellen looks down at her paint-spattered outfit.

                    RUTH
               (continuing; notices and
                understands)
          They're just fine, Hon You don't
          have to go back to your place to
          change. Not with that bozo lurkin'
          on you.
               (beat)
          This is gonna be real relaxed.
          You'll be sort of like our - what
          do you call it - bohemian guest.
          Real artsy fartsy, you know?

She indicates a bright yellow Volkswagon parked behind her
with a large picnic basket in the back.

                    RUTH
               (continuing)
          Come on. I've got the car all
          loaded.

The two women get in the car and start down the driveway to
the street.

EXT. APARTMENT HOUSE - DAY

As the car pulls out into the street, Propp comes out of the
apartment building. He spots the Volkswagon with Ellen inside
and sprints to the curb where his ND plainclothes car is
parked. Jumps inside and heads off after the women.

EXT. DOCKS - DAY

Ruth and Ellen pull into the parking lot next to the boat
slips. They get out and look around at all the yachts.

                    RUTH
          I wonder which one it is? He said
          it was called the Freebooter.

Ellen points to one of the nicest yachts in the cove. With
Freebooter painted across the side. It's the same boat we saw
earlier when Harry was partying with his nubile girlfriend.

                         ELLEN
                Is that it?

                         RUTH
                    (frowning)
                It's much too grand.

Sam comes out of the bridge. He spots them and waves.

                         SAM
                    (shouting)
                Hey, Ruthie! Over here.

Ruth puts a hand across her chest.

                         RUTH
                Oh, my heart!

She and Ellen grab the picnic basket and head for the yacht.

ON THE FREEBOOTER

Where Ruth and Ellen have joined Sam.

                         RUTH
                I didn't know you had friends like
                this, Sam.

Sam laughs at this clumsy remark.

                         RUTH
                    (continuing)
                I didn't mean that how it came out.
                Still-

                         SAM
                I move in classy circles these
                days, Ruth.
                    (grins at Ellen)
                Seriously, though. My buddy got
                lucky getting into the market - and
                smart getting out. He's big bucks
                city, now.

                         ELLEN
                    (looking around the yacht)
                So, I see.

Sam indicates the posh main cabin, which can be seen through
the windows.

                         SAM
                Why don't you ladies check out the
                amenities, while I get things
                moving?

The women start to go below.

                    SAM
                (continuing)
          Oh, one thing. Stay out of the
          cabin next to the wetbar. My
          buddy's got some stuff in there
          he'd like to keep private.

                    RUTH
                (rolls her eyes)
          Probably porn.

                    ELLEN
          As long as I can use the head, I
          don't care if he has Pamela
          Anderson and Tommy Lee in there.

ANGLE

Sam trots up to the bridge and opens the door. Craig is on
his knees, a mass of cables pulled from the control console.
He's stripping two wires. Craig looks up at him and grins.

                    CRAIG
          This is a helluva lot easier than
          stealing cars.

He touches the wires together and the engine roars into life.
Quickly, he twists them together then adjusts the throttle
until it steadies down. Gives Sam a thumbs up.

ANOTHER ANGLE

Sam hurries down the stairs to the main deck. He casts off
the lines. Then turns and cups his hands to his mouth.

                    SAM
                (shouting)
          Hit it!

Craig smoothly pulls out and heads into the channel.

ANOTHER ANGLE

Propp is standing on the dock, watching the yacht move toward
the open sea. He's got a cell phone glued to his ear.

                    SGT. PROPP
                (into phone)
          Hey, Susie? This is Sergeant Propp.
          I need you to check a boat
          registration for me...

INT. FREEBOOTER'S MAIN CABIN - DAY

Ellen and Ruth lounge on soft leather couches, sipping wine
and thoroughly enjoying themselves. Sam enters. He has his
cell phone flipped open as if he's about to call someone.

                    SAM
          Comfortable, ladies?

                    RUTH
          Are you kidding? We feel like
          queens.

                    SAM
          That's good. Because before we get
          too deep into this deal, there's
          something I want to discuss with
          Ellen. A little bit of business,
          then we can get on with our fun.

                    ELLEN
               (puzzled)
          What business?

                    SAM
          Hang on. Let me get my partner in
          here. He'll want to hear this.

He turns to the door.

                    SAM
               (continuing; raising his
                voice)
          Okay, Craig. You can come on in.

Ellen reacts when she's hears that name. And she has an even
bigger reaction when the grinning Craig enters the cabin.

                    ELLEN
          What's he doing here?

                    SAM
          That's what I want to discuss with
          you, Ellen.
               (beat)
          See, it's like this. Ever since we
          met I've had a good feeling about
          you. A feeling that you were going
          to make me a whole lot of money.
               (beat)
          Enough to share with my friends

He nods at Ruth, then at Craig. But Ruth is furious at this
turn of events.

                         RUTH
          I don't want any part of your
          scheme, Sam Barr. I took you on in
          good faith that you were gonna
          change your ways. No more crooked
          stuff. No more hurtin' people.
               (gets to her feet)
          You better turn around right this
          minute and take us home, you hear?

Sam shakes his head, then reaches out and gives her a push.
Not a hard push, just enough to tip her back into her seat.

                         SAM
          I'm disappointed that you feel that
          way, Ruth. But that's okay, it just
          makes the pie bigger for me and
          Craig to share.

Ellen has recovered her wits. She's not only unafraid, but
she's pissed.

                         ELLEN
          You must be crazy. I don't have a
          penny to my name. Except in trust.
          And my brother controls that.

                         SAM
          I know all about it, Ellen. And for
          awhile it had me stumped. I
          couldn't figure out how to get my
          hands on that trust money.

Sam gets to his feet and goes to the small cabin door next to
the wet bar.

                         SAM
               (continuing)
          But then I found my answer.
               (beat)
          Here, let me show you.

ANGLE

As he opens the door. Ellen gasps in awful shock. For sitting
there is her mother!

                         MRS. BERMAN
               (whining)
          Harry, where's the TV? It's almost
          time for Perry Mason.

Sam whips the cellphone up, aiming it.

                    SAM
          Smile, Mom. You're on Candid
          Camera!

And there's a click as he snaps the picture.

INT. HARRY'S OFFICE - DAY

Harry's on his running machine again, shadow boxing as he
trots on the endless belt. The speaker phone CRACKLES to
life.

                    SECRETARY'S SPEAKER VOICE,
          Mr. Berman? There's an urgent call
          for you.

                    HARRY
               (annoyed)
          I asked not to be disturbed, Linda.
          This is my personal time. Our
          clients are just going to have to
          learn-

                    SECRETARY'S SPEAKER VOICE,
               (breaking through)
          I'm sorry, sir. But, it's a man
          about your mother.

                    HARRY
               (jolted)
          Put him through, Linda.

Immediately, the phone buzzes. Harry leans over and taps a
button to activate the speaker.

                    HARRY
               (continuing)
          Harold Berman. How may I help you?

He resumes jogging.

                    SAM'S SPEAKER VOICE
          Hey, Harry. Sam Barr here.

                    HARRY
               (impatient)
          What's this business about my
          mother?

                    SAM'S SPEAKER VOICE
          Got your cell phone handy?

                    HARRY
               (Snorts impatience)
          Answer my question.

                    SAM'S SPEAKER VOICE
          Hold your horses, Harry. This'll
          only take a second.
                    (beat)
          Man, you sure have packed this boat
          with trick gear. Satellite
          tracking, sonar, a computer station
          and even a by-god state of the art
          cell phone booster.

                    HARRY
                    (puzzled)
          My boat? What are you talking
          about, Mr. Barr.

                    SAM'S SPEAKER VOICE
          Wait a minute...

Over on his desk, we hear Harry's phone chime into life -
playing the Rock theme.

                    SAM
          Now, go check your cell messages
          and come on back and we'll talk.

Harry dismounts and hurries to his desk. Grabs the cell and
flips it open. He fumbles up the message from Sam, the reacts
as his Mother's picture pops up on the screen.

                    HARRY
          Oh my God!

ANOTHER ANGLE

He races back to his workout station, glaring at the speaker
phone as if it is his deadliest enemy.

                    HARRY
          What the hell is this all about,
          Barr? I want an explanation. And I
          want one fast.

                    SAM'S SPEAKER VOICE
          I really do admire your style,
          Harry. I mean, we haven't even
          officially met and we're already on
          the same page.
                    (beat)
          Okay, now. Here's the deal. I want
          you to fix this into your mind...
                    (beat)
          Five hundred thousand dollars. Got
          it? Five hundred thousand dollars.

                    HARRY
          Why is that such a magic figure?

                    SAM'S SPEAKER VOICE
          Because that's how much is left in
          your sister's trust fund after you
          ripped her off for two and a half
          million.

INT. FREEBOOTER'S MAIN CABIN - DAY

Chuckling, Sam cuts the connection. Mrs. Berman has been
moved next to Ellen, who has a protective arm around her.
Mrs. Berman is oblivious. She's got her "book of secrets" in
her lap and is turning pages, muttering to herself.

                    ELLEN
               (to Sam)
          How did you find what Harry was up
          to?

Sam crosses the room to Mrs. Berman and Ellen.

                    SAM
          Didn't your mom try to tell you
          about her book of secrets?

                    ELLEN
          Well, sure, but-

Ellen stops in midsentence as Sam leans down and gently pulls
some loose pages from the back of Mrs. Berman's book.

                    SAM
               (to Mrs. Berman)
          I need to borrow these a sec, Mom.

Sam waves the documents at Ellen.

                    SAM
               (continuing)
          You should have listened to your
          mother, Ellen. She's got the whole
          deal spelled out right here.

He goes to a fax machine, sitting on a small, built in desk.

                    SAM
               (continuing)
          I have to fax these to your
          brother. He wants to make sure that
          I've got proof.

                    ELLEN
                  (outraged)
        Proof? What does the son of a bitch
        need proof for? You're holding our
        mother hostage.

Sam feeds the documents into the fax.

                    SAM
        No biggie. He's a businessman. He
        wants to see all the cards he can.

Ruth stirs in her seat. She's got a large drink in her hand
and is obviously under the weather.

                    RUTH
        So you're back to the old game,
        huh, Sam? A crook robbin' crooks.
                  (turns to Ellen)
        Sorry, but that's what your brother
        is.

Ellen shrugs. No apologies necessary.

                    RUTH
                  (continuing)
        They're gonna put you back in jail,
        Sam. And this time you ain't -
        aren't - ever gonna get out. I'll
        damn well see to that!

                    SAM
        I hope you're not thinking of doing
        something stupid, Ruth, hon. We've
        been getting along pretty well,
        haven't we? Why not go with the
        flow?

Ruth slugs back more booze and refills the glass from the
bottle beside her.

                    RUTH
        Yeah and we'll see how long that
        lasts. You were cheatin' when you
        were broke and needed me. What's it
        gonna be like when you've got some
        money in your jeans?

Sam sighs a weary sigh and shakes his head.

                    SAM
        You just keep hitting the bottle,
        Ruth. You're making yourself real
        attractive, you know?

Ruth mutters under her breath and goes back to drinking.

                    ELLEN
          What about Ma and me? Are you
          really going to let us go when you
          get the money?

                    SAM
          Sure, why not?

                    ELLEN
          Aren't you afraid that I'll blab to
          the police?

                    SAM
          You worry too much, Ellen. I've got
          it all figured so that the fewest
          people necessary get hurt. Lot
          cleaner that way.

He goes to the intercom, which is mounted by the main door.

                    SAM
               (continuing; raising his
                voice)
          Yo, Craig. Head for Paradise Cove.

                    CRAIG'S INTERCOM VOICE
          You got it.
               (giggles)
          I mean, Aye, aye, Capn'.

                    SAM
               (laughing)
          Isn't he a pistol?

ANGLE ON ELLEN

Protective arm around her mother, guarding her like a she-
wolf protecting her cub.

EXT. DOCKS - DAY

Harry's limo pulls up to the dock where his boat was berthed.
He gets out, lugging a heavy briefcase. He's dressed in fancy
workout clothes that show off his impressive build. Harry
looks at the empty slip and shakes his head.

                    HARRY
               (under his breath)
          The son of a bitch!

There's the OS SOUND of an outboard and Harry looks up to see
Craig guiding the Freebooter's little deck boat to the dock.
Harry raps on the driver's window, which comes down.

                    HARRY
                 (continuing)
            Take off, Joe. I'll make my own way
            home.

                    CHAUFFEUR
            Yes, sir, Mr. Berman.

And he reverses out of the dock area.

ANGLE

Harry stands over the motorboat, Craig peering up at him.

                    CRAIG
            Got the money?

                    HARRY
                 (impatient)
            Of course I've got the money. Why
            the hell else would I-

He breaks off, realizing he's arguing with a dimbulb.

                    HARRY
                 (continuing)
            You are obviously not the brains of
            this outfit.

Craig glowers, pissed at the insult. But Harry doesn't give a
damn. He jumps down into the boat and takes a seat, waiting.
Craig continues glowering.

                    HARRY
                 (continuing)
            Jesus! Let's get this over with,
            shall we?

Craig finally gives up trying to intimidate him and speeds
away. Beat, beat and then Sergeant Propp rushes into frame!
He reacts as he sees the boat quickly becoming a smaller and
smaller object on the horizon.

                    SGT. PROPP
            Shit!

Propp looks around, frantic. And then he spots:

A YOUNG BOATING COUPLE

Backing their 20-foot Wellcraft down a boating ramp. The
YOUNG WOMAN is driving the pickup, while her HUSBAND guides
the trailer into the water.

ANOTHER ANGLE

Propp starts running.

                    SGT. PROPP
                  (shouting)
              Hold it right there!

The woman and her husband turn and gawk at Propp as he races
up to the boat, splashing through water. He digs out his
badge and flashes it at the husband.

                    SGT. PROPP
                  (continuing)
              Police! I'm commandeering this
              boat.

The husband reacts in shock, reaching toward Propp.

                    YOUNG HUSBAND
              Hey, you can't do that!

                    SGT. PROPP
              The hell I can't!

He knocks the guy into the water. Quickly, he unhooks the
line and pushes the boat deeper into the water. In a flash
he's on board and starting the engine. Then he powers away at
top speed, the terrified couple watching him go and wondering
what the hell just happened.

EXT. FREEBOOTER'S DECK - DAY

Craig tools up to the Freebooter. Harry jumps for the ladder
and climbs up the side, the briefcase under his arm.

ANGLE ON DECK

Harry finds Sam waiting for him. Mrs. Berman sits next to him
in a deck chair, while Ellen hovers nearby. She's got her
beach bag, with the stun umbrella, within easy reach.

Ruth lounges in the cabin doorway, taking frequent sips of
booze and muttering to herself. She is one unhappy woman.

                    SAM
              Glad you could join the party,
              Harry.
                  (indicates Ellen and Mrs.
                  Berman)
              I'm afraid Mom and Sis haven't had
              such a good time.
                  (MORE)

                    SAM (cont'd)
        But now that you're here, I'm sure
        things will liven up.

Mrs. Berman peers at Harry, a deep frown furrowing her brow.
She turns to Sam.

                    MRS. BERMAN
        Why did you invite him, Harry? He
        doesn't look like our sort.

Sam is vastly amused by this. Ellen snorts in disgust. Then
leans over her mother, pointing at her brother.

                    ELLEN
        That's the real, Harry, Ma.
            (points to Sam)
        He's nothing but a common thug.

From her corner, Ruth toasts Ellen.

                    RUTH
        Common through and through!

She takes a hefty slug. Meanwhile, Mrs. Berman objects to
Ellen's remarks.

                    MRS. BERMAN
        Don't try to fool me, young lady. I
        certainly know my own son.

She reaches over and gives Sam's hand a squeeze.

                    MRS. BERMAN
                (continuing)
        Such a good boy, too. Buying me
        presents. Visiting me every day.

Ruth laughs - on the edge of drunken hysteria.

                    RUTH
        Good boy! Ha! Shoot, he's no better
        than a whore in the streets. 'Cept
        he lives off women.

Sam reacts, she's getting under his skin.

                    SAM
        Shut up, Ruth. You don't know what
        you're talking about.

                    RUTH
        Shut yourself up. I'm just
        truthin', that's all. You screwed
        over me. You screwed over Ellen and
        now you're screwing over that poor
        old woman.
                (MORE)

>   RUTH (cont'd)
>   (beat)
>   Wimp!

Sam takes a step toward her, raising his hand. But Harry is
growing impatient with all this quarreling.

>   HARRY
>   (to Sam)
>   Look, my friend. I'm a busy man.
>   You want to smack your woman
>   around, have at it. I'd smack her
>   myself, the way she's talking. But
>   please have the courtesy to wait
>   until we're through.

Harry offers the briefcase.

>   HARRY
>   (continuing)
>   Take it and go. You can have the
>   deck boat. A small, but handsome
>   bonus for your efforts.

Good humor restored, Sam takes the briefcase. He opens it and
looks inside. He reacts - pissed.

>   SAM
>   What the hell is this?

He pulls a single check-sized piece of paper out and hurls
the briefcase to the deck. Ellen reacts, stunned.

>   ELLEN
>   What are you doing, Harry? You're
>   going to get our mother killed.

Harry ignores her.

>   HARRY
>   (to Sam)
>   What you have there is a cashier's
>   check - made out to me - for two
>   hundred and fifty thousand dollars.
>   All I have to do is countersign it
>   and the check's in play. Good at
>   any bank anywhere in the world.

Craig blows high, wide and handsome. A gun suddenly appears
in his fist as he leaps across the deck. He shoves the gun up
against Harry's head.

>   CRAIG
>   Think you're a smart ass, huh? Well
>   I'll show you smartass.

And he cranks back the hammer. Harry's unconcerned.

                    HARRY
                 (to Sam)
          Is this how you negotiate?

Sam can't believe what he's hearing.

                    SAM
          You thought I was negotiating? What
          are you, crazy? What world have you
          been living in? I'm a criminal, you
          dumb son of a bitch.

Bitter laugh from Ruth.

                    RUTH
          Ain't that the truth!?

Sam shoots her a dirty look. But Harry soon has his attention
back again.

                    HARRY
                 (still calm)
          Everything's negotiable. You've got
          half the money there. Two hundred
          and fifty thousand dollars. A
          handsome sum. You can take it and
          go with little worry about police
          interference. Or, you can wait
          until I collect the rest and turn
          it into a cashier's check.
          Remembering, of course, that the
          longer this goes on, the more
          likely something will go wrong.

                    CRAIG
          You're damn straight. Like you
          bein' dead, kind of wrong.

But Sam sees Harry's point. Somewhat. He waves Craig aside.

                    SAM
          Let him go, Craig.

                    CRAIG
          But he's tryin' to make a fool of
          us, Sam.

                    SAM
                 (firm)
          I said, let him go.

Reluctantly, Craig does so. But he keeps the gun on Harry.

                    SAM
                 (continuing;)
          Okay, you wanted to negotiate.
                 (MORE)

                         SAM (cont'd)
             Get to it, Harry. My buddy there is
             getting damned impatient.

                         HARRY
             What's to say? I've already
             outlined my offer.
                   (indicates briefcase)
             Two hundred and fifty thousand
             dollars. Not a penny more.

Sam points to Mrs. Berman.

                         SAM
             One word and Craig will blow her
             away.

                         CRAIG
             Damn straight!

                         HARRY
             Okay, so you kill my mother. But
             that won't get you more money. And
             it sure won't get me to counter-
             sign the cashier's check. Making it
             worthless.

                         SAM
             You're betting that at some point
             I'm not going to lose my cool -
             like Craig over there - and blow
             you away out of sheer piss off.

                         HARRY
             That wouldn't be too smart.

                         SAM
             But damned satisfying.

                         HARRY
                   (scoffing)
             Nothing's more satisfying than
             money.

                         SAM
                   (amused)
             You think so?

He walks over to Ruth. Who looks up at him, alarmed.

                         RUTH
             What are you doin', Harry?

                         SAM
                   (ignoring her)
             Allow me to demonstrate the
             criminal mind for you, Mr. Berman.

He suddenly grabs Ruth by the scruff of the neck. Her glass goes flying, shattering on the deck.

                    RUTH
                 (shouting)
            Harry, don't!

Harry drags her kicking across the deck. Ellen freaks.

                    ELLEN
            Stop it, Sam. Please!

She jumps forward to help Ruth, but Sam pushes her away as if she were a child.

                    SAM
            Check it out!

And he lifts Ruth up over his head and hurls her screaming into the sea!

ANGLE ON RUTH

Kicking and sputtering in the water. Craig loves this. He runs to the side to watch.

                    CRAIG
                 (laughing)
            Swim, Ruthie! Swim.

Ruth recovers enough to swim toward the boat. She clutches at the side. Sam grabs a peeve pole and pushes her away.

                    RUTH
                 (screaming)
            Sam! Sam!

Ellen rushes over to Sam and tries to pull the pole away. But Craig pulls her off. Then he holds her, watching with much amusement as Sam teases Ruth.

                    SAM
            Come on, Ruth. Come on, sweetheart.

He holds the pole out for Ruth to grab.

                    SAM
                 (continuing; crooning)
            Daddy was only teasing, sweet pie.
            Only teasing.

But the minute Ruth gets hold of the pole he plunges it down, pushing her under.

                         SAM
                   (continuing; shouting)
               Psyche!

                         CRAIG
                   (laughing his head off)
               Do it again, Sam!

And Sam does it again. As soon as Ruth surfaces, he pushes
her under. And again. And again. Until Ruth can barely keep
afloat. Getting weaker and weaker.

                         SAM
               Enough! I'm bored.

He pushes her under a final time. Holds it there. And this
time when he lets go, Ruth does not reappear. Sam turns to
Harry, who is ashen.

                         SAM
                   (continuing)
               Get my point?

Harry just nods. Sam is back in good spirits. He rubs his
hands together.

                         SAM
                   (continuing)
               Okay, let's get to it.
                   (beat)
               Where's the rest of my money?

                         HARRY
               What are you talking about? The
               check - that's all of it.

But Ruth's death has cracked his facade. We - and Sam - can
tell that he's lying.

                         SAM
                   (chuckling)
               Don't try to con a con man. You
               can't tell me that a smart man like
               you would put yourself at the mercy
               of the likes of me without some
               kind of fallback.

Craig gets it. He grins and pokes Harry with the gun.

                         CRAIG
               Wanna get wet like old Ruthie?

Still, Harry hesitates.

> ELLEN
> For God's sake, Harry! Give him the
> damned money!

Grimly, Harry fishes another cashier's check from his pocket
and hands it over. Sam looks at it and his face lights up.

> SAM
> That's better!

He reaches into his pocket and gets out the other one.

> SAM
> (continuing)
> Got a pen?

Harry just shakes his head.

> SAM
> (continuing)
> How about you, Ellen? Got a pen in
> that bag?

He walks over and scoops up the beach bag. Ellen is
practically coming out of her skin as he fishes around. He
notices the umbrella.

> SAM
> (continuing; amused)
> Still expecting rain, Ellen?

Ellen just shrugs, hoping to hell he doesn't notice.

> SAM
> (continuing)
> Hey, here we go!

And he pulls out a pen. Drops the beach bag and goes to
Harry. Shoves it into's Harry's hand. Then he turns his back,
leaning over slightly to make a writing surface. Harry is
subdued. Almost frozen in place.

> SAM
> (continuing)
> Get to it, Harry.

Harry signs. Sam turns and plucks the checks from his
fingers. Waves them at Craig.

> SAM
> (continuing)
> Now that's what I call a good day's
> work. Two fifty for you. Two fifty
> for me. And Bob's your uncle.

                    CRAIG
                (frowning)
            How'd Bob and his uncle get in on
            this deal.

Harry's spirits are returning. And with them, his nerve.

                    HARRY
            Jesus! What a dope!

                    SAM
                (sighing)
            You just have to have the last
            word, don't you
                (beat)
            Okay, fine by me.

And he flexes his big muscles then strolls over to Harry,
motioning for Craig to follow.

                    SAM
                (continuing)
            He thinks he's Jesus Christ,
            himself. Let's see if he can walk
            on water, Craig.

Craig snickers and joins Sam. Harry backs up, holding out his
hands as if they could shield him.

                    HARRY
                (reacts - holy shit)
            Hey! We had a deal.

                    SAM
            Well, I just cancelled it.

Harry keeps back pedaling until he bumps against the rail.

                    HARRY
            Hold on! Maybe we can-

Desperate, he takes a swing at Sam. Sam slips the punch and
knocks Harry down. Then he grabs one arm of the dazed man.

                    SAM
            Give me hand, Craig. He's a big son
            of a bitch.

Laughing, Craig shoves the gun in his belt and grabs the
other side. Ellen pulls out the stun umbrella.

                    ELLEN
            Please, Sam! No!

She races over, fumbling for the trigger with nervous fingers. But before she can get a steady grip, Sam gives her a shove and she falls back on the deck.

Mrs. Berman thinks this is all great fun. She claps her hands.

>   MRS. BERMAN
>   (shouting)
>   Let's all go swimming!

Sam and Craig have Harry up and are getting ready to hurl him over the side. But then:

>   SGT. PROPP'S OS VOICE
>   Well, well. What are you good folks
>   up to?

Jolted by the voice, the two turn to see:

>   SERGEANT PROPP
>   In a classic shooter's crouch, gun
>   aimed straight at Sam.

Over his shoulder we can see the Wellcraft tied up at the bow.

>   SGT. PROPP
>   Now, you boys stay just like you
>   are. I don't want to have to do
>   anything hasty.

Ellen can't believe her good fortune.

>   ELLEN
>   Thank God!

>   SGT. PROPP
>   Never thought you'd be glad to see
>   me, huh?

Ellen smiles and shakes her head. But before she can say anything more, Propp comes out of his crouch and cautiously advances on Sam and Craig.

>   SGT. PROPP
>   (continuing)
>   You really should have been nicer
>   to me, Ellen.
>   (beat)
>   Now I don't really give a shit what
>   happens to you.

He wags the gun at Sam.

                         SGT. PROPP
                      (continuing)
                 Give!

                              SAM
                 Top pocket.

Propp nods and carefully reaches out with his left and digs
the checks from Sam's pocket. Fumbles them apart with one
hand and glances at the figures. He whistles in appreciation.

                         SGT. PROPP
                 Five hundred grand! Damn! I thought
                 that's what I heard you guys
                 talking about. But I figured it was
                 too good to be true.

He takes a step back.

                         SGT. PROPP
                      (continuing)
                 You can resume killin', boys.

Uses his gun to indicate Harry.

                         SGT. PROPP
                      (continuing)
                 Him first.
                      (indicates Ellen and Mrs.
                       Berman)
                 The broads next.
                      (grins)
                 Then maybe we'll have a last drink
                 together before I do you.

But Sam isn't going to go that easily.

                              SAM
                      (barking)
                 Get him, Craig!

And he drops Harry and lunges forward. Craig's only a half
step behind him! Drawing his gun and screaming at the top of
his lungs.

                             CRAIG
                 Fuck youuuuuu!

Propp gets off a shot at Sam, but it's too hurried and he
misses. Sam powers into him, knocking him flat on his back.

The cop tries to get up but Craig fires - and the bullet
slams him back down.

ANGLE

As Harry sees his chance and charges into the melee, swinging his big fists as he bulls into Sam and Craig. Sam's momentarily stunned, but Craig steps to the side.

He raises his gun to fire, but then Propp recovers enough to get off a final shot.

The bullet hits Craig in the chest and he topples to the deck, dead. Propp tries shoot Sam, but then falls back on the deck to breathe his last.

ANOTHER ANGLE

As Harry squares off with Sam, fists high, head hunched between his shoulders, dancing like a boxer.

> HARRY
> Now, we'll see who's boss, you son
> of a bitch.

Sam looks him up and down, then laughs.

> SAM
> Yeah, I guess we will.

And he advances on Harry, a sneer of disdain on his face, his hands mockingly down at his side.

Harry swings, but Sam slips the punch and slaps Harry across the face. Harry's eyes widen as he realizes this isn't going to be as easy as he thought.

He charges into Sam, delivering a flurry of blows, but Sam dances around, mocking him.

Then Sam stumbles over Propp's corpse and Harry leaps forward to deliver a pile driving blow. But Sam ducks his head and takes the blow on his skull.

His fist broken, Harry screams in pain. Sam laughs and slaps his face again.

> SAM
> (continuing)
> So, now who's boss, huh?

Then he slams a fist into Harry's gut, doubling him over. Another hammer blow puts Harry on his knees.

                          SAM
                    (continuing)
          I've always wondered if you really
          could kick shit out of a man.
                    (beat)
          And I aim to find out right this
          minute.

He kicks Harry in the side, knocking him on his back to paw
at the air helplessly. Another kick and another.

ANGLE ON ELLEN

She's horrified but at the same time she realizes this is her
last chance to save her mother and herself.

She snatches the umbrella from the beach bag and grabs Mrs.
Berman by the elbow.

                         ELLEN
                    (whispering)
          Come on, Ma!

                       MRS. BERMAN
                    (very upset)
          Why is Harry hurting that man?

                         ELLEN
                    (still whispering)
          Shhh, Ma. Shhh!

She coaxes her mother from the chair and the two women flee.
They find Propp's boat tied up near the bow of the yacht.
Ellen guides her mother to the ladder.

                         ELLEN
                    (continuing)
          Down there, Ma! Hurry.

Mrs. Berman obeys, climbing over the side and going down the
ladder. Meanwhile, Ellen grabs the rope and slowly pulls
Propp's boat closer to the yacht.

Mrs. Berman starts to step onto the deck of the other boat,
then hesitates. She looks up at Ellen.

                       MRS. BERMAN
          We have to help Harry!

But just then there are two loud OS SHOTS. Ellen jumps at the
noise. Then there's two more. She looks down at her mom.

                         ELLEN
          Harry's dead, Ma. Now we have to
          save ourselves. Okay?

Mrs. Berman shakes her head - this is all too much for her.

> ELLEN
> (continuing)
> Ma? Don't give up now. Please, Ma.

Suddenly Mrs. Berman's face clears - it's like a light dawning.

> MRS. BERMAN
> I won't, Ellen.

Ellen can't help but be rocked by her mother's sudden recognition of her. Tears stream down her face.

> ELLEN
> Go on, Ma. Hurry!

And Mrs. Berman drops to the deck of the Wellcraft and scrambles out of the way. She looks back up at her daughter.

> MRS. BERMAN
> Come on, Ellen. It's your turn now.

Ellen starts climbing over the rail so she can follow her mother down the ladder. But then there's an OS THUD above her. Gasping in fear, Ellen looks up.

ANGLE ON SAM

Poised on the flying deck above her.

> SAM
> Aren't you even going to say
> goodbye, Ellen?

Then he jumps lightly down to Ellen's deck. She holds the umbrella up to ward him off.

> ELLEN
> Don't come any closer.

> SAM
> (laughing)
> What are you going to do with that
> thing? Think you're Mary Poppins?

And he reaches out a hand. Immediately, Ellen jabs him. A long blue arc of electricity streaks out and Sam howls in pain as he's knock back by 80,000 volts of electricity. He sits up, gasping for breath.

> SAM
> (continuing)
> Jesus, what was that?

He jumps back to his feet.

>   SAM
>   (continuing)
>   You've been shopping for tricky
>   stuff, haven't you, Ellen?
>   (he raises his pistol)
>   Too bad you didn't buy a gun
>   instead.

But before he can fire, Ellen lunges forward again. This time she zaps the gun.

>   SAM
>   (continuing; shouting)
>   God damn!

In his agony, Sam reflexively pulls the trigger.

ANGLE

The bullet misses Ellen, but plows into FUEL CANS tied up against the side. Gasoline pours out and runs down the deck.

ANOTHER ANGLE

Sam lunges forward, but Ellen coolly zaps him again. This time the jolt knocks the gun out of his hand. Then she advances on him, the umbrella at ready. Sam backs away a few steps.

>   SAM
>   Screw this. I'm getting the other
>   gun.

He whirls and runs down the alleyway. Ellen immediately bolts for the railing. She starts to clamber over, but before she can escape Sam comes racing back.

>   ANGLE
>   He spots her and raises the gun.

>   SAM
>   Nice knowing you, Ellen.

But before he can fire Ellen stabs the umbrella into a pool of gasoline on the deck.

ANOTHER ANGLE

There's a long arc of blue electricity and the fuel explodes! Engulfed in flame, Sam screams in agony!

He fires wildly in every direction as he spins around and around. Ellen turns and dives into the water.

ANGLE

Ellen surfaces, then strikes out for Propp's boat. She grabs the ladder and climbs up on deck.

ON THE DECK

Ellen rushes past her mother to the Captain's Chair. She grabs the wheel and searches around for the starter.

> MRS. BERMAN
> Do you know how to drive one of
> these, Ellen?

> ELLEN
> (grim laugh)
> No, Ma.

Then she sees the key in the ignition and gives it a twist. The engine ROARS into life. She pulls on the throttle. Instantly the boat lurches backward, slamming into the yacht.

> ELLEN
> (continuing)
> Damn.

She pushes the throttle forward. The engine stalls. Frantic, she hits the ignition switch. Nothing. Another attempt and this time the engine roars into life. But suddenly:

ANGLE

A burning figure dives into the water. It's Sam! He surfaces, eyes crazy in his blackened face.

He lunges forward, grabbing one of the lines trailing behind the boat. He wraps a length around his wrist then pulls himself toward the Wellcraft, hand over hand.

> SAM
> (ghastly croak)
> Ellen!

Ellen throttles forward and the boat surges away but Sam clings to the line.

ABOARD THE BOAT

The line unravels from a coil on the deck, then just as we
see that it's attached to the anchor, Sam's weight pulls the
anchor across the deck. It starts to go over the side, but
then it jams against the rail.

ANOTHER ANGLE

Sam using his incredible strength to pull himself closer and
closer to the Wellcraft.

ON ELLEN

She rushes to the anchor. Struggles to free it.

                    ELLEN
          Help me, Ma!

Mrs. Berman runs to her daughter's side. The two women fight
with the anchor- Sam getting closer all the while.

Then it jerks free! The anchor splashes into the water.

ANGLE ON SAM

Suddenly finding himself treading water - Ellen's boat
speeding away. Then the anchor's weight starts to pull him
under. He gulps water and fights like hell to stay afloat.
His head goes under once - twice - three times. Then Sam is
no more. And at that moment:

ANGLE ON THE FREEBOOTER

As it explodes into flames.

ANGLE ON ELLEN

As she guides the boat through a hailstorm of fiery debris.

ANOTHER ANGLE

Then it's over and Ellen sags in relief as she realizes that
they're safe. Her mother gives her a hug.

                    MRS. BERMAN
          I'm so glad to see you, Ellen.

                        ELLEN
                 (laughing and leaking
                     tears)
              Me too, Ma. Me too.

Mrs. Berman glances at her watch.

                      MRS. BERMAN
              If we hurry, we can catch Perry
              Mason.

                        ELLEN
              I'm hurrying, Ma. Just as fast as I
              can.

And she throws the throttle forward and the boat zooms toward
the distant blue rim of land.

ANGLE ON BOAT

As it speeds into the setting Florida sun. Becoming a smaller
and smaller dot.

FADE OUT

                        THE END